CLAIMING HER BEASTS
BOOK THREE

DIA COLE

Claiming Her Beasts Book Three

All rights reserved.

Published by Black Diamond Press LLC.

Copyright © 2021

This book is protected under the copyright laws of the United States of America. Any reproduction, electronic sharing, or other unauthorized use of this book is prohibited without the express written permission of the publisher.

This is a work of fiction. Names, characters, places, and incidents are either a product of the author's imagination or are used fictitiously, and any resemblance to any persons, living or dead, business establishments, events, or locales is entirely coincidental.

ISBN: 978-1-946975-31-7

SUMMARY

I didn't think living through the apocalypse would be easy. I just didn't think it would be this hard...

My sexy beasts seem more interested in fighting each other than fulfilling my increasingly dark and twisted fantasies. Our scorching hot leader is trying to break me with his wicked punishments. And the secret my sister is keeping may destroy us all.

Even worse, our enemies are multiplying, and when our supply run goes south, the price for survival may be too high to pay...

GHOST

This was always one of my least favorite parts.

STARVING TO DEATH ON A METAL GURNEY IN A TOP-SECRET underground military research facility was about as fun as it'd looked in my prophetic visions.

Unfortunately, my preview of this time had done little to prepare me for the suffering I'd experience as my mind and body slowly wasted away in the darkness.

Minute by minute. Hour by hour. Day by day. Week by week.

If I didn't already know the scientists had evacuated due to the apocalypse, I might have assumed they were inflicting this torment on me intentionally. Those sadistic bastards enjoyed pushing me and their other unfortunate test subjects to the brink of death.

Dissections, amputations, incinerations, and electrocutions were the fun *du jour* in this hellish place they called the lab.

Dr. Zimmerman claimed he and his staff were testing our limitations so they could design stronger genetic hybrids for the military. But I knew the truth.

They wanted to better control their beasts.

My brothers' ill-fated rebellion in Afghanistan had shaken the General's confidence in the entire project and Dr. Zimmerman was desperate to save his life's work. I'd been tempted to tell the good doctor he should be more concerned with the diabolical plans of his research partner—plans that would nearly annihilate the human species—but I'd held my tongue.

I'd never share knowledge of the future with them again —not after what they'd tried to do to my anassa. What fools they were to think the future could be changed.

So it was. So it is. So it will be.

I tried to lower my head in prayer, but the thick silver band around my forehead prevented all but the slightest movement. The band and the silver chains wrapped tight around each of my limbs kept me weak, immobile, and unable to telepathically connect with my only surviving sibling.

Not that Hunter was in any position to help. He was too busy walking his own path of destruction. I'd tried to warn him off this course, but that too had been in vain.

His fate was written. So was mine. So was my anassa's...

And I'd seen it all. That's how I knew it was pointless to try to free myself from the silver or from the cloying darkness of this dank cell hundreds of feet below the earth.

In truth, I deserved this torture. Even though my actions had been preordained, I would eternally carry the guilt of betraying my anassa.

A vision of her as a giggling, mischievous child flashed through my mind. She'd loved telling knock-knock jokes and pulling pranks on her sisters. But because of me, she'd never be that laughing, carefree girl again.

And yet, the trauma of her childhood had turned her into a strong, fiercely independent female who was savagely protective of those she considered family. She needed those traits to triumph over what was to come.

I shuddered, wishing with all my might to see her. How incredible it would be to watch her destiny unfold in real time.

As if someone or something had granted my wish, my spirit suddenly burst free of my body. Stunned, I rose as an incorporeal mist, surging through the top floors of the lab before following the long elevator shaft to freedom.

❃

MARVELING THAT I'D SOMEHOW USED MY ASTRAL projection abilities despite the silver and my weakened state, I surfaced in an empty house in the middle of the army weapons training grounds. The heavily fenced off desert area, filled with empty homes, provided excellent cover for the lab and the weapons the army scientists really tested here.

Us.

Moving faster, I flew over the open desert. I was miles from the army base, miles from the city, and miles from her. But I'd have no trouble finding my anassa. Her spirit was a fiery beacon to my soul.

As I traveled over sunbaked basins and craggy red rock mountains, I scanned the empty two-lane road below. No caravan of Alpha Diaz's black SUVs were headed to the lab.

It must not be that part yet.

A mixture of relief and disappointment rippled through me as I continued my flight over the arid, cactus-studded landscape. The road expanded, and the sage green scrubs and dust devils soon gave way to human structures. Just a smattering of buildings at first. An empty gas station. A deserted fast-food restaurant. A motel whose only guests were rotting carcasses.

Eventually, the road bled into a highway, which became a freeway with looping overpasses that almost resembled cursive letters from above. A shame they'd be clogged with abandoned vehicles for the foreseeable future.

My aerial flyby took me through downtown Saguaro Valley where I noted hordes of infected gathering around several of the high-rise buildings.

People must live inside.

I felt a pang of sympathy for them. At some point in the future, their resources would run out and they'd starve or have to take their chances with the mob of infected outside.

Good thing they'll soon have a savior.

Anticipation burned through me as I flew north, passing over strip malls and clusters of pink stucco homes. *There!* Even if I hadn't felt my anassa's spirit, I would have recognized the Saguaro Valley Christian Academy from my past visions.

The private school looked exactly the same, down to the handful of soldiers and civilians fortifying the front gates.

The sound of a familiar shout had me jetting over the roof. There, at the back of the school, was a group of browbeaten looking civilians standing in a line. An imposing male dressed in camo paced up and down the playing field, barking orders at them.

Ah, Dominic. Some things never change.

The Titan soldier looked exactly as I remembered from my visions, but it took me a second to place the shifter standing near him. Avi looked so different, and yet there was no mistaking that furrowed brow.

Always so serious, that one.

What about my brother? Filled with the need to find Hunter, I flew around the side of the school and came upon my anassa's sister poking her head out of a storage shed. Eden gave an anxious look around before carrying out a small animal wrapped in bloody towels. Tears leaked out from under the large sunglasses she wore.

Oh, we're already at this part.

Feeling some relief at knowing precisely where we were in the timeline, I watched the slender brunette set the deceased animal down near several freshly dug graves. While she grabbed a shovel and began to dig, I looked over the grave markers.

So many more names will join these...

Deciding not to focus on that, I dove through the brick wall of the school and emerged in a locker room occupied by females in various stages of undress. Uninterested in them, I darted through the bathrooms and out into the gymnasium.

The basketball court and stage looked just as I remembered. And so did the large square windows at the top of the wooden bleachers. Dominic hadn't turned them into an escape route yet.

He better get on it.

Exiting the gym, I traveled down the hallways not bothering to stop in the principal's office where I knew my brother's body lay in stasis. It was only an empty shell now. Hunter's spirit was elsewhere.

A soulful, hypnotic singing voice drew me to the music room. Inside, a long-haired and bearded Reed sat on the floor strumming the strings of an acoustic guitar while Sai, still looking every inch the rock star he'd once been, belted out verses from his perch on the piano bench.

I didn't recognize their song—something about a ring of fire—but I immediately sensed my brother's spirit inside Reed.

"Hunter!" I called out telepathically.

Sai jumped, his arm plunking down on the piano keys. "Did you hear that?"

"Hear what, man?" Reed blinked a pair of brilliant blue eyes up at Sai.

"It sounded as if someone shouted." Sai laughed nervously. "I guess I'm spending too much time with you, Fruitcake. I'm starting to go crazy too."

"Not cool," Reed said, not looking the slightest bit offended.

Interesting. Sai heard me, but neither Reed nor Hunter had. I wondered why that was and if I could communicate with my anassa in this disembodied state. Not that I would. It was imperative I do not interfere with her destiny.

Moving on, I headed back into the hallway and floated down to the infirmary where I knew little Rosie lay fighting for her life. I was just turning to look in on the child when I felt myself being sucked back down the hallway the way I'd come.

No! I need to see my anassa.

Trying to rally my waning strength, I forced myself forward, making up lost ground and passing through the chapel doors. I didn't bother looking at the pews or admiring the large stained-glass window behind the pulpit. Instead, I flew straight through the wood panel wall into the chaplain's office where my anassa's spirit glowed like a bonfire.

She sat on a chair across from an oak desk.

For a moment, all I could do was drink her in—smooth golden skin, long dark hair, full red lips, and generous curves. She was, and would always be, the most beautiful female in all the realms to me. However, right now, she looked decidedly uncomfortable.

The moment I placed the man with the prematurely gray hair behind the desk, I understood the reason

She's meeting with Roger. I'd seen a few visions of her sessions with the psychologist, but not this one.

Roger steepled his hands under his receding chin. "So, Lee. Why do you believe you're a sex addict?"

Huh? I zeroed in on their conversation.

"Because I want it all the time," my anassa blurted out. *Morning, noon, and night.*

How am I hearing her thoughts? That shouldn't be possible yet.

"And does this distress you?" he asked her.

"Not really, but it's strange." She chewed her lower lip the way she always did when she was anxious. "Before the apocalypse, I'd never even been with a guy and now I'm screwing around with three of them."

"Three?" Roger looked down at the notepad in front of him. "Is there someone new? Someone besides Reed and Avi?"

"Um, this is confidential, right?" She gave Roger a questioning look. *This all better be confidential, dammit.*

Her unspoken thoughts amused me.

Roger nodded. "Anything you say here is just between us."

"Well..." She ran her hand through her hair. "... Dominic often watches Avi and I when we're... um... together."

I sensed her shame, embarrassment, and excitement. The last emotion was the one I hoped she'd embrace sooner than later.

I too enjoyed watching.

"Sergeant Rosario?" Roger's jaw dropped, but he quickly composed himself.

She frowned. "Avi knows. There's no way he could not know. But he hasn't mentioned it. And Dominic acts like nothing has changed between us. If anything, he's harder on me during training than ever. Did I tell you he transferred me to the laundry team? I've had to clean people's filthy underwear all week." She made a face.

"Mm-hmm. So does this arrangement bother you?"

"Yeah, I want to be back on the food prep team."

He chuckled. "I mean Dominic watching you and Avi?"

Her cheeks flushed. "It's actually a huge turn on." *Oh, God. I'm so messed up.*

No, you're not, I wanted to tell her. She didn't know she was under mind control. Alpha Diaz had compelled her to want sex during her last night at the strip club. Clearly, Javier hadn't predicted he wouldn't be around to tend to her needs.

His loss. Our gain.

"Do you want to know what I think?" Roger said after a long silence.

"What?"

"I think we've all been through a traumatic experience." Roger cleared his throat. "We're all *living* through a traumatic experience. And we're trying to cope as best we can. Sex appears to be one of your coping mechanisms. There's nothing wrong with that as long as it's consensual and you and your partners enjoy yourselves."

She nodded, looking relieved.

"Now, I was hoping we could pick up where we left off yesterday."

She gave Roger an exasperated look. *Not this again.* "What more is there to discuss? I already told you, my biggest fear is something bad happening to Eden and Reed."

Roger picked up his pen. "You view yourself as their protector?"

"I look out for them. I always have." She sat up straighter in her seat. "Neither one of them could make it in the world..."

"Without you?" Roger finished.

"Yeah, they need me. And... I need them. I mean, if

anything happened to them, I don't know if I could keep going, you know?"

Roger made a non-committal sound and jotted more notes.

She peered over the desk at his notepad and gave him an outraged look. "We're not enmeshed, and we don't have boundary issues. I was legally their guardian for God's sake."

"But now they are both adults and you're involved in an intimate relationship with Reed."

"Not currently," she said quickly. "He's been in no shape to do anything... since he stopped using."

"And I venture to guess that's why you've sought out these other lovers?"

"No. Yes. Um, Reed and I have an open relationship," she answered, seeming flustered. "Reed doesn't like the idea of me being with other guys, but he's dealing with it..." she trailed off.

"And you're okay with Reed seeing other women?"

I had to give Roger credit for asking the tough questions.

She looked down at her hands. "Um, yeah."

"Really?"

She looked up. "No, not really. It drives me crazy to see these stupid girls chasing my... chasing Reed around the school all damn day long, but I can't be a hypocrite."

"I see," Roger said, tapping his chin with the pen. "So, how has it been living in such close quarters with Reed? It's just you two staying in the music room, right?"

She nodded. "It's been fine. I only moved in to help him detox from the morphine. He quit cold turkey and hasn't used in a week." She smiled, clearly proud of Reed.

"That's impressive. It's nice of you to help him through such a challenging time."

"It's the least I could do," she mumbled. *I should have never made him take those drugs.*

"And now that he's in recovery, you'll be moving out?"

She picked at one of her fingernails. "I suppose. Dominic will probably make us move back into the classrooms with everyone else, but I won't let him separate us."

Roger looked from his notes to her. "You've said you're only able to sleep if you're lying next to Reed."

She shrugged. "It's the only time I can relax."

"Because you're in love with him?"

My anassa flinched. "No. I've already told you, I'm not capable of falling... of that emotion."

"Because of what happened with your father?"

She paled. "Yes. He and my mom were totally in love. I mean, you'd gag to see them together. Always hugging and kissing. And then he murdered her in cold blood before coming after me and my sisters."

That's my fault. Guilt swept over me.

"So, would you say you have trust issues?" Roger asked, making another note.

"That doesn't come close to covering it." She tried for a laugh, but it sounded hollow.

"Do you think Reed is like your father?"

She shook her head so hard, her teeth clicked together. "He's nothing like my father. He's kind, sensitive, and usually pretty chill. Both Avi and Dominic are much more like my father was. They're kind of alpha-holes, you know?"

"Hmm." Roger jotted another note. "Do you think Reed would ever hurt you emotionally or physically?"

No, she thought, chewing her lip thoughtfully. "He'd never hurt me. He... he's in love with me."

Roger's brow furrowed. "But you don't reciprocate the feeling?"

"I can't. I just can't." She wrapped her arms around her chest.

"Aren't you attracted to him?"

"I'd have to be dead not to be." She flashed Roger a wicked smile. "He's the best-looking guy here."

Roger chuckled. "I agree, but don't tell my husband I said that." He shared a conspiratorial grin with her before putting his pen down. "I think I understand what's going on here."

She blinked. "What?"

"You won't allow yourself to fall in love, not because you think Reed or your other partners will hurt you, but because you think you will hurt them."

A stunned expression crossed her face. "Y-you're right."

"However, by not allowing for a deeper connection, you are hurting them, intentionally or not."

She closed her eyes and trembled. "You know what my biggest fear really is?" Without waiting for the psychologist to respond, she said, "I fear becoming a monster like my father and doing what he did."

"You fear becoming a murderer?"

She gave a humorless laugh. "I'm already a murderer."

"You killed in self-defense," Roger clarified. "You killed to save the people you loved."

"But killing didn't bother me. It felt good." She took a ragged breath. "I carry this darkness—this rage that's been building all these years. Ever since that night when my father..." She shuddered and cleared her throat. "I have to fight so hard to keep those feelings in check. I have to fight to keep control."

My fault. My betrayal had planted those seeds of darkness.

"What would happen if you lost control?" Roger asked, not knowing the fate of our world hung on that very question.

She said nothing. But I heard her thoughts, and they sent a tremor of fear through me.

No! That can't happen!

My focus snapped, and I was suddenly being sucked back

to my physical body. As I hurled through the walls of the school and out into the city, I resolved to seek her out again as soon as I had the strength.

I couldn't interfere with her destiny, but I could share her pain and offer her hope.

I owe my mate that much...

❀　2　❀

L E E

"It's a good day to die," Zara said, pointing her semiautomatic assault rifle up at the cloudless sky.

My friend's words made the fine hairs on the back of my neck prickle. "Don't say that. Don't even think it." Keeping my fingers tightly wrapped around my tactical knife, I wiped away the sweat on my forehead. It was only New Year's Eve, but the stifling heat wave was a familiar prelude to a scorching Saguaro Valley spring—a spring we probably wouldn't live long enough to see.

Zara swiped her frizzy rainbow curls out of her face and flashed me a feral grin. "We all got to go someday. Why not today?" She moved farther out into the debris-covered street, her face shadowed by the Festival of Lights banner doing the splits between two palm trees overhead.

The banner was yet another reminder that the apocalypse had arrived two weeks before Christmas. Three weeks later, we were still battling the dead in a town forever festooned in the cheerful trappings of my least favorite holiday.

"Hush," hissed Zara's younger brother, Dev. He flattened his back against the abandoned Suburban we were using as cover and glared at Zara through his thick-rimmed glasses. "Get back here if you know what's good for you." At eighteen, he was only a few years younger than Zara and me, but when he acted like this, he reminded me of his bossy eldest brother.

My lips curled as Avi's rugged face flashed into my mind. Since Christmas, he and I had spent every free moment together. At this point, I knew every square inch of Avi's gorgeous, ripped body better than my own. And yet, I still ached for more of my willow tree's touch, something that was creating tension with my other lover, Reed.

Zara blew a raspberry at Dev. "You're fast becoming my least favorite brother."

"Should I care?" Dev ruined his comeback by sneezing.

As he wiped his nose with his sleeve, Zara snorted and bounced up and down on the balls of her sneakers like the overexcited puppies my sister Eden once rescued. Of course, that had been long before the canine flu vaccine brought about the zombie apocalypse. Now the human species needed rescuing far more than any animals.

"Calm down. You're making me nervous," Dev pleaded. "And I already have a headache. It must be from all the damn pollen." He gave a weak wave of his hand toward one of the Jacaranda trees whose purple bell-shaped blossoms were blooming a full two months earlier than they should. Even the foliage was confused over the crazy as hell weather we'd been having.

Zara rubbed her belly. "Well, I'm starving. Why did we have to skip breakfast for this stupid field training test?"

My stomach rumbled at the reminder of our missed meal. I'd given my sister most of my dinner last night, which made missing the single protein bar we were rationed for breakfast hurt more than usual.

"Shut up, Zara. They'll hear you." Dev jerked his acne

covered chin in the direction of the crowd gathering in front of the Euro Gift Shop down the street.

I tensed, glancing at the mob.

Even with their heads and limbs bent at odd angles, the shambling bodies could almost be mistaken for normal people. But a closer look at their milky eyes, uncoordinated gait, and rotting skin gave them away.

Biters. Zombies. Flesh-eaters.

The tattered army fatigues, hospital gowns, and Southern Arizona University sweatshirts fluttering against putrid flesh were evidence that the town's former citizens had been an eclectic mix of retirees, college students, and military families. In life, those groups may have rarely mingled, but in death, they were inseparable.

Zara scoffed. "They're all the way over there."

She can't be serious.

We all knew how dangerous Biters were when they gathered together, and that horde was one of the largest I'd seen since the day the world went to hell a few weeks ago. The memory of the undead mob smashing through my house had me shivering despite the warm temperature.

Zara held her fingers to her lips and mocked her brother by making loud shushing noises.

Neither the desert heat nor Zara's cavalier attitude was doing anything to thaw the ice water running through my veins.

Why did I volunteer for this? Oh wait. I didn't.

Sergeant Dominic Rosario, the ruthless leader of our group, ordered us to accompany him on this training mission. Before he'd left to scout ahead, he'd announced we'd be tested on our survival skills and our knowledge of his rules.

Ugh. He has so many goddamn rules.

Living under Dominic's command kept us alive, but sometimes I wondered if we'd embraced the devil to survive hell.

I rubbed a sweaty palm on my jeans. *I have to pass his test.* Those that failed were exiled or assigned the most menial jobs back at the school where we were staying. Although being shackled with the sanitation team wasn't the worst thing that could happen, being thrown out of the safe house without the protection of Dominic and his soldiers might be. Especially since I had a body snatching demon after me.

I shuddered at the thought of the comatose, ten-foot-tall beast lying on the floor of Dominic's office. Hunter was supposed to be under Dominic's control, but he'd somehow slipped the sergeant's leash to possess Reed and take my virginity.

A familiar wave of disgust and anger pulsed through my body. No matter how his touch had enflamed my body, Hunter violated my trust and I wanted to see him burn. Thankfully, Reed had vanquished him, but Dominic warned that Hunter would continue to stalk me, perhaps in the guise of a different body.

I shivered, bile rising in my throat.

As if sensing my fear, two of the Biters down the street lifted their heads and sniffed the air.

I froze, not daring to move a muscle.

After a tense moment, the creatures turned back to their shambling.

I let out a relieved breath.

"Those Biters have the right idea. We should get breakfast there." Zara pointed at the gift shop. "They have the most amazing fruitcakes. They're even better than sex." She smacked her lips. "Come on, Dev. Get one with me."

"No way."

"What about you?" Zara turned to me. "We all know you enjoy fruitcake." She winked, referencing Reed's nickname around the school.

Dev gritted his teeth. "No one is getting a fruitcake with you. Stop acting crazy."

Zara flipped him off.

Dev and I shared a troubled look. Although sassy as hell, the pixie-sized woman's survival skills and razor-sharp focus during training drills had earned her a spot on Dominic's coveted red team. Her strange behavior was only making my anxiousness grow.

"I'm getting breakfast." Zara spun on her heel and marched down the street.

❧

HAS ZARA LOST HER DAMN MIND?

"Stop her," Dev begged. "She listens to you more than me."

I wasn't sure that was true, but I ran after my friend and snagged the strap of her weapon with my free hand. "Do you have a death wish?"

Zara winked at me and mouthed, "Play along." The overpowering scent of rum wafted off her clothes.

I gasped in disbelief. *We're out in one of the deadliest parts of the neighborhood, and she's drunk? Great. Just great. She's going to get us killed.* I cast a quick glance at the Biters. Thankfully, they hadn't detected our presence. *Yet.*

"Let me go," she shouted, trying to shake me off.

Years of spinning around a pole, along with Dominic's daily defensive trainings, gave me the strength to reel the smaller woman in. I dragged her behind an overturned gray sedan, trying to ignore the blood-streaked windows. "Dominic ordered us to stay by the Suburban." *Rule of survival number one, follow Dominic's orders.*

Zara gave a dramatic eye roll. "He's been gone too long. He's probably been eaten."

My stomach dropped. *Not Dominic. He can't die.* Despite my conflicting feelings for the handsome sergeant, I couldn't bear to consider anything bad happening to him. I shook off her words. "Seriously? He can take out a horde with his bare hands. You don't want to piss him off."

Zara scoffed. "Just because you have the hots for one of the scariest mofos still alive on this planet doesn't mean I'm going to roast my lady balls off waiting for him." She whipped around and elbowed me in the gut.

I doubled over with a grunt, losing my grip on her. "Why the hell did you do that?"

She glared at me with her hands on her hips. "I'm getting that fruitcake."

"Not only is that suicidal, you know we're never supposed to travel anywhere alone." *Rule of survival number eight, always travel with backup.*

She arched a brow. "So, come with me."

Movement over her shoulder quickened my pulse. Two zombies peeled off from the pack and lurched our way. "Biters, eight o'clock!"

The closest flesh-eater was female. She wore teal medical scrubs and an ID badge linking her to the retirement home up the street. The shredded skin of her throat revealed a half-eaten trachea, the same color as her sunken white eyes.

Close behind Nurse Death shambled a hulking, male Biter, wearing a blue polo and bloodstained chinos. Maggots danced in and out of the gaping hole where his nose had once been.

I gulped. These Biters weren't like the toothless, armless ones we'd practiced fighting back at the school. *These monsters will fight us to the death.*

Zara spun around, her eyes narrowing. "I'll teach these cock blockers to get between me and my breakfast." She shouldered her rifle and pointed it at the female Biter.

"What are you doing?" I grabbed the weapon and ripped it from her hands. "Guns are only used as a last resort." *Rule of survival number five.* "The noise will attract the others."

"You're right. Damn, I forgot my spear. Can you handle them?"

Crap! I gave Zara her rifle back and shoved her behind me.

Nurse Death was only a few yards away. Seeing us, she clicked her bloodstained teeth together in frenzied anticipation.

Oh, God! My heart hammered so hard I thought it'd burst through my chest like some kind of alien monster. As fear consumed me, I felt myself starting to space-out. Darkness edged my vision as ghostly terrors of my past threatened to suck me in.

"Snap out of it, Lee!" Zara whispered hoarsely. "Do something or we'll die."

She's right. Forcing away the nightmares in my head, I turned my attention to the nightmares in front of me. I took a deep breath and immediately choked on the pungent, rotting-meat stench of the approaching zombie. Quickly switching to mouth breathing, I focused on Dominic's training. The words he'd drilled into my mind came back to me.

Attack. Don't react.

Stiffening my shoulders, I raised my knife and ran at the flesh-eater head-on.

Nurse Death opened her jaws and reached for me.

Avoiding the creature's long, jagged fingernails, I stabbed my blade straight through her milky eye. It exploded like an overripe grape.

Ugh. I ripped my blade free, and Nurse Death collapsed to the street, lifeless.

Before I could congratulate myself on the kill, the male Biter shambled over the corpse and tackled me to the asphalt.

Shit! The air whooshed out of my lungs and my knife flew out of my hand.

"Kick him off!" Zara cried.

Adrenaline roared through me as I fought to keep the Biter's snapping jaws away from my neck.

"You've got this, Lee. You've got this!" Zara chanted, suddenly becoming my personal cheerleader.

No, I don't. He's too strong. My arms shook with the strain of trying to hold off the freakishly huge creature.

He gnashed his teeth, and several writhing maggots fell onto my face.

Oh, God! I couldn't stop the impulse to shake them away. I lost my grip on the Biter.

He went for my throat.

Zara swung the butt of her rifle into the side of his face, knocking him off me.

I rolled away as she brought the rifle down on his forehead, crunching in his skull like an eggshell.

"Th-thanks," I stammered, wondering why she'd waited so long to help.

She let out a heavy sigh. "You may not thank me in a few minutes. Just remember whatever happens, it'll be okay."

I stared up at her in confusion. "What will be okay?"

Ignoring my question, she glanced up at Dev, who'd jogged over to join us.

He sneezed and offered me his hand.

"I'm good. Thanks," I said, pushing myself to my feet. Despite Dev's insistence he just had allergies, I suspected he'd caught the cold that was making its way through the safe house. Getting sick was the last thing I needed. Dominic's trainings kicked my ass as it was, and the sergeant didn't allow days off for sickness.

Dev coughed into his elbow. "Better luck next time."

"Assuming there is a next time," Zara added, shaking her head. "This was your field training test, girl."

I blinked in slow understanding. "Wait, you mean you guys staged this?"

They shared a guilty look.

"I don't understand. Aren't you being tested today, too?"

"We passed our field training already," Zara replied in an apologetic tone.

"Oh." I tried to smother the bitter feeling of betrayal, but I couldn't meet Zara's gaze.

"Please don't be mad. Dominic didn't give us a choi—" Zara broke off as an enormous shadow fell over us.

My breathing went choppy as I spied all six-foot-six muscular inches of Dominic standing a few yards away. His dark close-cropped hair, tactical vest lined with throwing knives, and shiny black combat boots marked him as the Special Forces soldier he was.

As always, the sight of him filled me with the insane urge to fling myself into his massive arms—arms that would sooner choke the life out of me than embrace me.

"You three, over here." His deep voice rumbled like thunder.

Not wanting to test the sergeant's limited patience, we hustled to follow him down the street.

A small gasp of surprise escaped my lips when I saw the carnage in front of the gift shop. The entire pack of Biters lay motionless on the ground—a single knife wound in the center of their skulls. Dominic's calling card.

As I stepped over the piles of bodies, I realized Dominic must've been inside the shop watching us the entire time. No wonder the Biters were gathering around it.

Way to be observant, Lee.

Dominic's black as pitch eyes drilled into mine as he propped the door to the shop open. The ever-present dark scowl on his sinfully full lips should've been enough to dampen my attraction. But despite his dangerous aura, or maybe because of it, he stirred my hormones the way few men ever had.

I boldly held his gaze, just as I did during his trainings, briefings, or when he watched me have sex with Avi. Truth be told, I didn't enjoy screwing Avi half as much if Dominic wasn't observing in the shadows.

What's wrong with me?

Dominic lived to browbeat people, and still I lusted after him. *Why?* It defied all reason. The one thing I knew was that I'd never let him, or anyone else, intimidate me.

As I stood there, refusing to give him the submission I knew he was seeking, Dominic's stare turned to a glare.

"Inside. Now."

A sinking feeling grew in the pit of my stomach. *Crap. I've failed his test.*

3

LEE

"Come on. I've cleared the shop," Dominic said, waving us inside. His massive shoulders filled the doorway.

I had to squeeze by him to enter the small store. The barest brush of my body against his was enough to heat my blood.

I tried to suck in a steadying breath, but it was spiked with the sweet cinnamon spice of his breath, which put my hormones into a dizzying tailspin. The man had a serious addiction to cinnamon candy, and as a result, I couldn't be around the aromatic spice without thinking of him—craving him.

Trying to clear my mind, I glanced at the rows of nesting dolls and colorful wooden bowls on display shelves around us, but my gaze kept going back to Dominic.

Even if the sergeant didn't hold my fate in his basketball-sized hands, it would be impossible not to stare at him. His sculpted cheekbones, chiseled jaw, and bronze complexion easily made him one of the most beautiful men I'd ever encountered in my life. Too bad he was also an asshole. A very deadly asshole.

He probably knew a hundred ways to kill someone. I looked at the knives sheathed in his vest. *Hell.* He probably knew a thousand ways.

I shouldn't want this man. But I did. My soul-deep, visceral attraction to him was only growing stronger over time, which made no sense.

What kind of idiot lusts after someone who treats them like shit?

Dominic was always punishing me for breaking his rules and failing his tests. I'd lost track of the number of times he'd forced me to go without meals or run laps until I collapsed. A week ago, he'd staged a fake zombie attack that drove another survivor to suicide and convinced me I was about to die. The hellish experience triggered my PTSD and resulted in one of the worst space-outs I'd experienced in years.

The bastard deserved nothing but my hate. Too bad my body disagreed. I had to cross my arms over my chest to hide my stiffening nipples. Not that he'd ever act on my obvious attraction to him. For all his voyeuristic tendencies, he'd made it clear that soldiers and civilians did not fraternize. It was even one of his damn rules.

"Attention," the evil son of a bitch called out.

Zara, Dev, and I fell in line, our backs against the cash register counter.

Dominic paced in front of us. "Did you wake with amnesia this morning, Miss Walker?"

I flinched at the ice in his tone. "No, sir."

"Then explain why you seem to have forgotten every goddamn thing I've taught you."

Sweat trickled down the back of my neck. "Um—"

Not giving me a chance to respond, he continued, "Your defensive skills are piss-poor, and you showed a complete lack of situational awareness out there. Do you want to be zombie chow, Miss Walker?"

"No, sir." My stomach knotted. "Did I fail the test?"

A muscle ticked in his jaw. "Of course, you failed the test. If Miss Sighn hadn't saved your ass, it'd be in pieces on the street."

Zara stiffened. "Lee did take out the first Biter, and she showed a good understanding of the rules."

I gave her a look of appreciation. I could almost forgive her for setting me up. *Almost.*

Dominic let out a cold laugh. "Like rule number nine?"

Never leave a weapon behind. Oh, crap. I looked down at my empty knife sheath.

"Looking for this?" Dominic held up my blade and waved it under my nose.

When I grabbed for it, he pulled it out of reach. "You won't need a knife like this where you're going."

"And where will that be?" I curled my hands into fists. *He won't exile me, will he?*

Dominic glanced over at Zara and Dev. "You two go on ahead. We'll meet you back at the safe house."

"Yes, sir," they said in unison.

Zara flashed me an apologetic look. "Lee, I—"

"Out." Dominic pointed at the door.

"Come on." Dev dragged his sister forward.

"Wait." Zara stopped at a row of gift baskets stacked near the door and snatched one.

"I saw that, Ms. Sighn," Dominic called out as Zara darted outside.

A moment later, the door opened, and Dev flung the gift basket back inside. "Sorry about that," he said before closing the door.

No fruitcakes for Zara today. I let out a choked laugh.

"Pull yourself together. Soldiers don't cry," Dominic chided.

As if. I met his scowl with my glare. "I'm not crying and I'm not a soldier."

"You'll become one or you'll die." Dominic's expression hardened. "I'm your commanding officer, you will address me as sir." He gave my knife an appreciative look and then slid it into his tactical vest.

"That's mine. Give it back." The blade was much more than a weapon. It symbolized me conquering the nightmares of my childhood and I intended to carry it until my dying breath.

"It's mine now. If you ever demonstrate sufficient skill to wield it, I'll return it to you." His mocking tone indicated how unlikely that was to happen.

Red crept across my vision. For the past several weeks, I'd been forced to abide by all his rules, eat tiny amounts of food, endure brutal trainings, and exist on meager bits of sleep. *For what?* The protection of this man who'd just taken the only item of value I had left.

Suddenly, the idea of being exiled didn't bother me. *Fine, let him throw me out. I might have to watch out for Hunter, but I'll have my freedom.*

Decision made, I let out a deep exhale. Since I had nothing to lose, I leveled Dominic with a hard stare of my own. "Give me back my knife, Sergeant Pain in the Ass."

He jerked his head around so fast he might've gotten whiplash. "What did you call me?"

"Are you hard of hearing?" I couldn't believe the words coming out of my mouth, but I wasn't about to back down. "Give. Me. My. Knife. Asshole."

His eyes glittered with challenge. He pulled my blade out and raised it over his head. "Make me."

I jumped for it, but he raised it higher.

Dammit. More games. I'd never get my knife from him that way. And the very idea of me trying to take the massive soldier on in hand-to-hand combat was ridiculous. *Unless I use an entirely different set of survival skills...*

Channeling my brazen stripper persona, I yanked off my T-shirt and let it fall to the ground. Since the air felt so amazing on my heated skin, I went ahead and slowly peeled off my sweat-dampened cami, too. That left me in only a sports bra and jeans.

He inhaled sharply. "What are you doing?" It might've been my imagination, but the pulse at his neck seemed to kick up a notch or two.

Excellent. The sergeant isn't immune to me. I lifted the bottom of my bra, giving him the X-rated view men had paid dearly for at the club. "Just getting comfortable. It's so hot in here."

"Put your clothes back on," he growled, his predatory gaze locking onto my bare breasts.

I lifted my chin in challenge and threw his words back at him. "Make me."

◈

DOMINIC LOOKED AS IF I'D SMACKED HIM ON THE HEAD with a two-by-four. His hand, still gripping my knife, dropped to his side.

A thrill shot through me as I let my bra snap back down over my girls. *It's working.* Making no attempt to take the blade, I sauntered over to him, wearing the come-hither expression that'd made me the headliner to one of the most popular strip clubs in town. "You've got to be burning up in that." I reached out and touched the front of his tactical vest.

He swallowed hard and stepped back toward the door. "Stop whatever this is right now."

"What do you mean?" I looked up at him through my lashes while raising the bottom of my sports bra.

He opened his mouth and closed it.

Biting my lip to keep from laughing, I released the bottom of the bra with a snap. "Why don't you show me some new moves? You said it yourself, my fighting skills are piss-poor." I stepped closer, forcing him to brush against me or step back.

He stepped back.

Something dangerous blazed in his midnight eyes. "You—"

"Shh," I whispered, feeling the heat between us. My breath caught as a hot rush of desire pooled low in my belly. *No. I can't let him affect me.* Battling my body's traitorous response to him, I aligned our hips and lifted my mouth toward his.

His breathing shallowed as he slanted his head over mine.

Now. Using the element of surprise, I yanked my knife from his hand at the same time I hooked my foot around his and swept it out from under him.

He fell into the gift baskets with a crash. Packaged food, crinkle-cut colored paper, and cellophane exploded around us.

I kicked aside a box of candied almonds and waved my knife over him in triumph. "Looks like your defensive skills need work too."

He said nothing for a moment. "You may be right." His lips quirked up.

My mouth fell open in shock. *Is he actually smiling?*

Dominic pushed pieces of broken wicker off his chest and sat up. "Your methods are unorthodox, but you got the job done. You can keep the knife."

"Thank you," I muttered. It figured he'd turn my act of defiance into one of his tests.

"Help me up," he ordered, holding one hand out.

I looked at him through a narrowed gaze. *Another test?* I could just imagine him yanking me to the ground to teach me a lesson. My breath caught as my inner tramp warmed to the idea. *Maybe he'll roll on top of me and...*

"No tricks," Dominic said, as if reading my mind.

I sheathed my knife and reached over for his outstretched hand.

His fingers wrapped around my wrist.

The sensation of his flesh against mine made goosebumps dance across my skin. As he rolled forward, I couldn't help noticing how the muscles in his neck flexed like rip cords. Unable to tear my gaze away, I watched the sleeve of his sand-colored T-shirt ride up. It revealed a blood-crusted oval on the side of his huge bicep.

What? No! The air froze in my lungs. The mark was unmistakable. *He's been bitten.* Horror had me twisting my hand free and shoving him back.

"What the—" Dominic broke off when he saw my gaze on his arm. He quickly tugged his shirtsleeve down.

"Is that a bite?" My voice shook.

An impassive mask fell over his face. "It's nothing for you to worry about." He pushed himself to his feet.

Like hell. "Were you bitten by a zombie?"

Confirmation was in the stiffening of his shoulders. "We should head back to the safe house."

I shook my head. Emotions blew through me—shock, denial, and unexpected anguish. The idea of losing the insufferable, stubborn, domineering sergeant gutted me. "S-safe house," I echoed weakly.

He nodded. "I'm briefing my squad in an hour."

Dominic's cardinal rule ran through my mind. *All infected must die.* Under no circumstances were any infected survivors to set foot inside the school. *He can't return. I can't allow him to endanger the safety of everyone else.*

Dominic bent down and picked something off the ground. "This must be one of those damn fruitcakes Zara was going on about. It looks safe to eat."

With shaking hands, I reached for my gun.

Dominic studied the cellophane wrapped loaf in his hand. "I'll send a team to gather the food here—" He broke off when he saw my weapon pointed at his face. "What are you doing, Lee?"

"I can't let you go back to the school with a bite. I'm sorry." My eyes burned as I released the safety. Every muscle in my body tensed. The gunshot would draw Biters. I'd have to run like a hell the moment I pressed the trigger.

"Christ, wait!" He licked his thumb and rubbed it vigorously over the bloody mark on his bicep. "Look." Tension rolled off him as he held out his arm.

I blinked in disbelief. There was nothing under the blood but pinkened flesh. "Thank God." Letting out a shuddering breath, I lowered my gun. The loss of adrenaline left my knees weak and rubbery. "That looked just like a bite." So much so I couldn't imagine anything else that would've left a mark like that.

Dominic's gaze narrowed. "You were ready to kill me."

"I-I'm sorry," I stammered. *Crap. Well, if I wasn't getting thrown out of the safe house for failing the field training test before, I certainly am now.* Bracing myself for his rage, I met his gaze.

"I'm not mad."

"Y-you're not." I searched his face, trying to translate his inscrutable expression.

"That was a very brave thing you did. You've passed the field training test."

"What? You're shitting me." I'd nearly killed him in cold blood, and he was giving me a compliment?

He pressed his lips together as if fighting a smile. "I assure you, I'm not."

A wave of dizzying relief swept over me. Despite my bravado, the idea of trying to survive out here on my own terrified me.

Dominic cleared his throat. "Today, you've shown resourcefulness under pressure and a solid understanding of the rules of survival. Here." He pressed the fruitcake into my hand. "Go ahead, have some breakfast, you deserve it."

Eyeing him warily, I opened the wrapper. I'd never been a big fruitcake fan, but the scent of candied fruit and spices made my stomach rumble. It'd been weeks since I'd smelled something so divine.

I bit into the moist cake and moaned. *Holy crap! Zara is right.* Each bliss-filled bite was better than the last. Only when I was licking the boozy aftertaste from my sticky fingers did I realize Dominic was watching me with rapt attention.

A flash of self-consciousness had me wiping my mouth with the back of my hand. "Did you want one?" I gestured down at the scattered loaves on the floor. "They're amazing. Zara claims they are even better than sex."

Dominic's gaze fell to my lips. "I doubt that." His voice was low and rough. He took a step forward, closing the distance between us.

"Why do you watch me and Avi?" I blurted out breathlessly.

He went motionless, and for a heartbeat, I thought my question had killed the moment. And then he said, "Because you want me to watch you."

My denial was swift. "No. I don't."

Dominic's deep chuckle made my mouth dry. "You're right. You don't want me to watch. You want me to join in."

Ah, hell. I did.

He reached out and cupped my chin in one of his huge hands. "Why do you have such power over me?"

My heart skipped a beat and the fruitcake wrapper fluttered from my hand. Suddenly, all I could think about was pressing my mouth against those cupid's bow-shaped lips of his. Unable to stop myself, I tilted my head up at the same time he lowered his.

His cinnamon breath ghosted my skin.

My eyes fluttered shut. When nothing happened after a few moments, I opened my eyes.

Dominic now stood several feet away.

Disappointment and confusion rushed through me. "I thought you were going to kiss me."

"That will never happen. You and I will never be together." It sounded as if he was trying to convince himself of that.

Then why do you stalk me around the safe house? Why do you punish me more than anyone else? Why do you watch my sexcapades with the intensity of a jungle predator?

Before I could ask any of those burning questions, a Biter slammed into the window behind the cash register. The creature's rotting face left a revolting trail of zombie goo on the glass.

Dominic cursed. "Get your clothes on and your knife out. You're going to put this one down. This time, remember your training."

Welcome back, drill sergeant. With a deep sigh, I yanked on my cami and shirt. By the way Dominic averted his gaze as I dressed, it was clear whatever connection we'd temporarily made was gone.

Bang.

The Biter hit the glass again.

I eyed the creature without a trace of fear. How could I be afraid of that skeletal husk when I'd just gone toe-to-toe with Sergeant Pain in the Ass and won. Smiling, I drew my knife.

Dominic eyed my weapon. "You'll have to keep proving you're deserving of that blade, Ms. Walker."

"Oh, I will, sir." I returned his challenging stare with one of my own. *And you'll have to keep proving the safety you offer is worth putting up with your bullshit.*

His dark eyes flashed with something I could've almost sworn was approval. "Let's move out." He shoved open the shop door and led me back into hell.

✺ 4 ✺

R E E D

"**R**eed and Dawn, you're doing great," Enrique called out from across the playing field. "Two more laps to go."

As the yellow team leader clapped his hands together in encouragement, the curly-haired woman running beside me sped up. "Eat my dust, Fruitcake."

Even though Dawn's tone was flirtatious, I flinched at the nickname. Apparently, I'd never live down my crazed, naked rampage through the gymnasium on our first day at the school.

In my defense, I'd been possessed by a genetically engineered monster. Thankfully, Hunter and I had learned to coexist semi-peacefully in the weeks since then.

"Pick up the pace, cocksucker," the asshole growled inside my mind.

"Screw you. I'm doing my best." Which was surprisingly well considering a week ago I'd been jacking morphine day and night in a futile attempt to banish him. Just one week of being a junkie had turned my body into mush.

Doing some jumping jacks and running a few laps for the

yellow team tryouts should have been no big deal. But the muscles in my legs spasmed painfully as I struggled to keep up with Dawn Barnum, the nineteen-year-old who just had a cast taken off her ankle last week. It was embarrassing as hell.

The only saving grace was that my girl, Lee, wasn't here to witness my humiliation. Unfortunately, the same couldn't be said for most of the members of red team and yellow team seated on the sidelines.

At least Avi had instructed them to be quiet.

"Push harder," Hunter yelled loud enough to make my skull throb. *"We can't look soft in front of that dickwad."*

Hunter's words drew my focus to the swarthy guy with the shaved head standing among the other survivors. Avi wasn't looking at me, though. His scowl was aimed at Grady and Mario. The burly biker and the tattooed former gang member were trying out for red team.

Bruce Richardson, the red team leader, was putting Grady and Mario through an obstacle course of horrors that included crawling through ditches, scaling the side of a school bus, and putting down three restrained zombies with their bare hands. So far, the men were still struggling to get over the bus.

As if feeling my stare, Avi glanced over and sneered at me.

"He's definitely a dickwad," I muttered. It gutted me that the woman I loved was running off to screw Avi when I was so desperate for her affection. An unwelcome rush of jealousy made my chest tighten. *"What does Lee see in that guy?"*

"He's a Lykos, not a guy." Hunter reminded me.

It must be Avi's shifter nature that attracted Lee. It certainly wasn't his surly demeanor. And it couldn't be his menacing appearance. He looked like the kind of guy who'd slit your throat in some dark alley and then piss on your corpse. But although I was easy-going and better looking, I couldn't shift into a wolf like he could. *"How can we compete with that?"*

Hunter scoffed. *"Lykos are pussies. Let me take over and I'll show him who's alpha."*

"No way in hell." The last time I'd allowed Hunter to possess my body, he'd betrayed his promise not to touch Lee. I still hadn't forgiven him for having sex with her. Besides, Hunter wasn't known for his subtlety and if he revealed himself again, Dominic would kill us. Or rather, Dominic would kill me, hoping to return Hunter to his original body.

I shuddered at the thought of facing the business end of one of Dominic's knives. I had to keep Hunter's presence in my mind a secret from him and Lee. She'd flip her lid if she found out Hunter was still knocking around inside my head.

"Watch it!"

Despite Hunter's warning, it took me two seconds too long to realize Dawn had stopped short in front of me. I swerved to avoid her and ended up colliding with the soccer goal post.

Thwack.

My skull exploded in pain. Disoriented by the gong-like ringing in my ears, I fell into the net, where I thrashed around like a fish out of water.

"Reed!" Dawn shrieked, running over.

Enrique joined her a second later, and the two tried unsuccessfully to untangle me.

Hunter groaned. *"Seriously, cocksucker? You're about as useful as a football bat."*

I didn't need Hunter's running commentary right now. Not when the peals of laughter from the crowd on the sideline were burning my ears. Even more mortifying, two additional members of my fan club raced over.

"He smashed his gorgeous face," Kelsey, Bruce's sixteen-year-old daughter, wailed as she pushed Enrique out of the way.

"Oh, no! Poor baby," crooned Jacquie Stoltz, the raven-haired daughter of the safe house EMT. I hoped no one summoned her dad, Isaac, even though my nose was probably broken.

"It's not," huffed Hunter. *"Stop acting like a pussy."*

"Whatever, man." Hunter always minimized every bit of pain and discomfort I experienced. Apparently, nothing I went through ever came close to his suffering as a military science experiment or the brutal combat trainings and missions he'd endured.

I struggled harder to free myself, but only became more entangled. *Shit!* I gritted my teeth and closed my eyes in frustration. *"I told you we weren't ready. We should have never attempted tryouts today."*

"Our body is fine. You've just got to get your head out of your ass so you can see where we're going," Hunter snarled. *"Let. Me. Drive."*

"For the last goddamn time. No!"

Hunter let loose with a volley of expletives that made my head ache even more.

"He must be hurt really bad," Kelsey cried.

"I'm fine," I croaked. Peeling my eyes open, I found her, and the other two girls crouched next to me.

Dawn batted the other girls' hands away. "I'm helping Reed."

"Reed needs my help, too," Kelsey insisted.

"And mine," Jacquie added. "I'm good with rope." The eighteen-year-old winked at me through the net.

"Ladies, give Reed some breathing room," Enrique pleaded, to no avail. My fan club wasn't budging, and I was trapped, unable to shake off their wandering hands.

"What's wrong with these females?" Hunter exclaimed, as someone rubbed my crotch.

I had no idea. Women had been chasing me all my life. Not that I ever returned their interest. The only one I wanted was Lee. She was my sun, moon, and stars. Although she insisted we have an open relationship, I'd never consider getting involved with any other woman.

Hunter made a sound of disapproval. *"Don't they know you've found your mate? Once mates find each other, they don't stray."*

"Then why is Lee straying her ever loving mind out with Avi?"

Hunter had no answer to that painful question. Then, to add insult to injury, our stony-faced rival stomped over.

"Out of the way," Avi barked at my fan club.

The three girls immediately scurried away.

Avi unsheathed a hunting knife and cut the net. Once I was free, he scowled down at me. "You're not ready for action."

"I'll show you some motherfucking action, little Lykos," Hunter seethed.

I would have been angrier if I didn't agree with Avi. *"He's right, Hunter."* It was going to take more than one week of sobriety to rebuild my strength.

I lifted my hand, but Avi didn't grab it to help me up.

Instead, the bigger guy shook his head and muttered, "What the hell does Lee see in you, Fruitcake?"

"A hell of a lot more than she sees in you," I snapped.

Avi's eyes narrowed. "Excuse me?"

"Whatever you think you have with her will soon be over," I said, using the goal post to pull myself up.

Avi glowered. "She has me. She doesn't need you anymore."

His words cut right into my worst fear, but I wasn't about to show him that. I forced a laugh. "If that's what you think, you're kidding yourself. She sleeps in my arms every night. She loves me." Problem was, she wasn't *in love* with me, but he didn't need to know that.

I must have hit a nerve because he flinched. "Keep talking shit, Fruitcake. Let's see where it gets you."

Avi then turned his glare on Enrique. "Dawn promotes. Reed stays on green team permanently."

My stomach sank.

❧

"He permanently assigned us to green team!" Hunter shouted in my head. *"Motherfucker! He can't do that."*

"He just did." Maybe I should have been nicer to Avi, but I resented the hell out of the fact that he'd started something with Lee, knowing she was with me.

Avi nodded at the men, still struggling to get over the side of the bus. "Grady and Mario stay on yellow team."

Avi's announcement was met with boos from the audience on the sideline. I quickly added unpopularity to Avi's growing list of sins. The shifter didn't seem to care as he clapped his hands together. "Everyone, back to your assigned teams for drills."

Enrique gave me a sympathetic look as he strode by. "Sorry it didn't work out, Reed. I'm sure you'll get another chance to tryout."

I forced a smile. "Yeah, hope so."

"There's no hope so. We're getting on the team. Screw yellow team. We're going for red team. Just let me take over for fifteen minutes and we'll make mincemeat out of that joke of an obstacle course. Then we'll stuff it in that little Lykos' face and show Dom that—"

I groaned. *"Jesus. Don't get started on Dominic again."* Hunter had an unhealthy love-hate obsession with the sergeant.

"Fuck off," Hunter grumbled.

I was about to return the insult when I caught sight of Eden standing by the graveyard at the far back of the school.

Damn. She'll tell Lee about my horrible performance. *Ah, well.* There were no secrets around the school anyway.

I waved at her, but she didn't seem to see me. Eden and I hadn't spoken much this past week, which wasn't our norm. *I hope she's doing okay.*

Hunter snickered. *"She's probably just missing her daily dicking since Mike is MIA."*

"Stop! She's like my little sister." And right now, she didn't look so good. Eden's complexion was chalky, her clothes were rumpled and stained, and she wore a pair of men's darkly tinted aviator sunglasses that took up half her face. Even her stance looked off. Her head was tilted to the side and her foot was slightly raised off the ground, as if her muscles had locked up mid-step.

Weird.

"I've seen weirder," Hunter announced.

"Of course you have." Turning my attention back to Eden, I shouted, "Hey, Edie!"

She didn't move.

"Reed!"

I spun around to find a striking, dark-haired guy dressed in tight slacks and an unbuttoned red silk shirt calling my name from across the field.

An overwhelming feeling of shock and awe hit me the way it did every time I saw my idol.

Sai Sighn.

The Sai Sighn. Even after a couple weeks, I was incredulous that the rock star I'd hero-worshiped for years was staying at the school with us. Even more unbelievable, the lead singer of the Cocktail Kings seemed to want to be my friend. It was so incredible, I almost wanted to pinch myself.

I waved at him, and he jogged over.

Sai moved with an almost predatory grace, sunlight reflecting off the gold chains roped around his neck.

A thrill went through me. *He's coming over here!*

Hunter harrumphed. *"Why don't you suck the guy's dick already?"*

"Shut up. Sai is a big freaking deal." Years ago, I'd watched Sai compete and win America's Top Singer. It'd blown my mind that a kid from my same town could become a superstar. Since then, I'd cyberstalked the guy, who hadn't been much older than me, as he transitioned from geeky kid to multi-platinum rock god.

Wanting so much to be like Sai, I'd begged my mom for a bass guitar for my fourteenth birthday. I'd even formed my own band with my friend Ronnie. I'd thought if one kid from Saguaro Valley could become a Grammy winning music artist, maybe I could too.

Hunter let out a cruel laugh. *"Hate to piss on your parade, but music has no place in the world now."*

"Screw you, asshole," I shouted back, realizing too late I hadn't used my inside voice.

Sai stopped a couple of feet away, looking confused.

"Not you, man. An ant just bit me," I said, hoping he would buy it.

"Ah, yeah. Fracking ants." He gave me the same dimpled grin that had earned him the title of sexiest celebrity alive in the gossip magazines Lee used to read.

My heart beat faster. Ronnie and I used to joke that Sai Sighn was the one celebrity we'd go gay for. The guy had a kind of raw magnetism that captivated everyone around him. Me included.

Sai leaned in to study me. "You took quite the facer. Did you break your nose?"

"No," Hunter huffed.

"I'll be fine. It's not even bleeding." I ran my fingers over the throbbing bridge of my nose. "Definitely not one of my finest moments."

Sai slapped me on my back. "Don't beat yourself up. You just need a little more time to train."

"Your brother doesn't seem to think so. Avi made my assignment to green team permanent." It still surprised me that Avi and Sai were related. They couldn't be more opposite. Sai took nothing seriously and was always laughing. Avi, on the other hand, never cracked a smile.

Sai snorted. "Buzzkill acts as if he makes the rules around here. He doesn't. Impress Dominic and you're golden."

"We can do that," Hunter said quietly.

"No, we can't," I replied, using my inside voice this time.

Janelle, a former stunt woman who was built like a brick house, motioned at us. "Sai, get your sexy ass over here and show me what you've got."

"We're sparring partners this week," Sai explained as he cupped his hands around his goatee and called out, "Coming!"

"Not yet, but that can be arranged," Janelle shouted back, thrusting her hips. "I'll do you all night long."

"Oh yeah, baby!" Casey, a stacked blonde, shouted. "Sai's the king. The Cocktail King!"

Murielle, a pencil-thin brunette, laughed and joined Casey and Janelle in their cat calls to Sai.

Sai shook his head. "See what I have to deal with around here?"

"Tell me about it," I said, thinking of my annoying fan club.

Sai's expression went wistful. "Ironic, isn't it? Your woman is the only one I want, and she won't give me the time of day..." He trailed off. "No offense."

Hunter snarled. *"Punch the pretty boy in the face."*

"No." I didn't know why, but Sai's interest in Lee didn't bother me. Besides, Lee seemed to have shoved me back in the friend zone anyway. I sighed, feeling defeated. "Lee is more your brother's woman than mine these days."

Sai shook his head. "And Avi has never been good at sharing. You're a total idiot for letting him and Lee happen." Sai saw my expression and winced. "Sorry."

"No, you're right, man." If I hadn't gotten strung out on morphine, I never would have lost Lee to Avi.

"We haven't lost Lee," Hunter grumbled in the back of my mind. *"We just need to show her we aren't a worthless pussy by getting on red team."*

That seemed as likely as me sprouting wings. "There's got to be another way to get her back."

Sai's slow nod made me realize I'd spoken out loud again. "The secret to seducing anyone is to find out what they desire most and be the one to give it to them."

The concept was simple, and yet profound. *Yes! Of course. No one knows Lee better than I do.* I knew what she desired most. Feeling my mood brighten, I nodded back at Sai. "That's an awesome idea. Anyone ever tell you you're a genius?"

Sai laughed. "Never. That's why I like you so much, Fruitcake."

I returned his grin, already making plans. "I can set up our room with all Lee's favorite things." Or at least the things I could find on short notice.

"Yeah, good idea. We can get her that vanilla perfume she likes," Hunter added.

"It's a body wash," I corrected, *"We could ask Jacquie to check the girl's locker room to see if there's some in there."* I frowned, looking up at the sun, "I'll need to have it ready by the time Lee gets back from her laundry shift." It usually ended around noon. That gave us a few hours.

A shadow passed over Sai's face as if he knew something I didn't.

"What is it, man?"

Sai shook his head and grinned. "You know what? Screw

sparring practice. I'm going to help my main man out. You tell me what you need, and I'll help you get it."

"Wow. Thanks," I said, stunned by his dazzling smile and generosity.

The rock star slung his arm around my shoulder, giving me an intoxicating blast of his bay rum cologne. "So, tell me, what does Lee desire most?"

❧ *5* ❧

SAI

I strode toward the cafeteria, wondering how my life had gotten so utterly fracked. Last year, I'd spent New Year's Eve having drunk, tantric sex with super models on my yacht. This year, I was spending it running around this shitty school acting as Reed's little errand bitch. All morning I'd been begging, borrowing, and stealing to get the items on his wish list. But I guess it would all be worth it if it made him and Lee happy.

Just listen to me. I sounded like some lovesick teenager, not the lead singer of one of the biggest bands in the country.

Frack. How the mighty have fallen.

I used to be the guy with a harem so big, I never even bothered learning my lovers' names. Kind of a dick move, but whatever. It wasn't as if any of those models and groupies meant more than a good time. And it wasn't as if they cared about me, either. They just wanted a meal ticket and to tell their friends they were doing Sai Sighn the Cocktail King. It was totally transactional—they got what they wanted, and I got what I wanted—and everyone was cool as cake with that.

Besides, it wasn't as if I ever wanted to hitch my dick to one pussy or make a stupid move like getting married. Only suckers and fracking idiots did that. Or at least that's what I'd believed until I'd met Lee. Since then, I couldn't so much as whack off to the idea of anyone else.

Well... I guess that wasn't entirely true.

Fruitcake was really growing on me, and it wasn't just because he was hotter than a brush fire. Reed was also legit a nice guy, and I hadn't run into many of those in a long time. I also had mad respect for him being in recovery. I'd met shit-tons of addicts in the industry who never had the balls to get clean. But he just up and cold turkeyed last week. *Who the hell does that?*

And he seemed to have some raw talent, unlike most motherfrackers who begged me to listen to their demos. His voice and his self-taught guitar skills impressed me during our jam sessions. Reed was a natural, like I'd been.

It also didn't hurt that he stared at me with those worshipful eyes that were so blue they practically glowed. Just being around him was a full-on ego stroke and the more time we spent together, the more I wanted him to stroke more than that. Which was odd because while I was open to bumping and grinding with an occasional dude, I preferred my all-female harem.

Although right now, I'd trade every last one of those models for a single dark-haired female with an ass I could bounce a quarter off of and a rack that made me sing soprano. Lee had me so worked up, I'd started having fracking wet dreams about her. It was embarrassing as shit. I'd even had to toss the Versace leather pants I'd slept in last night. No way would I risk Lee getting a hold of that mess during her laundry duty.

But damn. That dream last night, of Reed and me tag

teaming her, had been off the fracking chain. After we'd taken turns with Lee, Reed had his way with me. Which was fracking insane, because I never bottomed. *Ever.* But in the dream, I'd been game, and it had been fracking incredible. So much so, this morning I'd been willing to ditch red team training to help him out.

What the frack is wrong with me?

I never acted this way. I didn't do favors for people. They did favors for me. And I never chased after lovers. They chased after me.

So why was I acting like such a fool for Reed? Why did his happiness matter so much to me?

Maybe my attraction to him was a byproduct of my desire for Lee. The woman I wanted was into Reed, so I was into Reed. That kind of made sense in a twisted way. What didn't make sense was that Lee was also into my buzzkill brother.

Frack me. I mean, I had guitars with more sexual experience than Avi. And it wasn't like Mr. Stick in the Ass was interesting or had a way with the ladies. He was the most basic guy here. *Why would she frack him when she could have Reed, or better yet, both me and Reed?*

Scowling, I shoved the cafeteria door open with a little too much force. It cracked against the wall.

Hannah Richardson, a horse-faced, skinny brunette, who was setting the tables, let out a startled gasp, while her seven-year-old daughter squealed.

"It's him, mom! The guy from TV is back!" Amy, a younger version of her mom, jumped up and down, clapping her hands together. She wore a glitter-encrusted party hat on her head and every time she bounced off the ground, a silver shimmer dusted the air.

I schooled my face into an apologetic smile. "Sorry, ladies."

"You never need to apologize, Mr. Sighn," Hannah said in a breathless voice. She reached a hand up to fluff her hair and accidentally knocked into a stack of paper cups that exploded onto the floor.

"Mom, you're making a mess," Amy shouted at her red-faced mother.

"Here, let me help." I knelt down to gather the cups. When I set them on the table in front of Hannah, the woman's eyes glazed over.

"Can I have your autograph?" Amy asked, grabbing my arm.

Hannah snapped out of her daze and gave her daughter a stern look. "Amy, stop bothering Mr. Sighn."

"Call me Sai," I said with a smile that had Hannah flushing and fanning herself. "And yes, you can have an autograph." I grabbed one of the Happy New Year napkins off the table and pulled out the pen I always carried. "To a special girl. Rock on. Sai," I said, writing the words down on the napkin.

When I handed it to Amy, she beamed and showed it to her mom. "Now you can ask him to sign your tits?"

"Amy!" Hannah looked horrified.

"What? I heard you tell Aunt Tori you wanted him to—"

Hannah slapped her hand over her daughter's mouth and gave me an embarrassed smile. "Paula's in the kitchen."

"Great. Thank you." I made a beeline for the kitchen door before things got any more awkward.

The mouthwatering scent of ham and baked beans greeted me as I stepped inside.

The heavy-set older woman standing near the generator-powered ovens didn't notice me until I cleared my throat.

"Sai!" Paula exclaimed, spinning around. "You're back!"

"Just checking in on my wish list, doll." It'd been an hour

since I'd originally swung by with my requests. She should have had plenty of time to get things together.

"Well, I've got everything you asked for." Paula motioned at an overfilled box in the middle of the kitchen counter.

I peered inside. "And it looks as if you added a few other things too. Aren't you as sweet as a beehive full of honey."

Paula's face flushed, turning nearly the same shade as her badly dyed hair. "Well, you need some protein and fruit with all that junk food."

"Thank you, doll." I didn't mention it wasn't for me. Paula wouldn't be so willing to break Dominic's rules if she knew the food was for another woman.

"Anything for the Cocktail King." She fluttered her eyelashes. They were so clumped with mascara they reminded me of tarantula legs.

"You know, I'm your biggest fan."

How many times have I heard that? Still, it didn't hurt to be appreciative. I flashed her my signature dimpled smile and watched her breathing go ragged.

"Are you sure there isn't *anything* else I could get you?" She pointed at her teeth. "I've got full dentures. Have you ever had a gum job before?"

Frack no! I hid my revulsion with a smile. "I don't think your hubby would be on board with that."

"What Errol doesn't know won't hurt him." She giggled and her saggy breasts heaved under the floral apron she was wearing.

So used to people throwing themselves at me, I didn't miss a beat. "I'm beyond flattered, doll. But I have a rule about messing with married women." *Listen to me. I sound like fracking Dominic.*

Paula pouted and looked away. Something seemed to catch her eye. "Oh, I almost forgot. I think I have a solution to that bath you wanted."

If she suggests I strip so she can handwash me, I'm running, not walking, out of here.

Paula motioned me to follow her to the sink and pointed at a large covered plastic storage bin sitting under it. "The soldiers filled several bins like that with chlorinated water they got from one of the residential pools nearby. I guess they thought I could use it for dishwashing, but we're set right now with all the rain we've been having lately. Would you want the water? It's been filtered, so it's pretty clean."

"Hell, yeah. That's fantastic." Forgetting myself, I gave the old bird a hug. Getting Lee a bath had been the first item on Reed's list, but we'd run into nothing but roadblocks trying to pull that together. It didn't help that Dominic had recently ordered all water rationed. Every liter of drinking water was tracked, and green and yellow team members were only allowed sponge baths every other day. Red team members could still bathe daily, but I didn't imagine that would continue for long.

"You smell amazing." Paula pressed her lips against my neck and tugged on one of my necklaces.

Ugh. Clearly, today hadn't been her day to bathe. Trying not to gag on her old lady B.O., I gently stepped away. "How much of this water do you have?"

"Well, there's another bin this size in the pantry and there's a sixty-gallon bin that's half full outside." She motioned at the open kitchen windows.

At first, I couldn't see anything besides the generators used to power the stoves, but then I looked over at the outdoor eating area and saw the large covered black plastic tote by the picnic tables. "Perfect! It's even big enough to be a bathtub."

"And the water will be warm from being outside," Paula added, giving me a wide smile. "There's no one out there now. Why don't you take a dip? I'll keep watch."

I just bet she will. "Nah. I'll bathe inside. I have a thing about bugs." I gave a mock shiver.

She pursed her lips in disappointment. "Suit yourself. There are buckets in the storage room, but it'll take you forever to move all that water."

"I'll get my friend to help. Thank you again, doll." Giving her another dose of my thousand-watt smile, I picked up the box she'd packed and carried it out into the cafeteria. Thankfully, Hannah and her daughter were too busy setting plastic forks near the buffet to get in my way as I stepped out into the hallway.

I'd almost made it down to the double doors by the library when a familiar voice called out, "Hey, idiot. Why aren't you training with the rest of your team?"

⚜

I SPUN AROUND AND GLARED AT MY TALLER AND MUCH balder brother. "Hey, Buzzkill." Avi always hated when I called him that, but he deserved it. The dude wouldn't know fun if it bit him in the ass.

"You're this close to losing your place on red team." Avi held one hand up with his fingers an inch apart.

"No one wants to see the size of your package, bro," I said with a snicker. "And Bruce loves me." The red team leader was a huge fan of mine and he'd sooner throw one of his own brothers off the team than me.

Avi scowled. "Is that contraband?" He tried to peer in the box, but I swung it away.

"It's none of your fracking business, now if you don't mind." I tried to walk around him, but he moved in front of the doors, blocking my path.

"I do mind," Avi growled. "And I'm not putting my ass on the line to save you if you break Sarge's rules and get exiled."

"Good to know."

Avi stabbed a finger into my chest. "You need to get it into your head that you're not a big shot anymore. No one cares about your stupid band or your gold albums now."

"They're platinum, by the way. But thanks for your support, bro."

"Put that shit down and join your team outside." Avi stood there as if he fully expected me to follow his orders.

Why does he still think he can boss me around like I'm a child?

I huffed in frustration. Knowing that arguing with him would get me nowhere, I decided to tell him the truth. "I'm working on a project with Reed. Trying to keep the guy busy so he doesn't realize his girl is out on her field training test." I felt guilty for keeping Reed in the dark, but Lee must not have wanted him to know.

"She's not his girl," Avi said darkly.

"Oh, but she is. How does it feel to be a homewrecker, bro?"

Avi ground his molars together. "You're just jealous that she didn't fall for Sai Sighn's famous charm."

He was right, but I wasn't about to admit it. "Nah, bro. Even rock stars have lines we don't cross. You don't kick a man when he's down and you don't steal his woman while he's trying to get clean." I gave Avi the same disapproving look he was always giving me.

Avi looked stricken.

Wow. It felt good to knock the self-righteous prick down a few notches. All my life he'd lorded over the fact that he was older, stronger, and even had fracking superpowers. I mean, he could shift into a wolf whenever he wanted, not that he ever did. *What a waste.* Avi also got nearly all of mom's attention when she was around. I guess her all too human second son wasn't interesting enough for her. Neither she nor Avi gave a single shit about my fame and fortune.

Frack them.

Giving Avi another disapproving look, I pushed past him. Then I marched through the double doors and down the hallway until I got to the music room.

The door was closed. I had to kick it a couple of times before Reed finally heard me and opened it.

"Hey, man. Looks like you scored." The grin he flashed me took my motherfracking breath away. He had a face that could sell out stadiums the world over.

"Yeah." *Wish I could score with you and Lee.* Stepping into the large room, I set the box down next to the piano where we'd been setting up the gifts for Lee.

"Did Paula deliver?" he asked, digging through the box with an eagerness that made me laugh.

"For me, of course."

Reed lifted a bag of nacho chips in the air. "Yes! We have almost everything now. I wish we could have gotten the bath, but—"

"Oh, I've arranged that, too," I said, interrupting him. "Although we're going to have to carry a shitload of water here."

Reed's brows shot up. "Seriously? You got her a bath?"

"And the bathtub to go with it." I flashed him a cocky grin. "I'm Sai Sighn, I can make anything happen."

Reed ran over and hugged me. "Man, you're the greatest!"

I had to bite back a groan as he pulled me flush against him and slapped my back. *Frack.* The press of his lanky body against mine made my dick jump to attention. He was a few inches taller than me, but we fit together perfectly.

Why do I feel such a strong pull toward him? It was almost as strong as my attraction to Lee. I mean, even his scent was appealing. Earthy and slightly herbal. I pressed my nose into his long hair, still damp from his sponge bath, and inhaled deeply.

Reed jerked away, an adorably confused expression on his face. His lack of experience was such a turn on. Earlier in the week, he'd confessed that he'd only ever been with Lee.

"I like your shampoo. What do you use?" I asked, pretending I didn't see the impressive tent he'd pitched in his jeans.

Reed shrugged and crammed his hands into his pockets. "Whatever I find lying around. I'm not picky like you and Lee." He turned to look at the pile of items we'd gathered. "Once we get the bath set up, we'll be ready for Lee."

"Are you sure that's everything she desires?" I teased.

"Yes, except for the damn threesome she wants with me and Avi," Reed said in a bitter voice.

Threesome? You better believe I didn't let that slip by. "If it's a threesome she wants, I'm game." I kept my tone light in case he took offense.

Instead of glaring at me or laughing, Reed gave me an assessing look.

Is he considering it? Frack me. My heart sped up and my palms grew clammy. "I've had plenty of experience with group stuff. You just tell me what you're comfortable with and I'll make it happen." I knew I was rambling, but I felt as if I was suddenly in the middle of a job interview, and I didn't want to blow it.

But I do want to blow him. My mouth watered as I gave the gorgeous guy another once over.

Reed gave a slow nod. "Okay."

"Okay?" I repeated slowly, trying to stay calm. *He probably doesn't mean what I think he means.*

"Yeah, why the hell not, man? I mean, if Lee has her heart set on a threesome, I'd rather do it with a dude I wan... I like, than Avi."

He wants me. Frack. Reed and Lee... together! It was literally my dream come true.

"It'll be epic," I promised. Suddenly, I was as giddy as a fat guy at an all you can eat buffet. *Screw last year. This New Year's Eve is going to be off the motherfracking chain.*

※ 6 ※

LEE

Dominic was as talkative as a statue as we made our way back to the school. I tried several times to engage him in conversation, only to earn the sergeant's signature icy glare.

So much for our little truce and so much for trying to get to know the guy. Although now that I thought about it, maybe the mystery was part of his appeal. I really knew nothing about him. Not his age. Not his interests outside of ordering people around. Not even what his personal life was like.

He could be married for all I know.

My stomach twisted as an unpleasant wave of jealousy rolled through me. The feeling was ridiculous and completely unfair since I already had two other men in my life and neither Avi nor Reed were happy about sharing me. *Tough shit.* I'd never commit to only one person. Forming that kind of exclusive attachment could set me up for falling in love— something I refused to do. Romantic love was toxic. It warped people into monsters. Just look at what my father did.

I swallowed back the echoes of grief, wishing my sister

had learned from our mother's fatal mistake. Instead, Eden had fallen hard and fast for Mike, Dominic's second in command. She even wore one of Mike's dog tags on the collar around her neck to show her commitment to the soldier.

I'll bet Dominic is thrilled about that.

Maybe Dominic is in a committed relationship, too. It would explain his refusal to act on the crazy chemistry burning between us.

I glanced down at the bare fingers on the massive soldier's left hand. He wasn't wearing a ring, but that didn't mean anything. I could fill a warehouse with the number of married ringless men who frequented the club where I'd worked.

Thoughts of Eros had me glancing behind us. We were only fifteen miles north of the club and my home, not that I would dream of venturing through downtown to go back there. If we were seeing bigger hordes of Biters here, I could only imagine the legions of dead congregating there.

Something caught my eye. If I peered hard enough, I could just make out plumes of smoke darkening the sky in the distance. *What the hell?* The smoke seemed to be coming from the south valley, which was primarily known for its luxury resorts, hiking trails, and exclusive spas.

"Come on," Dominic called back, looking annoyed that I'd stopped.

I scurried around an abandoned, blood-covered scooter to catch up with him. "What do you think is burning back there?"

I didn't expect him to answer me, but he said, "The Calaveras are lighting fires to drive the dead north."

I shivered at the mention of the deadliest gang in the southwest. Unfortunately, I was well acquainted with its leader. Not only had Javier Diaz attended my shows at the club, but he'd also made me an indecent proposal. Even worse, he'd sent his men after me the day the world went to hell. Those goons had killed my uncle and beat Reed unconscious.

I tightened my fingers around my knife. What I wouldn't give to bury the blade deep in Javier's chest. *No one hurts my family and walks away.* If I ever crossed paths with him again, I'd make the drug lord pay.

"Ms. Walker," Dominic said in a low voice.

I slowly realized I was holding my knife above my head. Trying to act as if I hadn't just spaced out, I lowered my hand and cleared my throat. "How do you know it's the Calaveras? Anyone could be lighting fires." *Hell. If it repels zombies, maybe we should light some fires, too.*

"Mike did some reconnaissance on his way back to base," Dominic answered.

"So that's where Mike went," I muttered. Eden had been wallowing around like a sad sack of potatoes since her lover disappeared.

Dominic grunted. "Mike said the Calaveras are using drones to scan for female survivors."

I blinked. "What, like to save them?"

Dominic's dark look was answer enough.

"That's horrible." I clasped my knife even more tightly in my hand. *Crap.* Now, in addition to zombies and body-snatching demons, I needed to watch out for rapist gang members.

"This is war," Dominic said, his voice edged in bitterness.

He's right. We are at war. With the dead. With the virus. With each other.

Taking a deep breath, I tried to look unshaken. "Did Mike make it to the army base?" *And more importantly, are we finally getting rescued?*

Dominic's expression could have been carved from granite. "He's gone radio silent."

That didn't sound promising. "When was the last time you heard from him?"

"Nearly seventy-two hours ago. I'd ordered him to get a closer look at the Calaveras' compound." Dominic scrubbed a hand over his close-cropped hair. "At this point I have to assume he's been captured or—"

"Killed," I finished for him.

"Yes." Although his face was impassive, I sensed the fate of his soldier really bothered him. And Dominic wasn't the only one who'd be bothered.

Dammit to hell. Eden was going to lose her mind when she found out. Although the fallout from her imminent heartbreak would be minor compared with the frightening consequences of this new threat. If the Calaveras kept driving zombies north, we'd be overtaken or find ourselves trapped inside the school.

Anxiety formed a ball in the back of my throat. It evaporated when I remembered Eden's recent suggestion that we move the safe house. Earlier in the week, she'd mentioned how much nicer it'd be to ride out the apocalypse in one of the palatial estates in the foothills.

I turned to Dominic. "We should all head further north. There are mansions in the foothills equipped with water, solar power, and hard-core security."

When we were kids, Gran worked for a luxury house cleaning service. Sometimes she'd bring Eden and me to her jobs. Although we were supposed to stay out of trouble, once Eden and I had gone exploring and accidentally opened the door to a hidden panic room. The amount of food, weapons, and supplies inside had amazed us.

I bet we can find that house again.

"It's only another ten or so miles north. We'd be safer up there." The estate with the panic room was enclosed by a twenty-foot-tall stone wall. I'd much rather bet my life on that than the school fence.

Dominic frowned. "We're not moving."

"What? Why?"

"My orders are to keep you and the others on the list at the school until we're evacuated. That's where we will remain."

I frowned at his mention of the mysterious list his superiors had given him. He and his squad had been ordered to locate and rescue everyone on it. Most of the people on the list included the family members of soldiers from the nearby military base. It made sense for the army to bring their loved ones to safety. But the only soldier Eden and I were related to was long dead.

May he rot in hell.

Needing answers, I said, "Why is my name on your list? I don't have any army connections."

Dominic ignored my question. "We're not moving the safe house and that's final."

"No one's coming to save us." There'd been no contact from the army base and the evacuation date had come and gone. Yet, Dominic insisted on waiting for help that would never arrive. "If we don't go somewhere safer, we'll all die."

The hard line of his jaw told me I might as well be arguing with that twenty-foot stone wall in the foothills.

Dammit. I hated that he unilaterally made all the decisions —decisions that could mean life or death for the people I cared about.

Feeling uneasy, I glanced back at the smoke in the distance. I'd need to share this with Eden, Reed, and Avi.

Seeming to read my mind, Dominic said, "You'll not discuss this with anyone. That's an order."

What the hell? "People need to know what's going on."

He shook his head. "The last thing we need is civilians

panicking. Besides, we have much bigger problems than the Calaveras driving the infected north. Now keep up." He took off so fast, he was almost a blur.

How can he move like that?

Wondering if he was genetically engineered like Hunter, I jogged through the empty strip mall and found him crouched down near the bus stop across from the school.

I gave him a dirty look. "How am I supposed to keep up if you—"

Dominic held up his hand, silencing me. Tension rolled off him in waves as he pointed in the direction of the rioting mob in front of the school gates.

Crap! I clamped my mouth shut, even though the shambling corpses couldn't possibly hear me over their own deafening chorus. The cacophony of their rattling moans and gnashing teeth filled the rancid-smelling air.

❦

I KNELT DOWN NEXT TO DOMINIC, WATCHING DOZENS OF our ravenous enemies claw at the school fence. Even with the front gates reinforced with school buses, an even larger horde could easily smash their way through.

Which is why we need to leave...

But this wasn't the time to try to change Dominic's mind about relocating. This was the time to focus on getting back inside the school without getting torn apart.

Oh, God. If I screw this up, we'll both die. My stomach flipped and I broke out in a cold sweat.

"Ready?" Dominic asked in a low voice.

No! As my heart took up a frenzied beat inside my chest, I reminded myself that Dominic trained me for this. What's more, I had the deadly sergeant as my escort.

He won't let anything happen to me.

I don't know why I was so sure of that, but I was willing to bet my life on it. Taking a deep breath, I rolled my shoulders like an athlete preparing to compete. And in a way, we were competing. Us versus them. Life versus death.

"Lee?" Dominic's cinnamon breath caressed my skin, warming my insides.

"Let's do this," I whispered.

Dominic signaled Darcy, the dark-skinned soldier standing on the roof of the school. She called down to the soldiers and red team members manning the gates.

Bang. Bang. Bang.

In a shark frenzy of movement, the mob rushed around the side of the school, following whichever soldier was banging a metal pipe against the fence.

"Now." Dominic grabbed my arm and dragged me across the street.

What the hell? I stumbled, trying to keep up with his huge strides.

Although I'd trained for this dangerous maneuver, none of those scenarios involved reentry to the school while in his death grip.

"Let me go."

Ignoring my request, Dominic hauled me into his arms and raced to the school bus parked closest to the fence. Then he all but threw me onto the hood. "Go. Go. Go."

Trying to catch my breath, I clambered over the cracked windshield and onto the roof of the bus with Dominic on my heels.

Apparently, I wasn't moving fast enough because he grabbed me around the waist and swung me over onto the roof of the school bus parked inside the school grounds.

Several soldiers and members of red team gawked at us from the schoolyard. Avi was among them.

Embarrassed, I tried to push Dominic away. "Dammit. I don't need your help."

"I disagree." The sergeant's shockingly warm fingers clamped down on my hips. He seemed in no hurry to release me.

"Let me go." I rammed my elbow into his lower stomach, which wasn't protected by his tactical vest. I rejoiced at the sound of his grunt, but then his thick biceps tightened like bands of steel around me.

"Don't bite the hand that feeds you," he snarled into my ear.

Oh, he wants to see biting. Anger and a streak of recklessness had me dropping my head and clamping my teeth down on his bare forearm just above the strange device that seemed grafted to his skin. I bit down, not hard enough to do any damage, but hard enough to show I wasn't to be manhandled.

Instead of releasing me, he clenched me so tightly the knives strapped to his vest dug into my back. "Harder," he groaned, his voice thick and husky.

Suddenly, I was hyperaware of him crushed against me. Everything around us—the blazing sun, the grim chorus of the dead, our audience below—faded away. Every one of my senses zoomed in on the rasp of his hot breath on my ear and the massive erection pressed against my ass.

Holy crap. He does have a monster cock.

A rush of desire slammed into me so fast and hard, my knees nearly gave out. Good thing there was a muscular body to support me—a very aroused body. My breathing went choppy as the proof of Dominic's attraction throbbed between us.

He wants me.

My nipples tightened under his arm, and heat pooled between my legs. Unable to help myself, I bit down harder and rocked back against him. His smooth bronze skin broke under my teeth, and I tasted the coppery tang of his blood on my tongue.

"Christ, Lee." Dominic thrust against me.

It seemed pain was a major turn on for the sergeant. *Why is that hot as hell?*

The banging on the side of the fence stopped. Without the sound to distract them, the Biters rushed back to the gates below us. We were in no danger though, and the sounds of their moans and clicking teeth didn't dull my arousal for a second. My blood turned to wildfire as I bit down harder.

"What are you doing to me?" Dominic groaned.

"Let her go!"

Dominic snapped his head around to see Avi running over.

Avi's hazel eyes sparked with fury. "Get your hands off her. She's mine."

Shocked that Avi would make that kind of possessive claim, I tore my mouth from Dominic's arm.

Avi bounded onto the bus roof in front of us.

There wasn't time to process the impossibility of my lover jumping eleven feet straight off the ground because Dominic moved in front of me and shoved me back so fast I fell.

The unflattering sound of my ass hitting the bus roof was drowned out by an unearthly growl.

"Calm down, soldier," Dominic ordered.

"Get. Away. From. Her." The rumbling growl grew louder.

What the hell is going on? I couldn't see past Dominic's legs.

"Move the civilians out of here!" Dominic shouted to his soldiers.

On the ground, Ren and Jace hustled the red team members into the school.

In front of me, Dominic slowly unsheathed a knife and moved into a defensive stance that allowed me a direct view of Avi.

But my willow tree was nearly unrecognizable. His hazel eyes glowed with an eerie light, and coarse black hair sprouted across every inch of his rapidly expanding body. Even more horrifying, his nose protruded into a snout and his jaw elongated and filled with sharp fangs. "Get away from my mate," he snarled.

What is happening?

I bit back a hysterical scream as Avi's muscular chest burst through his T-shirt and he fell forward onto hands that morphed into claw-tipped paws.

As I shook my head in denial of what I was seeing, Avi tore off his pants and boots. There was a loud crunching noise as his bones and muscles contorted. A moment later, the largest wolf I'd ever seen in my life stood snarling in his place.

Holy crap! He's a werewolf. I've been screwing a werewolf!

�֍ 7 ֍

AVI

Rage gripped me as I stared down the male threatening my female.

Lee's my mate.

The realization staggered me. She was human. I was Lykos. It should have been an impossible pairing. But the moment I saw her fighting to escape Sarge's punishing hold, I knew with a primal certainty she was mine and I'd kill anyone who hurt her.

Including my commanding officer.

My razor-sharp claws scraped the metal roof as I stalked closer to Sarge.

I no longer cared he was a Titan soldier genetically engineered to be my alpha. He'd abused my female for the last time.

The fake zombie attack Sarge staged last week triggered Lee's PTSD and put her into a comatose state for hours. And now, after forcing her through a punishing field test—a test my sister told me Lee failed—Sarge dared attack my female again.

He'll die for hurting her.

I dropped my gaze to Lee, who stared out at me from between Sarge's legs. Her eyes were wide with fear and her lips were streaked with blood.

She's bleeding.

My chest rumbled as my growl deepened. All higher-level thinking faded under the onslaught of my wolf's primitive urges.

Kill him. Protect her.

All my life I'd kept my beast suppressed by wearing silver. Although chained, it had always been there, pacing just under the surface. Since I'd cast off the cursed metal to mate with Lee, it had grown strong—strong enough to take over.

Instead of fearing the loss of control, I felt powerful and whole for the first time in my life.

My snout peeled back as I bared my teeth at Sarge. It was the only warning I'd give him.

Sarge blinked at me as if coming into some kind of realization. He glanced at Lee and then back at me. "You think Lee is your mate?"

Unable to answer, I crouched down, readying for my attack. From an early age, my mother had instilled in me a healthy fear of the Titan handlers like him. They used military technology to bind shifters. She'd warned me that if I removed the silver, I'd risk being enslaved by them.

But I was no longer afraid. Sarge was the only handler here and, since he was already paired with another beast, he couldn't bind me. Besides, after the line he'd just crossed with my mate, I was done respecting his authority.

He's no longer my alpha.

Sinking back on my hind legs, I prepared to lunge.

"Avi, I didn't hurt her," Sarge said in a low voice. He sheathed his knife and motioned Lee to come closer. "Lee, tell him."

Lee slowly stood and peered out at me from around

Sarge's arm. "Dominic didn't hurt me. He was trying to help." She paused and glared at Sarge for a moment. "Although, I didn't need his help." She sounded annoyed, not terrorized.

"We'll agree to disagree." Sarge sounded exasperated, not angry.

As my inner wolf whined in confusion, the red haze in my mind slowly cleared and I saw the situation in a new light.

Sarge hadn't been attacking her. Rather, he'd been trying to assert his dominance the way any alpha would. But my oak tree was too stubborn to submit to him. She was just as alpha as he was. And when forced into close proximity, two alphas of the opposite sex either fought to the death or...

Mated...

I sniffed the air, picking up the sweet musk of her arousal through the stench of decay.

Shit. She desires him.

Not that it should be any surprise. The two of them had been eye-fucking each other for weeks. I gnashed my teeth together, wanting to hurt Sarge even more.

"Avi?" Lee whispered. Her terrified expression arrowed me in the heart.

She fears me. Ah, hell. That was the last thing I wanted. If she claimed me, we'd be able to telepathically communicate through our mate-bond, and I could tell her not to be afraid. But I'd never heard of a human claiming a shifter.

Even worse, the soul-deep connection I had with her appeared to be one-sided. Not only did I have to share her affections with her fruitcake boyfriend, Lee only wanted me to touch her when Sarge was watching.

I'd never let on that I knew he was there or that I'd repeatedly heard her cry out his name instead of mine. Like an idiot, I'd thought eventually she'd get bored with whatever twisted game she was playing with the already mate-bonded sergeant, and then she'd fall for me as hard as I'd fallen for her.

Obviously, I'd been wrong.

As Lee moved closer to the other male, my hackles rose.

Sarge reached back and anchored her tightly against him while she clenched his arm in a white-knuckled grip.

The legendary Titan hated people touching him. Everyone knew that. And yet, here he was, allowing her to seek comfort from him while he shielded her with his body.

How fucked is that? She's mine, not his. Sarge had already been claimed by his Titan wife. They'd even formalized their bond with a human ceremony. Although females occasionally claimed multiple mates, it was unheard of for a mate-bonded male shifter or Titan to do so. Sarge should have been the last guy I had to worry about.

So why is he acting as if Lee is his mate? I let out a low whine and sat back on my haunches.

"Glad you came to your senses." Sarge motioned at the Titans who'd surrounded the bus. "At ease, soldiers. Back to your posts."

Jace and Ren slowly lowered their weapons. Darcy, who was peering down the scope of her sniper rifle, took her finger off the trigger.

I let out a ragged breath, realizing how close I'd come to dying. The three Titans would have blown me to pieces the moment I attacked their sergeant.

If I die, who will look out for my family?

Sai, Zara, and Dev were still too young and reckless to survive in this new world. Unlike me, they were human, and they hadn't spent their formative years being trained to fight like a Special Forces soldier. My mother entrusted me to protect them, and I couldn't very well do that if I was dead.

"You fucked up, Avi," Sarge said, leveling me with his dark glare.

Isn't that the understatement of the year? Not only had I broken a dozen military laws by attacking my commanding officer, but I'd also shifted in front of a human. The penalty for that alone was death. But even the threat of dying paled compared to an even greater worry.

Lee won't want me now.

Hanging my head, I took a deep breath and shifted back to my human form. It'd been so long since I'd done that, I'd forgotten how amazing it was to have every single ache and pain vanish. The scar on my hand from an old hunting accident disappeared, along with the niggling soreness in my lower back and right knee. But I couldn't enjoy the sensation of being fully healed when I was filled with dread.

What happens now?

❧

"Cover yourself, soldier," Sarge barked.

Not about to push the Titan handler further, I grabbed my shredded pants and tied them around my hips. Then, bracing myself for rejection, I finally looked at Lee.

She twisted out of Sarge's grip and stared at me. "You just turned into a motherfucking wolf."

"Surprise," I said, lamely.

Lee glanced down at the soldiers who'd sauntered back to their posts. "But they don't look surprised." She turned to Sarge. "And you don't look surprised, Dominic. Why? Did you know about him being a werewolf?"

When Sarge didn't respond, her eyes widened. "Are you a werewolf too? Are they?" Her breath came in gasps as she motioned at the soldiers.

Sarge sighed deeply. "No. Avi is the only Lykos here."

"Lykos," Lee mouthed, looking completely shellshocked. "You've called him that before. It means werewolf?"

It was my turn to give Sarge a sharp look. Sharing information about our species was forbidden.

Seems I'm not the only one breaking military law.

Sarge returned my glare. "We'll discuss this in my office. Both of you meet me there in five." Then, without another word, Sarge jumped off the bus and strode over to where Darcy now stood on the school steps.

That left Lee and me staring at each other across the bus roof in awkward silence.

Hating the distance between us, I took a step forward. She didn't back up which I took as a good sign.

Holding my hands up in front of me in the universal sign of peace, I said, "You don't have to be afraid. I'm still the same guy. I'm still your willow tree."

"Are you?" she asked softly. "You don't look the same. You're a lot bigger."

She was right. I felt taller. My shoulders were broader, my biceps were thicker, and my abs were more defined than before.

She patted the top of her head. "You've got hair now."

I reached up, surprised to find a thatch of dark curls instead of my smoothly shaved skull. "Weird."

She let out a hysterical laugh. "Weird doesn't even cover it. Why didn't you tell me about this?"

I shrugged, trying to get used to my larger frame. "It's not something I'm allowed to discuss. And I've only shifted a couple of times before. The silver band I wear keeps this side of me suppressed."

Lee motioned at my bare arm. "The pretty armband?"

I nodded. "I stopped wearing it so you and I could... be together."

She blinked, clearly trying to take it all in. "This is crazier than Reed being possessed by a body-snatching demon."

It was my turn to give her a strange look. "What?"

She waved her hand dismissively and slowly crossed the roof toward me. "You're not going to bite me, are you?"

I couldn't resist saying, "Not unless you want me to."

Her laugh was weak, but I welcomed it anyway. She was handling this way better than I could have expected.

"Your eyes are a pretty amber color now." She stopped a few feet away, her gaze slowly moving up and down my body. "I have to say I like the changes."

"I'm glad." I wondered why this shift had dramatically changed my human body. Maybe I was always meant to be this size, but suppressing my wolf had stunted my growth all these years.

"Did every part of you get bigger?" Lee asked, glancing down at my crotch.

The heat in her eyes filled me with so much relief, my knees nearly buckled. *Thank fuck. She still wants me.*

Playing it cool, I said, "I don't know. Maybe you should come over here and check it out."

Giving me a coy smile, she crossed the distance between us.

I dragged her into my arms, savoring her closeness. "I'm sorry I scared you. I thought Sarge was hurting you and it triggered my beast."

"Beast. That's kind of sexy." She playfully pinched my nipple. "Maybe you can show me your... beast later."

"Yeah." My shaft thickened.

She pushed away from me as if thinking of something. "Better yet, show my sister."

I blinked at her. "What?"

"Eden is going to lose her mind. You know how nuts she is about animals, and dogs are her absolute favorite."

I pulled away, slightly offended. "I'm not a dog."

She wrapped her arms around my waist. "Of course not. You're a big, ferocious wolf. My big, ferocious wolf."

Her teasing tone worked to ease the tension from my body. I kissed the top of her head, feeling damn grateful for her acceptance. Maybe me losing control had been a good thing. Now there were no secrets between us. *There's nothing keeping us apart...*

"You two, my office!" Sarge shouted.

Except him.

I twisted around to see Sarge glaring at us from the school steps. His menacing expression told me I would pay a heavy price for my insubordination.

Fuck. What's he going to do?

⚓ 8 ⚓

LEE

"Move it," Dominic called out from the school steps.

"Asshole," I mumbled against Avi's bare chest. So what if Dominic tried to protect me from Avi a few minutes ago? That didn't change anything. The sergeant was still a pain in the ass, and he could wait a goddamn minute.

Avi's significantly more muscular arms tightened around me for a moment before he released me. I stared up into his face, marveling at the changes in his appearance. His rugged jaw was thicker, his cheekbones more angular, and his eyes were now a beautiful burnished gold.

Wow. If Avi had been attractive before, he was panty incinerating now. He might even give Reed, Sai, and Dominic a run for their money, and that was saying something.

Do werewolves get better looking every time they shift? If so, I was going to encourage him to wolf-out all the damn time.

Oh, God. What am I thinking? He's a werewolf.

"This is so crazy." I shook my head, still trying to wrap my mind around it. It was too unbelievable. And yet, I'd seen him transform with my own eyes.

My hands trembled, and I sucked in a deep, steadying breath. It was spiked with Avi's familiar woodsy scent. Immediately, my pulse slowed.

It's still Avi. He's just bigger. Hotter. And wolfier... Is that even a word? I'm going to make it a word.

I straightened my shoulders, deciding that after living through the past month, I could deal with this. *Hell*. The apocalypse had already shattered my concept of reality. Avi being a werewolf was just par for the course. It was one more crazy thing that I'd have to accept, like body-snatching demons and the mob of zombies rattling the fence below us.

"So, when do the vampires show up?" I joked, trying not to sound as shaken as I felt.

Avi scoffed. "Thankfully, the military scientists never engineered those."

"But they engineered you?" I asked, running my hand over the impressive swell of his pectoral muscles. According to Dominic, the military scientists had been genetically engineering super soldiers like Hunter.

Just what the hell were those army scientists doing, and how is any of it legal? I mean, there were laws against experimenting on people. *Aren't there?*

Avi shook his head. "Not me specifically, but my kind and other shifter species."

My jaw dropped. "They are other shifters? What like bears? Cats? Raccoons? How cool would a raccoon shifter be?" My recently deceased best friend, Cami, would have had a field day with this.

Avi's deep laugh rumbled against my ear. "The army designed us as bioweapons. So, sorry to disappoint, but there are no raccoon shifters."

I faked a pout. "A raccoon shifter would be totally badass."

"I'm waiting," Dominic shouted, sounding even more annoyed.

Avi sighed. "I've got to pay the piper."

"What do you mean?"

"There are military laws against shifting in front of civilians."

"But you're not in the military, are you?" I'd thought he'd worked in private security, but then I'd also thought he was human.

"No, but my mom is and any offspring of hers are subject to the same laws."

Gears clicked together in my mind. "Are Sai, Dev, and Zara wer—Lykos like you?"

"No, we all had different fathers. I got my shifting abilities from mine, whoever the hell he was."

"Right." I remembered Sai, Dev, and Zara mentioning they'd never known their sperm donors. Apparently, their Special Forces mom didn't like being tied down to any one guy. She and I had that in common.

Avi bent down to grab the boots he'd discarded and flashed me a mouthwatering view of his muscular ass.

While I hummed my approval, Avi made a sound of disappointment. His boots now appeared several sizes too small for his feet.

"I don't have all day," Dominic groused from the bottom of the steps.

"Coming," Avi shouted. In a blur of motion, he jumped off the bus roof and landed smoothly on the ground below. "Come on, Lee."

Feeling apprehensive, I looked over the edge of the roof. It seemed like a big drop.

Avi held up his arms. "Jump, I'll catch you."

His words triggered a memory of my father. Years ago, back before... before that night, my father would often play a trust game with my sisters and me. He'd set us on top of our old clothes dryer and order us to jump off into his arms.

Angel and Eden always jumped without hesitation. But I refused, much to his frustration. My father had always assumed it was because of a fear of heights, but maybe I'd sensed the darkness inside him even then.

"Come on. I won't drop you. Look at these guns." Avi flexed his impressive biceps. They'd gained a few inches, along with his height. He was easily as tall as Dominic now.

Damn. I'd always found tall guys sexy and now it seemed I was surrounded by them. The sudden mental image of me sandwiched between a naked Dominic and Avi took my breath away.

How can I make that a reality?

"Christ, what's taking so long?" Dominic marched around the side of the bus, his scowl destroying my fantasy.

"I think she's afraid to jump," Avi answered.

"I heard that." I rubbed my damp palms on my jeans. I'd just faced down a freaking werewolf and a pissed off Dominic.

I can handle this.

Dominic, who looked as if he was about to lose whatever shred of patience he had left, shouted, "Get down here."

"Where's the ladder?" I looked around the schoolyard for the ladder. It was normally set against the side of the bus.

Lifting his arms higher, Avi said, "I've got you. Trust me."

"Lee," Dominic said, his midnight eyes locking on mine. "Don't think. Just jump."

In a move that surprised even me, I vaulted over the side of the bus and crashed into Dominic.

He sprawled back on his ass with me on top of him.

"You were supposed to catch me!" I shouted.

Dominic shoved me off. "And you were supposed to jump to him." He motioned at Avi.

"Well, you should have been clearer," I snarled, rolling to my feet.

"I would have caught you," Avi said, trying to mask his

disappointment. At that moment, I felt as if I'd failed another important test.

Trying to ease the sting, I walked over, rose on the balls of my feet, and kissed Avi's cheek. "I know you would have, willow tree."

That earned me a smile.

Avi laced his fingers through mine as we followed Dominic across the schoolyard, up the steps, and through the glass doors of the school.

I'D NEVER HELD HANDS ROMANTICALLY BEFORE. IT FELT strangely nice and comforting to have Avi's fingers entwined with my own. Even so, I yanked my hand away once we stepped inside the school.

Reed was already sensitive about the whole open relationship thing. I definitely didn't want to throw it in his face. Thankfully, neither Reed nor anyone else was in sight. The hallway was quiet as Dominic led us around the front desk, through an admin area, and into the principal's office he'd claimed for himself.

It'd been a week since I'd last been in the oversized space, but it looked the same. Shiny framed diplomas competed for wall space with imposing floor to ceiling bookcases. An obscenely long black leather couch sprawled next to a table decorated with a pretty, but completely useless, stained-glass Tiffany lamp.

The expensive-looking ebony desk in the back was still blanketed in knives. However, now there was a single round unlit candle resting in the center of those wicked-looking blades.

Damn. I'd forgotten all about that vanilla candle. I'd brought it with me when I'd broken into Dominic's office last week. At the time, I'd been desperate to find the demon who'd possessed Reed. Only I hadn't found a demon. I'd found something else.

Hunter.

Unable to help myself, I scanned the area behind the desk until I spotted the outline of Hunter's ten-foot-long muscle-packed body underneath a green blanket.

He's still here. Or at least his body is. None of us knew where Hunter's consciousness was. If there was any justice in the world, he'd been vanquished to hell where he belonged.

I'd never forgive the bastard for possessing Reed's body and taking my virginity. *Our virginities*, I amended. Reed had been as inexperienced as I before Hunter intervened.

Mistaking my shudder, Avi wrapped his arm around my waist and pulled me into his side. "Cold?"

I shook my head, my gaze on Dominic.

The sergeant closed the door and stalked to the back of the office. "I have a problem."

I snorted. "You have a lot of problems."

He gave me a frosty glare as he leaned against the desk. "Silence, Ms. Walker."

Oh, so we are back to titles now.

He turned his scowl on Avi. "You just broke every rule in the book, soldier."

Avi dropped his gaze to the floor. "I'm sorry, sir. My only defense is that I thought you were attacking my..." he glanced at me and then back at Dominic, "... Lee."

"You said she was your mate."

Avi tensed and gave me an unfathomable look. "Yes."

Mate?

"Are you his mate, Ms. Walker?"

I didn't even try to hide my confusion. "What does that even mean? I like screwing him, but you already know that.

Don't you, sir?" I intended my tone to be mocking, but it came out flirtatious.

Dominic's eyes flared with hunger. Then, seeming to get a handle on his emotions, he cleared his throat. "I can't have a rogue shifter in the school. Avi, you have two options. Wear silver or become my beast."

"No!" Avi shouted.

I looked between the two men, feeling as if I was missing something big. "What's he talking about?"

Avi glanced at me, his body thrumming with tension. "He's threatening to enslave me—bind me to him so I'm forced to obey everything he says."

What? "He can do that?"

The tic in Dominic's jaw twitched. "I'll do whatever is necessary to ensure the safety of the civilians under my protection."

"You're not making him your slave." I turned to Avi. "Can't you just wear the pretty armband?"

Avi's expression tightened. "It makes me unable to fu..." He trailed off, but I got the drift, and I didn't like that one bit.

"There's another option." I gave Dominic a mutinous look. "We leave. It's actually the safer option anyway since the Calaveras are driving all the zombies in Saguaro Valley here."

Avi gave me a confused look. "Calaveras?"

"It's a gang," I explained.

Dominic scowled at me. "I gave you an order not to discuss that, Ms. Walker."

Screw him. I'd had enough. Enough tests. Enough rules. Enough Dominic. "I'm sick of your damn orders."

Dominic grimaced. "And I'm sick of your lack of appreciation. There's the door. Go. Both of you. And take your families with you. As of this moment, you're all exiled from the safe house."

Wait. What? It was one thing to leave on my terms. It was another to be thrown out.

"Go," Dominic said, pointing at the door.

Wow. Obviously, he doesn't give a crap about me. Feeling stung, I lifted my chin. "Fine. We'll get packed and—"

"You take nothing. No food. No weapons. No supplies. Just your family members and what you're wearing."

"That's not fair. Avi is practically naked!" I shouted.

Dominic pushed off the desk and stepped into my face. "What's not fair is working day and night for weeks to protect and train an entitled bitch who doesn't follow orders or show an ounce of gratitude. You don't even realize how good you have it here. But you'll learn soon enough."

Did that asshole just call me a bitch? I rose on my toes so I could glare back at him. "We'll be fine without you and your stupid rules."

"You'll die—"

Avi interrupted Dominic. "I'll wear the silver, sir."

Outraged, I spun around. "No, you won't—"

Dominic strode over to his desk, grabbed something off it, and tossed it to Avi.

Avi caught it over my head. It was the silver armband he'd thrown on the floor of the computer room the first time we'd had sex.

"Don't remove it without my permission," Dominic warned.

"Yes, sir." Avi fit the piece of jewelry around his arm and winced.

"Does it hurt?" I asked.

"It saps my energy," he answered, lines of strain bracketing his eyes and mouth. Addressing Dominic, he asked, "Now can we stay?"

"That depends on your... mate." Dominic dragged out the word, turning it into a taunt.

I put my hand on Avi's shoulder. "You don't have to do this. We can make it on our own. We don't need him." I glared at Dominic.

Such a cold-hearted bastard. How can he just exile us?

Avi shook his head. "I alone can't keep us safe."

"You wouldn't have to. Your sister and brothers are badass—"

Avi cut me off. "Dev is still a teenager, Zara refuses to listen to anything I say, and Sai will get distracted by the first pair of zombie tits he sees."

"But I can—"

"You failed your field test, Zara told me. She and Dev beat you back home by a half an hour."

"I didn't fail." I glanced at Dominic, hoping he might come to my defense.

The sergeant only glared back at me.

Avi continued, "And Fruitcake couldn't even get through tryouts."

My heart sank. "Reed didn't make yellow team?"

"He ran into the soccer post."

Dominic's cough sounded suspiciously like a laugh.

I gasped. "Is he okay?"

"He's fine, but he won't last an hour out there." Avi stabbed his finger at the mini-blind covered window. "Our best chance of survival is here."

"Your only chance," Dominic added.

Avi and I ignored him.

"But we won't be able to be together." My midnight sexcapades with him and Dominic were the only thing keeping me sane.

Avi gave me a pained look and opened his mouth to say something.

Dominic interrupted. "As of now, I'll allow you and your families to remain here. Don't give me a reason to change my mind. You're dismissed."

I stepped away from Avi. "That's it?" *Dominic isn't going to discipline us for insubordination?*

Dominic gave a curt nod.

"No punishment?" I couldn't help asking.

Avi gave me a what-the-hell look, but I didn't trust Sergeant Pain in the Ass to let us off so easily. Not when Avi full on attacked him and I practically chewed his arm to the bone outside. I glanced at Dominic's arm, but I couldn't find a mark on it.

Strange. Maybe I hadn't bitten him as hard as I remembered.

Dominic's top lip curled. "I've neutered your lover, Ms. Walker. I think that is punishment enough."

Dammit. Yes. It was. Now there'd be no stolen moments in the computer lab—no Avi ravaging my body while Dominic's searing gaze ravaged my soul. My mood plummeted to the carpeted floor, but I didn't want Dominic to think he'd bested me.

He doesn't know who he's dealing with. Tossing back my hair I said, "I guess there'll be no more midnight shows for you, sergeant."

Dominic stiffened, seeming to realize he'd punished himself too.

Point for me.

Clenching his jaw, he pointed at the door. "Corporal Ross is waiting to do your bite check, Ms. Walker. Best not to keep her waiting."

"Right." I wasn't about to argue with that rule. We had strict bite check protocols to prevent the infected from getting inside. But my inner tramp made me blurt out, "Why don't you just do it?" Without waiting for him to respond, I dragged my shirt and cami over my head and tossed them at Dominic's shiny boots.

Avi tried to grab my arm. "What are you doing?"

"My bite check." I shook him off, kicked off my sneakers, and yanked down my pants. "Also, I'm kind of hoping one or both of you throws me down on that desk and screws me senseless."

Both men went motionless.

"Put your clothes back on, Ms. Walker."

"But what about my bite check, sir?" I said, fluttering my eyelashes.

Tension in the room thickened as I slowly shimmied out of my panties and tossed them at Dominic.

His lightning-fast reflexes must have been taking a nap, because the tiny scrap of lace hung on his nose a moment before falling to the ground.

Yay! Another point for me.

Lee peeled off her sports bra and unleashed the sexiest breasts I'd ever seen. And I'd been alive for a very long time. "See, there are no bites anywhere. But I think you both should do a closer inspection. A much closer inspection."

Christ. I swallowed hard as she ran her hands up and down her body.

At least Avi had some presence of mind. "Stop this." He grabbed her arm again.

"Why?" Lee licked her lips. "I'm just giving us all what we want. You want to screw me. I want to screw you and... him."

Christ. Hearing her say that set me on fire.

Avi shook his head. "No. I don't—"

"This is how we can be together, willow tree. This is the only way we can be together."

"Fuck," he groaned, stealing the words from my mouth.

"Yes. That's what we're going to do." Lee pulled her arm from Avi. "But first you're going to take off that pretty armband. And Dominic is going to tell us what to do."

I opened my mouth to reprimand her, but her sultry look stopped me along with the raw truth.

I do want this.

My hunger for this female bordered on pain. And a week of watching her bang Avi had only deepened my desire for her. It didn't help that she held my gaze and shouted my name every time she orgasmed. It didn't help that she resisted me at every turn. It didn't help that she'd just threatened to leave me.

As if I'd ever let her go.

Oh, I'd put on a good show of pretending not to care. I'd even acted as if I'd exile her. But the truth was if she ever left, I'd drag her back kicking and screaming. I'd already imprinted on her lush scent, so I'd be able to track her to the ends of the earth.

Never had I been so captivated by a female. She'd pushed me, tempted me, and infuriated me past the point of reason. Even so, I was obsessed with her husky laugh. Her curvaceous body. Her rebellious spirit.

I'd thought if I could make her submit, I'd break her hold over me. But I was only kidding myself. Every day, the connection between us grew. Every day, it became harder to resist her.

So, I was considering doing the one thing I'd never done in the history of my military career.

Surrender.

I watched her stand there unabashedly naked and forgot how to breathe.

Christ.

Lust short-circuited my brain. Decades of military training and programming burned away, and my formerly ironclad control came perilously close to snapping.

Logically, I knew she'd weaponized her sexuality and was

using it against me. But my combat training hadn't prepared me for this... for her.

I couldn't stop my eyes from traveling over the perfection of her body. The smooth as satin skin. The soft swells of her breasts. The curves of her hips and ass. The tempting bare cleft at the apex of her thighs.

My cock throbbed painfully against the fabric of my pants as she sauntered over to my desk. Then she swept her candle and my knives over to the computer monitor as if she owned the place.

The tilt of her pouty lips drove me crazy. She knew she'd won. She'd conquered two of the deadliest males in the safe house without words, fists, or weapons.

Avi and I were both speechless and spellbound as she lifted herself onto the desk and parted her thighs.

Christ. That intoxicating view drove every thought except her from my mind.

As she slowly leaned back, the sweet musk of her desire teased my nostrils, driving me closer to the line I'd swore I'd never cross.

"Well..." she drawled. "Who is going to fuck me first?"

And just like that, my control splintered. In a blur of motion, I'd flashed across the room, rounded the desk, and shoved the office chair aside.

She let out a startled sound as I grabbed her arms and yanked her flat across the desk with her legs dangling over the other side.

Responding to her distress, Avi rushed over.

"Stand down, soldier," I ordered.

Avi looked between me and Lee. I could see the play of emotions across his face. He was torn between his instincts to protect his mate and his need to show his loyalty to me.

"It's okay," Lee said breathlessly. "We'll do it however Dominic wants." She relaxed against my grip.

Christ.

Her submission only cranked my lust higher. But I was still bound by the rules.

Mating with civilians was forbidden. Mating with humans was forbidden. And Lee was both.

As much as I craved her, I couldn't afford to break any military laws. The last time I had, it'd cost me my freedom and the one thing in the world I cared about. I glanced down at the beast sprawled out near my feet.

A deep wave of regret and longing hit me. I missed Hunter. Although I never would have admitted it to him, he'd kept me in check as much as I'd kept him in check. But I suspected if he were present, he'd be as lost for Lee as I was.

Hunter thinks she is his mate. That confused me even more. *How can she make both of us desire her when we're already*—I stopped that train of thought in its tracks as an even more disturbing thought occurred to me.

Maybe she isn't human. Maybe our attraction to her isn't natural at all.

My suspicions grew as I looked down at her. Her flawless face and body looked as if it'd been sculpted for a male's pleasure. Pouty red lips that begged to be kissed, breasts large and firm enough to fuck, toned legs that were long enough to throw over even the broadest shoulders, and a pussy that looked wet enough to sheath a cock as big as mine.

She can't be human.

Needing confirmation, I shackled her wrists and used my free hand to grab the closest blade from the cluttered pile of weapons near the computer monitor.

Her eyes flared with surprise and a glimmer of fear as I held up a sixteen-inch bowie knife. Knowing knives were one of her triggers, I expected her to freak out, but she only took a deep breath and relaxed in my arms.

She trusts me. Damn. That shouldn't have packed such a punch, but it did.

Avi let out a warning growl, but I gave him a hard look. "I need to know if she's part of the project."

Avi shook his head. "She's human," he insisted. But there was enough uncertainty in his gaze that I knew he wouldn't challenge what I was going to do next.

I drew the clip-pointed blade lightly over her chest.

Lee hissed in a breath of air. "Ouch."

When the tiny cut welled with blood instead of instantly healing, Avi gave me a smug look. "I told you, she's human."

"Wait, you think I'm a shifter too?" Lee asked, looking confused. "I'm not. I'm totally normal."

"There's nothing normal about you." I licked my thumb, intending to heal the small wound. But as I dropped my hand back to her breast, a dark part of me wanted her wearing my mark. I rubbed my thumb across her nipple instead.

It stiffened under my touch.

"More," she begged, arching off the desk.

A violent storm of lust thundered through me. I glanced at Avi to see if he was game.

The beast growled softly, his eyes glowing with hunger.

We'll give her more. We'll give her everything she can take. Human or not, she needed to learn the consequences of seducing monsters like us.

And I couldn't wait to teach her.

❦

IN A MOTION BORN OF DECADES OF PRACTICE, I FLIPPED the bowie knife. Excitement thrummed through me as I brought the rounded brass pommel down on her chest and drew the smooth metal over each of her nipples.

She shivered, her stiff brown peaks swelling even more.

I wanted to touch them again. But I didn't trust myself to stop touching her. *If we're going to do this, we need rules.* I gave Lee and Avi a hard look. "Rule one, I won't touch either of you. Rule two, neither of you will touch me."

Lee gave a pointed look at my hand clamped around her wrist.

"That doesn't count, and neither does this." I drew the pommel down her flat stomach, making lazy circles around her belly button ring. Then I ran it over the top of her sex.

Lee's breathing shallowed.

So did Avi's. The beast's gaze locked on the bowie knife as I dipped it between her thighs.

The moment the pommel contacted her swollen nub, Lee screamed and arched off the desk.

I tightened my hand around her wrists and forced her flat. "Don't move."

She relaxed back, and I rewarded her by working the rounded metal against her clit. Slowly at first. Then faster. And faster until the knife was a shiny blur.

"Oh, God!" Her thighs quivered, and I knew from watching her with Avi that she was close to orgasming.

I yanked the knife away.

"Dominic," she howled, her hips undulating in search of the friction she craved.

"Rule number three, you'll orgasm only when I give you permission. Now lift your legs and put your heels on the edge of the desk."

She moved into the position that opened her to Avi's transfixed gaze.

"Hold her legs apart," I ordered him.

Avi obediently pressed his hands against the inside of her thighs, spreading her even further apart.

"Yes. Just like that." Reaching between his arms, I slid the knife handle down through her slick wet folds and poised it right at her entrance.

She sucked in a breath as I slowly penetrated her inch by inch until the entire hilt was buried inside her.

"How does that feel?"

"Good. But not enough," she gasped. "I need more."

"How about this?" Fisting the blade, I yanked the handle out and thrust it back inside her.

"Yes! Yes!" she cried. "Faster."

Forgetting that I was supposed to call the shots, I fucked her hard with the wooden handle, loving how she chased each thrust with her hips.

Her pleasured cries grew louder. "Oh, God!"

Wetness coated my fingers, and I felt a stinging pain in my palm, but I didn't stop. Not when she was so close.

Avi made a choked sound. "Sarge."

I looked down to see blood dripping between her thighs. *Christ.* The razor-sharp steel of the blade had sliced my hand nearly to the bone.

"Don't stop," Lee pleaded.

"You don't make the orders," I growled. "Close your eyes."

The moment she did, I withdrew the bloody knife, careful not to nick her or Avi. Then I tossed the blade to the floor and wrapped my already healing hand in a clean shirt. I'd clean the rest of the blood off later. Right now, I needed to finish her off. Or rather, Avi did.

"Take off the silver and fuck her," I instructed the beast.

As if he'd been eagerly awaiting my command, Avi tore off the armband and the fabric from around his waist. Letting both drop to the floor, he grabbed his shaft and rubbed it over her opening.

Christ. She was so slick with my blood and her desire.

"Oh, yes," she hissed as Avi lined himself up and slowly pushed inside.

How I wished I was the one claiming her... stretching her to the border of pleasure and pain.

Lee's eyes flew open and rounded. "Holy hell. Avi, you're freaking huge now."

If she thinks that's big, wait until she sees me.

"No nice normal cock, anymore, huh?" the beast said, withdrawing and plunging into her again.

"Don't hold back." She made an inarticulate sound that made my balls tighten and my cock throb.

"Never with you, oak tree." He drove into her faster and faster, never taking his eyes from hers. It was obvious he was pretending I wasn't standing across from him.

Lee didn't screen me out, though. Instead, her nails dug into the flesh of my arm. The pinpricks of pain heightened my desire to the point I had to reach down to readjust myself.

Lee tilted her head back and stared at my crotch, only inches from her face. "I want you in my mouth, Dominic."

Christ. Imagining her hot, wet lips sucking on me nearly made me cum in my pants.

Yes. No. As lust and responsibility waged war inside my head, Avi tried to draw Lee's attention back to him.

"Look at me, oak tree." Avi thrusted his hips feverishly, his cock slamming into her so hard the desk quaked and my knives rolled to the carpet.

Lee threw her head back, her gaze seeking mine. "I'm so close."

"I'm going to cum," Avi roared.

The fuck he is. "Both of you freeze."

Lee and Avi went motionless, their chests heaving. My blood and their sweat glistened from between their joined bodies.

"Dominic, please," Lee whimpered, her eyes frantic with need.

I leaned down and whispered in her ear. "This is your

punishment." She wanted it, and now she had it. Releasing her wrists, I straightened and scowled at Avi. "Put on the silver, find some damn clothes, and return to your duties."

The beast's body shook, but he pulled out of Lee, reached for his silver armband, and slid it around his bicep. In an instant, his erection deflated.

Lee twisted around. "Dammit, Dominic. If you won't let him get me off, then you fuck me."

If she only knew how much I wanted to do just that. "No. You're going to suffer the same way I've suffered." So many nights watching her. Aching for her.

"No one needs to suffer," she whispered. "I want you. I need you."

Her words undid me.

"Why?" The question slipped out before I could stop it. I wasn't worthy of her desire. My treatment of her bordered on abuse. I was intentionally harder on her than any of the others because I resented the power she had over me and the power she had over my m—

My office door flew open and Lee's hippie boyfriend rushed into the room, his long ass hair whipping around his bearded face.

I need to start locking that door.

"Reed!" Lee gasped.

"Jesus!" Hippie's eyes widened as he took in Avi standing naked beside the desk, Lee naked on top of the desk, and me standing over her fully clothed. His gaze bounced between her blood-streaked thighs and Avi's blood-smeared cock. Then, as if a switch had been hit, his entire demeanor changed.

"You hurt her!" he roared, clenching his fists.

Avi scoffed. "No one's hurting anyone, Fruitcake. Get the fuck out and knock next ti—" He didn't finish because Hippie rushed across the office, grabbed the stained-glass lamp from the side table and smashed it against Avi's forehead.

Shards of rainbow glass flew everywhere.

I quickly lifted my arm to shield Lee.

"What the hell?" Avi shouted, swiping the glass from his bleeding face. "You're going to regret that—"

Hippie kicked his legs out from under him so hard I heard Avi's kneecap shatter.

Letting out a grunt of pain, Avi dropped like a stone.

Hippie quickly noosed the lamp cord around his neck and yanked it so tightly Avi's eyes bulged.

"Reed, stop!" Lee cried, scrambling over the desk.

Avi tried to break Hippie's hold, but the smaller male easily evaded the beast's grasping hands.

"If you hurt her, you die," Hippie snarled in Avi's ear.

Avi clawed at the cord, his face turning purple.

"You're strangling him. Let him go." Lee yanked on Hippie's arm.

As entertaining as this was to watch, I had to put a stop to it. "Release Avi."

Hippie immediately loosened the cord and shoved Avi onto the carpet.

Avi collapsed in a fit of coughing.

Lee rounded on Hippie. "What the hell is wrong with you, Reed?"

Hippie blinked as if waking from a dream. He looked down at the lamp cord in his hand and then at Avi, wheezing on the floor. "I-I ran into Zara who said you all just got back from your field training test." He gave Lee an accusatory look. "So, I went to find you. I heard you screaming. Then I saw the blood..."

"It's just a tiny cut," Lee insisted, looking down at her chest. She did a double take when she saw her blood-smeared thighs. "Whoa. I don't know where that came fro—"

"It's my blood," I interjected, holding up my bandaged hand. "Nicked myself during our knife play earlier."

"Knife play?" Hippie gave Lee an incredulous look. "You're screwing the sergeant too?"

Her face reddened. "Reed, I—"

"Like I said, Fruitcake, Lee doesn't need you anymore," Avi wheezed from the floor.

Hippie looked as if he'd taken a direct hit to the solar plexus.

Lee shook her head. "That's not true. Reed, don't listen to him."

"Whatever. Sorry, I interrupted your fuck-fest." Hippie flung the broken lamp on the floor and stormed out of the room.

Hmm. Even though he'd made a mess of my soldier and my office, Reed's fighting skills impressed me. Few humans could take down a highly trained Lykos in less than sixty seconds.

I can use him...

"Reed, wait!" Lee cried, grabbing her clothes and rushing after him.

"Fruitcake broke my leg." Avi groaned, using my desk to drag himself up. "Can I take the silver off to heal, sir?"

I gave him a disapproving look. "Yes. Then you can explain why the hippie who just handed you your ass is still on green team."

❧ 10 ❧

LEE

ammit. Why did Reed have to be the one to walk in on us?
"Honey, wait!" I shouted as he stalked through the admin area just outside Dominic's office.

Reed stepped out and slammed the door in my face.

Crap. I'd never seen him this angry before. In fact, I could count on one hand the number of times he'd ever gotten physical with someone. Once in high school, he'd punched Bryce Mitchell when the jerk spread rumors about me sleeping with the entire basketball team. Then last year, he beat the snot out of that creepy guy who'd followed me home from the strip club, and a few weeks ago he'd attacked Javier's goons when they tried to abduct me.

But none of his attacks were as violent as this one. If Dominic hadn't ordered him to stop, he might have strangled Avi to death. I couldn't reconcile that kind of savagery with the easy-going guy I'd grown up with.

Maybe he's still possessed by Hunter…

My blood chilled as I briefly considered the possibility. But then I remembered the pained look in Reed's eyes when he realized what was really going on in Dominic's office. That devastated look was the same one he'd worn at his mother's gravestone after her funeral and the same one he'd given me across Gran's hospital bed after her stroke.

No. Reed wasn't possessed. He'd just always been super protective of me, and that protectiveness kicked in when he'd thought I was being abused. Now that he knew the truth, he was most likely hurt and embarrassed. It didn't help that he'd found out I'd hid my field test from him.

I'd thought I was protecting him by keeping him in the dark. I didn't want him to worry, or worse, insist on coming along to be tested with me.

I have to make things right with him.

My hands and legs shook as I threw on my clothes. My weapons and shoes were still in Dominic's office, but I didn't want to go back in there and face those guys until I'd processed what just happened in there.

The three of us had taken things to the next level. And what a freaking level it had been. I couldn't wait to do it again. Although next time I wouldn't let Dominic pull the plug. With a little more seduction on my part, I was sure he'd forget about his stupid rules and fully unleash himself.

Am I ready for that?

No doubt the sergeant's brand of loving would be dark, intense, and likely to bring as much pain as pleasure.

Hell yeah, my hormones answered. I shuddered with excitement before reminding myself I needed to focus on Reed. The guy who didn't understand my need to explore the dark edges of my sexuality. The guy who wanted what I couldn't give.

Did I care about Reed? *Yes.* He was family. I'd die for him and kill for him. But I was also incredibly attracted to Avi and Dominic and I didn't want to give them up either.

Resting my head against the glass windowpane of the admin door, I debated what to do.

Maybe the kindest thing would be to let Reed go. The thought made my throat tighten and my chest ache. If Dominic was my darkness, Reed was my light. The way he looked at me, as if I was the most precious and beautiful creature in the world, made me feel special. And when he held me, I felt at peace in a way I'd never felt with anyone else. There was a reason I could only sleep if I was in his arms.

Reed is home to me.

And I couldn't kid myself that my feelings for him were platonic. It'd been so hard keeping my hands off his scarred body this last week. But he'd needed me to hold his hair back while he puked, not tear his pants off so I could ride his magnificent, pierced cock. And now I might never get a chance to be with him again.

Crap. How do I fix this?

The rising sound of arguing male voices in Dominic's office had me cursing. *Why couldn't the guys just get along?* Life would be so much simpler without all the testosterone-fueled jealousy, competition, and aggression.

Not for the first time, I wished I was into women, like my best friends in high school. The two of them never dealt with drama like this.

Letting out a frustrated sigh, I opened the admin door and stepped out into the school entryway. I thought the area was empty until I rounded the front desk.

Darcy stood in the doorway of the teacher's lounge across the hall, sniper rifle balanced across her broad shoulders. Even with her severe crew cut and heavily muscled physique, she was one of the most beautiful women I'd ever met. She was also one bad ass bitch who could hold her own against the rest of her all-male squad. Too bad she had it out for me.

"Finally. I don't have all day, Hooker," she called out, her tone dripping with venom.

I scowled, hating her nickname for me. "Dominic already did my bite check."

"I just bet he did," she sneered, her honey-colored eyes sweeping over me in barely veiled contempt.

I fought the urge to finger-brush my hair and instead gave her a taunting look. "Jealous?"

"Please." She snorted, dropping the rifle to her side. "Whores like you make me want to shoot something."

Feeling defensive, I crossed my arms across my chest. "I'm not a whore, bitch." I'd stripped to pay the rent and put food on the table, but I'd never had sex for money.

"No, you're something much worse." She moved closer until she loomed over me. "And much more dangerous."

"Dangerous?" I hated having to crane my neck up to maintain eye contact with her.

Why the hell were all these people so damn tall?

"I've seen what your kind can do. Turning soldier against soldier. Turning beasts against their handlers." She jabbed her finger at my chest, hitting Dominic's cut.

I slapped her hand away. "Don't touch me."

"I'll do far more than touch you if you keep messing with Sarge's head," she snarled, her teeth flashing white against the smooth ebony skin of her face. "I'll kill you."

Trying not to look as shaken as I felt, I lifted my chin. "You wouldn't—"

She got up right in my face. "Oh, but I would. And I'd be doing the entire world a fucking favor. You Siren bitches bring nothing but chaos and death."

Siren bitches? She sounded as crazy as Vincent, the schizophrenic bum who lived in the chapel.

"Go ahead. Put your siren spell on every male here but stay away from my best friend's mate."

Whoa. "Dominic has a..." I stumbled over the m-word, still not really understanding what it meant. "... a mate."

Darcy gave a sharp nod. "Jen loved him. Married him. Waited years for him. And it makes me sick to see him panting after you... challenging a Lykos for you... when she's only been dead a few weeks."

Oh, wow. Dominic had a wife, but she'd recently died. No wonder he was reluctant to touch me.

Poor guy is probably in mourning.

"Besides, you're pushing Sarge to the edge and we can't have him losing control with all the shit we're dealing with."

Great. Now I'm responsible for Dominic's state of mind. Like I really needed that weight on my shoulders.

"Do we understand each other, Hooker? You stay away from Sarge, and I won't have to end you." She gave me a threatening look that would have made any mentally sound person piss their pants.

But I was far from mentally sound. And I'd never done well with bullies and ultimatums. Letting some of my ever-simmering rage bubble to the surface, I said, "Don't threaten me with death, bitch. I've danced with that motherfucker. I'm not afraid of him and I'm not afraid of you."

I stepped right into her face. "What goes on between me and Dominic is none of your damn business. And I'd suggest you back off before I decide to use my siren spell on you." I rose on my toes and flicked my tongue over her cheek.

She reared back, panic flaring in her eyes.

Hah. Even smaller and weaponless, I'd won our pissing contest. *Sometimes it pays to be bat shit crazy.*

"Glad we had this talk. Bye now!" Blowing Darcy a kiss, I sashayed down the hallway as if I didn't have a care in the world.

That was so far from the truth.

THE FLOOR FELT AS IF IT WAS SHIFTING WILDLY UNDER MY bare feet. *How in the world did my life become some twilight zone episode?* I mean, death threats, zombies, werewolf lovers, sergeants who knife-fucked me, and boyfriends who strangled other people with serial killer finesse...

It was too bizarre to be real.

Dammit. What I wouldn't give to go back to a time when my biggest stressor was paying the bills.

The sound of rustling snapped me from my thoughts. Vincent was digging through the trash can outside the music room.

Can't I catch a break today?

The crazy bum pulled his head out of the bin and stared at me through the matted hair covering his gaunt face. His skeletal frame, soiled clothes, and overpowering stench had resulted in me mistaking him for a zombie more than once.

"The Queen is coming," he announced, brandishing an empty soda can. "She'll conquer this realm and rule the Kindred for eternity. We must prepare!"

I sighed. "Vincent, you're supposed to stay in the chapel. Does Roger know you got out?" The psychologist was supposed to keep a close eye on Vincent.

Vincent waved his can in my face. "The Queen is coming for you, Heaven. She'll destroy you and all who stand against her."

Ugh. It gave me chills when Vincent said crap like that. Roger told me to ignore Vincent's schizophrenic ravings, but that was easier said than done.

"Go back to the chapel, Vincent," I shouted, stepping around him to open the music room door.

Reed stood inside by the piano, his back to me.

Taking a deep breath, I walked in and locked the door behind me. Things were tense enough without adding a raving lunatic into the mix.

When Reed didn't react to the sound of me clearing my throat, I said, "Hey, honey. Can we talk?"

It wasn't the greatest opening, but it sounded better than the alternative—*Hey, honey. Sorry you walked in on me messing around with two other guys.*

Reed tensed but didn't turn around. "I don't feel like talking right now, Lee."

I rubbed my suddenly clammy hands on my jeans. "How are we going to fix things if we don't talk about them?"

Reed stared down at the piano keys. "I don't think things can be fixed. I also don't think there is a we."

"Honey…" I took a step forward and something crunched under my bare foot. I glanced down to see a line of dried rose petals leading over to the piano. "What's this?"

"There aren't any rose bushes around, so I pulled those from the bouquets in the chapel," Reed answered tonelessly. "I remembered the pink ones were your favorite."

I slowly followed the line of petals around the piano and discovered a huge plastic storage tub filled with water. Next to the tub was a small bottle of my favorite body wash, a brand-new razor still in the package, and a dog-eared copy of a gossip magazine I used to read. "Is this for me?"

"You said you miss baths."

"Reed!" I shook my head, overcome with emotion. "This must have taken hours to set up."

"We were going to boil the other half of the water, so it'd be hot, but we hadn't gotten that far."

"We?" I gave him a questioning look.

"Sai has been helping me. He scored most of the food." He pointed behind the tub.

I walked around it and found a basket filled with my

favorite chips, chocolates, and even my favorite blue sports drink. My mouth watered. It'd been weeks since I'd had any of those treats.

"Wow. This is incredible."

"And I traded my last pack of cloves for this." He set a small bottle of sparkling wine on top of the piano. "For your New Year's toast."

So moved by his kindness, I had to swallow back tears.

"Thank you." I walked over and put my arms around him. "This means so much, honey."

He shrugged out of my embrace. "I wanted to give you what you desired most. Apparently, I should have stabbed you instead."

The coldness in his voice had me taking a step back. "It's not like that. It's—"

"I don't want to hear about the kinky shit you're doing with those assholes." He finally looked over at me, his blue eyes flashing with hurt and anger. "I've been in love with you all my life, Lee."

I held out my palm as if to ward off the impact of those words. "Reed I—"

He stood. "No. It's my turn to talk."

I blinked in surprise. Reed never raised his voice to me.

"You told me you had laundry duty all morning."

"I didn't want you to worry about my field test," I said softly.

"You outright lied to me, Lee." His injured look cut me deeper than Dominic's knife. "Growing up, I was always too much of a chicken shit to tell you how I really felt. My greatest fear was that you'd reject me and then I'd lose you forever."

I shook my head. "That will never—"

"But I finally get it. You were never mine to lose. You'll never be mine to lose."

A pit opened in my stomach. *Is he breaking up with me?*

Reed strode over to the door and unlocked it.

"Where are you going?"

"Don't pretend you care," he said, stepping out and slamming the door behind him.

LEE

Reed's parting words hollowed me out. I stumbled over to the piano bench and sat down on the fluffy brown towel he must have laid out for my bath.

Don't pretend you care? Of course, I cared. When we were kids, I'd protected him from bullies. When he desperately needed a transfusion after the car accident, I'd made Gran sign the waiver so I could donate my blood to him. After he moved into our house, I'd given up my bedroom and bunked with my sister, so he'd be comfortable. And later, when Gran died, I'd left school and worked any job I could find to support him and Eden. I'd even moved my shifts around to attend his baseball games and band gigs.

He has to know I care for him. He's just pissed about finding me with Dominic and Avi.

I sighed, rubbing the cut Dominic had given me.

Why did Reed even agree to an open relationship?

He knew what it would mean. But then again, there was agreeing to something, and there was seeing it in action.

Just remembering what Reed walked in on heated my

blood. I couldn't believe I'd actually stripped and propositioned Dominic and Avi like that.

What was I thinking? Oh, yeah. I wasn't.

Ever since the apocalypse, my libido, not my brain, had been calling the shots. It seemed as if overnight I'd gone from rarely thinking about sex to being bombarded by sexual urges.

Roger thought it was my way of coping with the end of the world. But that still didn't explain why anything and everything turned me on lately. Dominic's scowl, check. Avi's sneer, check. Reed's lame jokes, check. Even Sai's shameless flirting, check.

Can people go into heat? Because that might explain my constant need to be touched and pleasured. Even now, my nipples tingled, and my clit throbbed, reminding me I hadn't gotten off today. Nowadays, if I didn't have an orgasm every few hours, I ended up in physical pain. Apparently, lady blue balls were a thing.

Deciding a cold bath might help, I stripped and dropped into the big plastic tub. Unfortunately, the chlorine-scented water was room temperature and did nothing to dim my unquenched desire. *Dammit.* Well, it was worth a try.

Time for plan B. After quickly washing my hair and soaping myself with my favorite body wash, I slid a hand between my legs and closed my eyes. As I pleasured myself, I replayed the encounter in Dominic's office. This time I imagined Dominic ripping off his pants and feeding me his monster cock.

Dominic jerks my head back and fucks my mouth while Avi ruthlessly pounds into me. Then Reed bursts into the office, rips Avi off me and rails me with his pierced cock.

Suddenly, my erotic fantasy morphed into all three men taking turns with me. *Oh, yes!* Sweet pressure built deep inside me. I rubbed myself hard and fast, not caring that water was sloshing all over the floor.

I was almost there. *Almost.* My muscles went taut as I

hurled toward a glorious release. A second before reaching the finish line, I heard someone inhale sharply.

Who's that? My arousal crashed and burned as my eyes flew open.

Sai stood a few feet away, holding a bucket of water in each hand. His hooded eyes burned with hunger as he brazenly stared at me. "Don't stop on my account, darling."

Oh, God. My face heated as I grabbed the towel from the piano bench and threw it over myself.

"I knocked, but no one answered," Sai explained, flashing me his sexy dimpled grin. As usual, the rock star looked like a walking sex god with his swarthy skin, curly dark hair, and rakish goatee.

"Um, yeah, I didn't hear you."

"I can see why." Sai set the buckets on the floor, bringing my attention to the beautiful tattoos sleeving his muscled forearms. Then he prowled to the end of the tub. "Would you like a hand with that?"

❧

As I blinked back at Sai, sexual tension filled the air. I'd been attracted to Avi's younger brother since the moment we'd met. And it wasn't just because of his fame, panty-drenching good looks, or smooth charm. I liked that I always knew where I stood with Sai. He'd made it clear he wanted me. He'd also made it clear he didn't do monogamous relationships.

With him, there would be no rules, no drama, and no claiming I was his mate or whatever. Just steamy sex with no strings attached. Right now, that sounded perfect.

Sai dipped his hand into the tub and caressed my leg. "I'm all about helping my friends in need today. What do you say?"

Yes! Excitement raced through me, only to fizzle out. If

Reed was furious over finding me with Avi and Dominic, how would he feel about me being with his rock idol?

"I-I don't think that's a good idea," I stammered. "You're Reed's friend and..."

"And he invited me to have sex with you two later on today."

My mouth dropped open. "What? No way. Reed would never..."

"He wants to make you happy." Sai nodded his head toward the basket of food. "He said you want a threesome. He'd rather the third person be me than..." His face tightened. "... Someone else."

I was speechless.

"You'll act surprised later though?" Sai winked.

Wow. Reed hated the idea of me with other guys. And yet he was willing to share me with Sai. That was freaking huge of him, and it spoke to his level of trust in Sai.

Seeming to misunderstand my silence, the rock star's cocky smile slipped. "Reed is okay with us being together, but if you don't want to—"

"No, I do," I said, interrupting him. No way would I miss out on this opportunity. "But maybe we should do a test drive right now." I flung the wet towel down on the floor and spread my legs.

Sai's smoldering gaze lit my body on fire. "That's an excellent idea, darling." He leaned over the tub, giving me a hit of his bay rum cologne, and then kissed me. *No.* Kissed wasn't the right word. He seduced the ever-loving shit out of my mouth with his lips, tongue, and teeth.

Holy crap. By the time we came up for air, the room was spinning, and I was a millisecond from orgasming. And that was just from a single kiss.

"I could spend an eternity worshiping you," he said, nibbling my lower lip. "Every part of you." He slowly licked his way down my neck and chest. "Hey. What happened here?" He tapped his finger near Dominic's cut.

"It's nothing," I said, pushing his hand lower.

He strummed his fingers over my nipple as if it were a musical instrument, and then lowered his head.

The moment his hot, wet mouth latched on, I arched out of the tub.

"Oh, God. Yes!" I wrapped one wet arm around him and practically dragged him into the water.

He jerked away, his red silk shirt dripping wet. "Slow down, darling. I've been dreaming of this for weeks." He whipped his shirt over his head and tossed it aside.

My mind blanked as I got an eyeful of the lean whipcord muscles of his chest and abs. That, combined with the gorgeous tattoos sleeving both arms, had me panting with desire.

"I'm going to take my sweet time," he promised, moving his lips back to my neck.

I felt as if I was going to self-combust. "Just get me off one time. Then you can take forever," I pleaded.

"Deal. But you have to stand up."

I practically jumped to my feet, sending water sloshing down the side of the tub and all over him.

Thankfully, he didn't seem to care. Giving me a wicked grin, he motioned at the piano bench. "Put your foot on that."

I did as he asked. "Like this?" The position, one leg in the tub and one on the bench, spread me wide open to his gaze.

"Yes." His groan brushed across my wet skin like a caress. "Frack. You're so beautiful, darling." He moved underneath me. "I could stare at this view for hours."

Hours? "Sai, you said you would—" I broke off as he gripped my ass and buried his head between my thighs.

"Oh, God!" I shuddered at the first swipe of his masterful tongue over my clit.

He worked his entire face between my legs, spreading me wider. His goatee tickled the inside of my thighs, but it couldn't distract me from the earthquake building inside me.

"Yes!" I cried when his tongue thrust deep inside my channel.

"I love how you taste," he murmured against my flesh. "Like the sweetest honey."

Needing less talking and more licking, I ground myself against his lips.

He chuckled. "I love a woman who knows what she wants—"

"Sai!" I begged. My fingers tangled in his soft curls, urging him on.

He pulled his mouth away and thrust two fingers inside me.

"Oh, yes!" I rocked my hips as he found my G-spot. "Right there!"

"What about here?" He slipped his other hand between my buttocks and rimmed my back hole. "This is where I want to frack you."

I stiffened with shock and desire. "I've never—" I gasped as he slowly penetrated my ass with a wet finger. There was a slight burn as he pressed all the way in and then inserted another finger. But it was followed by a strangely erotic sensation that sent tremors of rapture through me.

"How does that feel, darling?" Sai asked, thrusting the fingers in my pussy in time with the fingers in my ass.

"Like I'm a bowling ball," I tried to joke, but it came out as one loud, incoherent whimper when white-hot pleasure overloaded my senses.

He moved his fingers faster. "Just imagine me and Reed both inside you like this…"

The mental image had me gasping and tossing my head from side to side. "Oh, God! Don't stop. Don't—" My plea turned to a fevered cry as he sealed his lips around my clit and suckled hard.

The orgasm hit with the force of a tsunami, drowning me in waves of ecstasy. My legs gave out, but Sai was right there, bracing me with his body.

"I've got you, darling," he said, over and over. Although it was a full minute before I could hear him through the pounding of my heartbeat.

As I slowly caught my breath, he slipped his fingers out and wiped them dry on the towel. Then he looked up at me with smokey eyes. "So, what did you think of our test drive?"

"Wow, just wow," was all I could manage to say.

He grinned. "Just wait until I introduce you to my dragon."

"Dragon?"

He winked, leaving me to wonder if he was referencing something sexual or if he actually had a freaking fire-breathing dragon. Given my day so far, I couldn't rule either option out.

"What the fuck?" a deep voice shouted from across the room.

Sai groaned. "Frack. Buzzkill is here."

I twisted around to see Avi standing by the door. He tossed my sneakers and weapons on the floor, an expression of outrage on his face.

Sai gave him a wave from between my legs. "Hey, bro. What the hell is that on your head? A wig?" He pointed at Avi's thick brown curls.

Avi swung his gaze from Sai to me. "You're fucking my brother?" His thunderous roar was so loud it shook the music stands in the corner of the room.

Seriously? Did none of these guys know how to share?

"We haven't gotten to that yet, bro. Just warming her up." Sai rubbed his hands over my ass.

Avi cursed. "I never thought I'd feel sympathy for Fruitcake, but I do now. What sad motherfuckers we are to fall for a whore."

Whore? I flinched as if he'd slapped me. It was one thing for Darcy to call me that, quite another for my willow tree to say it.

"Apologize," Sai shouted. He jumped to his feet and stalked across the room to confront his much taller brother.

Avi sneered down at him. "What happened to not stealing Reed's woman?"

Sai curled his hands into fists. "I got permission from him first, bro. What happened to treating women with respect? And have you forgotten mom and Zara have harems? Are they whores too?"

Avi opened his mouth, then closed it.

Sai stepped right into Avi's face. "And what right do you have to..." He trailed off as he craned his neck up to stare at Avi. "... Frack, bro. You're like a foot taller than you were this morning. What happened to you?"

"I lost control and shifted... over her. It won't happen again." Avi gave me a scathing look.

My mouth felt full of sand. Call me stupid, but I really hadn't expected this kind of reaction from Avi. He'd gone from declaring I was his mate to slut shaming me in what felt like zero to sixty. It made my head spin and my chest ache.

A normal woman might have cried or fumed in silence. My crazy ass lashed out. "That's fine wolfman, because this whore has no use for your limp dick. You've just been replaced by a much better lover." I blew Sai a kiss.

A pained look crossed Avi's face before he blanked his expression. "I didn't come to trade insults. I came to bring the stuff you left in Sarge's office and tell Fruitcake he's been promoted to red team."

"Frack!" Sai exclaimed. "You're kidding?"

Red team? Reed is being promoted to red team? The group of highly trained fighting experts that were always going off on supply runs and dangerous missions. "No! He can't!"

"He impressed Sarge back there." Avi jabbed his finger in the direction of Dominic's office. "His training starts ASAP. Do you know where he is?"

I shook my head. *Oh, God. How can I protect Reed if he's on red team?*

"I'll help you look for him." Sai jogged over to grab his wet shirt from off the floor and flashed me a dimpled smile that would normally make my heart race. "I want to be there when Reed gets the good news."

Good news? This was anything but good news.

Sai leaned over and pressed his lips to mine. "I can't wait for our threesome later, darling." Then he strode out the door with his brother, leaving me to freak the hell out all by myself.

❧ 12 ❧

HUNTER

"*What the fuck are you doing, cocksucker?*" I shouted at Reed. "*Go back there and make this right with her.*"

It killed me that I'd blown my chance with Lee. My dirty dancer thought I was a monster. She hated me. *How can I ever earn her forgiveness if she and Reed aren't together?*

Ignoring me, Reed continued stalking down the hallway toward the gymnasium. "*Shut up, Hunter. And if you ever hijack my body again, I'll find some way to silence your ass for good.*"

I sensed his steely resolve. Reed's anger at me for taking over in Dom's office was inflamed by his hurt and jealousy.

"*I don't know what happened,*" I confessed. "*I just saw the blood on Lee and...*" And in a rush of anger, I'd barreled into the driver's seat of our body and lay the hurt down on that wolf shifter.

Garroting Avi had released some of my pent-up bloodlust and given me a rush I hadn't felt in ages. And yet, I'd immediately obeyed Dom's command to stop. *Fuck.* After so many years of being bound to him, I automatically followed his orders. It'd take time and effort to break that conditioning.

"Do you know the danger you put us in?" Reed seethed. *"If Dominic realized you're still in me—"*

"He didn't," I said quickly. There had been no suspicion in Dom's gaze. Probably because once I realized I had my former handler's attention, I'd ceded control back to Reed.

"Your emo-bullshit guaranteed that." Just thinking about the way we'd stormed out of Dom's office made me cringe.

Reed made a sound of frustration. *"It was bad enough when Lee was running off to screw Avi, but now she's banging Dominic, too. And he's cutting her with knives. How am I supposed to react? I'm certainly not turned on by it like you were."*

My denial was swift. *"I wasn't."*

"Lie to someone else, man. I felt your excitement. Why in the world would you want Dominic and Lee together?"

Good question. And I didn't have an answer. I hated Dom for killing my brothers. I'd sworn to avenge their deaths and yet... Dom and I had trained and fought together for so long. And for all that time, we'd been bonded... inseparable. Even though the connection between us had been artificial—manufactured by army scientists trying to emulate an alpha bond— it'd felt real. And it had gone much deeper than the typical handler-beast bond. Deeper than anything I'd ever felt in my life until I'd met Lee.

Reed wouldn't leave it alone. *"You call Lee your mate and you call Dominic your enemy. So, tell me, man, why does your mate screwing your enemy turn you on?"*

Refusing to dig through emotions that were best left buried, I hit back with some uncomfortable truths of my own. *"Why are you pretending like you can walk away from Lee? She's our mate. Instead of getting pissy about her being with other males, let's figure out what they are doing for her, so we can do it better. If she wants knife play, we'll give her fucking knife play."*

Hell. I had claws and a barbed cock in my old body. I could cut her up all she wanted if she was into that.

Reed shook our head. *"I've tried making myself into her ideal man for years. I got these because I thought she was into inked guys."* He held up our arm, flashing the tattoos running down our scarred forearms. *"I grew my hair and beard out because she liked that look. Jesus. I got my cock pierced because I overheard her saying she was into that."* He let out a bitter laugh. *"Turns out she'd only been joking."*

"Shit." I had to give Reed points for self-sacrifice.

"And the joke is on me," Reed shouted, startling Eric Miller, who was leaving the restroom.

The firefighter threw us a pitying look before stepping around us.

Making a sound of frustration, Reed slammed through the bathroom door.

The sanitation team hadn't been through yet, but Reed didn't seem to notice the stench as he marched us over to the nasty hair-filled sinks.

Reed searched the toiletry bags lying on the counter until he found a battery-operated electric shaver.

He flicked it on and lifted the buzzing machine against the side of our head.

"What are you doing?"

He answered with a swipe of the shaver.

A while later, I barely recognized the reflection staring back at us in the mirror. With our shorn hair and clean-shaven face, we looked like a new recruit.

"Guess Dom can't call us a hippie anymore."

"Guess not." Reed used a paper towel to wipe shaving cream off the straight razor he'd taken from a different bag.

The door swished open behind us.

"There you are. I've been looking for you, Fruitcake," Avi growled.

We met the wolf shifter's angry gaze in the mirror.

Shit. Reed and I thought in unison.

"I GOT THIS." WITHOUT EVEN THINKING, I FLUNG REED'S consciousness to the back of our mind and jumped into the driver's seat. As my adrenaline spiked, I quickly made a threat assessment.

There was only one exit, and Avi blocked it. The dickwad had the height and weight advantage, so I'd have to take him down hard and fast.

The good news was that I didn't see any weapons on him and the sleeveless black T-shirt he wore showcased the silver band around his bicep. The Lykos would be weak and unable to shift or heal injuries.

Dom's mantra ran through my head. *Hit first and hit hard.* Gripping the razor tightly, I rushed straight at the Lykos.

"Whoa!" Avi threw up his arms.

I slashed them with the razor and then dropped to the floor, preparing to slice his femoral artery.

Avi tried to kick me.

I turned to the side, barely avoiding a boot to the head. But he'd made a fatal mistake. Grinning, I grabbed the back of Avi's leg and used his momentum to bring him crashing down onto the tile floor.

Then I rolled on top of him. Pinning his arms with my knees, I lifted the razor over his throat, planning to end the fucker's life for good.

"Stop!" Avi shouted. "Sarge promoted you to red team. He sent me to tell you."

Hiding my surprise, I pressed the edge of the razor against his carotid. "Maybe I don't want to be on red team. Maybe I should just kill you and take your place on Dom's squad."

Avi growled and tried to throw me off. But I'd been killing

far longer than he'd been alive and even in Reed's smaller, weaker body he was easy to subdue.

I laughed. "You're pathetic. I almost want to tear your silver off so we can have a real fight, little Lykos."

His eyes flared in surprise. "How do you... Did Lee tell you?"

I bared my teeth. "Don't speak my mate's name."

"Your mate? What are you?" he shouted, struggling again.

"Something that's a hell of a lot older and stronger than you, dickwad." I dug the razor deep enough into his throat to draw a line of blood.

Avi's eyes widened. He went motionless.

"If you touch Lee again, I'll make a eunuch out of you," I warned.

His weak laugh took me off guard. "Too late." He looked down at the silver band on his arm.

"Why are you wearing that?" I blurted out. No shifter in their right mind would wear our version of kryptonite.

"If I don't, Sarge will make me his beast," he answered.

His words hit like an electric shock. "But he's already paired with a beast." *Me.*

Avi grunted. "Maybe it's an empty threat. But I'm not taking the chance."

Hmm. Handlers could pair with only one beast at a time. To bond with Avi, Dom would have to break his connection to me.

I felt Reed rousing in the back of our mind. He wasn't completely aware yet. But he would be soon.

Fuck. I was tired of being trapped inside Reed. It was a living hell to watch the emo cocksucker screw up our life and our relationship with Lee. And having to endure his growing man-crush on Sai was more than I could take. *But what if there is a way out?*

What if I can escape Reed and still have my freedom? If I was back in my old body, I could protect Lee and take her somewhere safe. I could explain everything. She'd forgive me and then I could give her what she craves.

Wild and kinky sex.

My mind whirled as I glanced down at the razor blade. I didn't understand my soul jumping abilities, but I suspected if Reed died, I might escape his body and return to my old one. But that would only work if Dom and I were no longer paired —there was no way I would willingly become the Titan's attack dog again.

Avi can take that on.

"It's your lucky day, little Lykos. I'm not going to kill you." I rolled off the male and stalked back to the sinks.

Avi slowly pushed himself up. "You really are insane. And that's my razor, by the way."

"It's dull. Don't you know, the sharper the knife, the quicker the kill?" It was something Dom used to say. I tossed the razor down on the counter, closed my eyes, and summoned Reed.

"Reed, false alarm. Avi isn't a threat."

Reed surged into our consciousness. *"Jesus, man. You can't keep doing that."*

"You told me it was okay if we were in a life-or-death situation," I reminded him. *"I thought dickwad was here to kill us, but he's only here to promote us to red team."*

Reed met the terrific news with a rush of panic. *"I can't be on red team. I don't know anything about fighting."*

"But I do," I said calmly. *"Now talk to the little Lykos so he doesn't get suspicious."*

Reed opened our eyes and blinked out at Avi, who was blotting the cuts on his arms with paper towels.

"Why is he bleeding, Hunter?"

"Not important. He's waiting for your answer on the promotion."

Reed cleared our throat. "Uh, thanks, but no thanks on the red team opportunity, man."

Avi scowled at us. "It isn't an offer you can refuse. You'll start training with the team immediately."

Reed shook our head. "No. I—"

The door swung open, and Sai stuck his head in the bathroom. "There's my main man! Congrats on promoting, Reed! Love the new do!"

Avi twisted around to glare at his younger brother. "Why don't you tell him how you were just eating his woman out?"

Reed's shock melded with my fury.

Sai grinned. "I was just warming Lee up for our threesome." He winked at us. "Can't wait for tonight."

"I'm going to kill the motherfucker," I shouted, trying to force my way back into the driver's seat.

"No. You're not. Lee probably came onto him," Reed said, sounding resigned. *"Seems she's jumping on any guy these days."*

"Well, you can't blame her. We weren't there to take care of her needs and Alpha Diaz's compulsion turned her into a nympho."

"What?" Reed's shock took me off guard.

"I thought you knew that." Surely, I must have mentioned it at some point. *Didn't I?*

"Definitely not, man. What the hell is going on?"

I sighed. *"Do you remember how I told you that alpha shifters can use mind control on humans and weaker shifters."*

"Vaguely."

"Well, one of those alphas used his ability on Lee. He basically commanded her to want sex all the time."

Reed reeled in shock. *"Jesus. When did this happen?"*

"Her last night dancing in the club. The same night we got together." I was still pissed I hadn't been strong enough to break Javier's compulsion.

"Wow, man. This—this explains so much."

"Reed," Sai called out, beckoning us over to the doorway. "Come on. Let's start the New Year's Eve celebration." He lifted a bottle of bourbon in our direction.

"Tell him no, cocksucker. We need to get back to Lee." I didn't like that we'd left things so negative with her.

"I need a minute before I see her again."

I cursed in frustration. *"You're such a pussy. I hate that I'm stuck with you."*

"You and me both, man."

Avi gave us a disapproving look as we strode over to Sai. "Don't be idiots. Remember what happened on Christmas Eve?"

Reed's mood bottomed out as he remembered that fat bitch dying on us in the cafeteria. Even I thought Dom had gone too far with that surprise tactical training exercise.

"You both need to keep a clear head," Avi warned.

As much as I disliked the wolf shifter, he had a point. *"The dickwad is right. Keep your head or you're dead."*

Sai scoffed. "Lay off, Buzzkill. It's New Year's fracking Eve and Dominic said in briefing he wasn't planning any drills today. Besides, we have to celebrate Reed's promotion and his fresh new look." The pretty boy grinned at us. "Every woman in the school is going to cream their panties when they see him."

"Nice going, cocksucker. There will be even more annoying bitches chasing us around now."

"Ah, hell." Reed reached for the bottle Sai was holding. "Can I have some of that?"

Sai pressed it into our hand. "Consider it your welcome to red team present. And on that note, let me show you where our team hangs out."

"Okay," Reed said, taking a swig from the bottle. The grainy alcohol burned our throat as Sai slung his arm around our shoulders and ushered us out into the hall.

"Lee won't like this."

Ignoring me, Reed took another swallow.

"At least stop drinking. I can't talk to you if you're drunk," I pleaded.

"That's the point, asshole."

❧ 13 ❧

LEE

eed is on red team. Crap!

I had to do something. Maybe I could convince Dominic to change his mind. *Yeah, right.* I'd have a better chance of changing the planet's orbit.

But Dominic can't make Reed be on red team if he refuses, right? A sinking feeling in my stomach told me I was wrong. Dominic didn't take no for an answer.

Dammit. Our only other choice was to leave the school. I mean, it wasn't even a question anymore. Reed's life was at stake.

And who cared about Avi's objections now? The rat bastard had lost his invite to come with us.

I rubbed my chest, still feeling the sting of his words. *Where does Avi get off calling me a whore?* He already knew I was with Reed, and he didn't seem to mind our threesome with Dominic.

So why lose his mind over me and Sai?

Maybe it was because Sai was his younger brother. I chewed on my lip as I considered the whole sibling aspect. I probably wouldn't have enjoyed walking in on Avi with another woman, but I'd deal. However, if I'd walked in on him with Eden...

I'd go postal.

Ugh. Maybe I had crossed a line. These open relationships were a lot more complicated than I'd anticipated. And a little more uncomfortable. I shifted my legs, feeling the lingering soreness between my thighs and ass. Sai's loving, as incredible as it had been, was going to take some getting used to.

But I definitely wasn't about to pass up my opportunity for a threesome with him and Reed. We could still make that happen before we left. It'd take at least a couple days for Reed, Eden, and I to get our supplies together anyway. Despite what Dominic said, there was no way we were walking out of here empty-handed.

I went over to the pile of clean clothes I'd stashed near the music stands. With shaking hands, I threw on a black G-string and sports bra, followed by a pair of black jeans and a black shirt. I'd learned early on that most stains were far less visible on dark clothing. So, even though being on the laundry team allowed me to wash my stuff more than the once a week we were mandated, it made sense to go with a Johnny Cash look.

Being on the laundry team gave me another advantage. I could swipe plenty of clean clothes for us before we left. Additionally, because of my stint on the food prep team, I knew where Paula stockpiled the canned and dried food. *I'll pack at least three days of meals, too.*

We'll also need our weapons, I thought, strapping on my knife sheath along with my gun holster.

Eden can get medical supplies from the nurse's office just in case we run into trouble.

My stomach curdled before I mentally shook myself. *No. We're going to be fine. We don't need medical supplies.* The three of us would hike up to the foothills estates. There, we'd have everything we'd need to hole up for the foreseeable future.

Our quality of life would be so much better up there. *No zombies. No moody shifters. And no infuriating sergeants bossing us around all the time.*

What about Sai? I felt a pang of regret about leaving the rock star after we'd just upgraded our relationship. I wondered if Reed would be open to inviting him along.

It wouldn't hurt to add one more to our traveling party. There was strength in numbers after all. And Sai was as skilled with his war hammer as he was with his tongue.

Liking the idea more and more, I put on clean socks and my sneakers and went in search of my sister. After I went over the plan with her, I'd talk to Reed. Hopefully, he'd have calmed down by then. He never usually stayed upset very long. Although I'd never seen him this mad before, he was usually so easygoing.

Avi, on the other hand, was moody as hell and although he was frequently pissed off about something, he'd never lost his temper at me before. As I passed the computer lab where Avi and I had our midnight trysts, my heart lurched.

Crap. I was going to miss that stubborn werewolf. In just a short time, Avi had become my rock. He was the one person I could go to with my problems, no matter how insignificant. He didn't criticize me the way Dominic did, or idolize me the way Reed normally did, or make a joke out of everything the way Sai did. Avi just accepted me as I was and offered his support. He'd helped me dig graves, fold laundry, and even given me advice on how to reach Eden, who seemed to be avoiding me lately.

Avi knew what it was like to be the oldest sibling, and he got me in a way few other people did. Or at least I'd thought so.

I stopped to stare at the small glass pane in the computer

room door. Dominic must have stood in this exact spot watching Avi and me every night. A shiver ran through me as I remembered the hunger in his midnight gaze.

Dammit. I'm going to miss Sergeant Pain in the Ass too.

Wondering if either of those alpha-holes would miss me, I turned into the hallway that led to the nurse's office. The sight of half a dozen people lined up against the wall wearing medical masks brought me to a halt.

"Remember, stand six feet apart from anyone not in your immediate family," Olivia called out as she walked the length of the line.

"What's going on?" I asked the blonde nurse wearing medical scrubs.

"New protocol. You need to wear one of these if you're interacting with the medical team." Olivia handed me a mask. "Are you having cold or flu symptoms?"

I fitted the blue mask over my face and shook my head. "No, I was looking for Eden. Is she working?"

Olivia sighed. "She's always working."

I motioned at the people in line. "Are all these people sick?"

She nodded.

"Oh, wow." I didn't know so many people were catching that cold.

At the back of the line, Kiara coughed and rubbed her heavily pregnant belly. "Figures. I survived a zombie apocalypse only to die of the canine flu."

My heart skipped a beat. *Did she say canine flu?*

Grady, a burly, greasy-haired, biker-looking guy with a horseshoe mustache, spun around. "You don't have the canine flu. Do you see any goddamn dogs here?" He swung his bloodshot gaze to Olivia. "Why the hell do I have to wait in line with this stupid spic? I want to see my daughter."

"Lower your voice," Olivia hissed. "I've already told you. Sharon needs to speak with you."

"About what?" Grady crossed his arms over his brawny chest. The wife-beater and sleeveless motorcycle vest he wore showcased the confederate flag tattoo on his muscular bicep. "Is she going to explain why Rosie is getting worse instead of better? What kind of doctoring are you whack-jobs doing, anyway?"

"If you'd rather wait in the chapel, I could send someone to get you—" Olivia broke off as Grady cursed, tore off his mask, and stomped down the hallway.

"I'm going to find Sergeant Rosario and report this shit," he shouted back.

"More likely he's going to find some booze," Olivia grumbled. "Guy can't stay sober for more than a few hours."

"This *isn't* the canine flu, right?" I asked her in a low voice.

Olivia gave me a shuttered look. "Officially no. Unofficially..."

Shit. We'd all thought this was just a winter cold. If this was the same virus that took out a quarter of the world's population last spring, it'd spread like wildfire through the school.

A cough from someone in line made me jump. "Does Dominic know?"

Olivia nodded. "He doesn't want the word getting out."

"Why?" *That's the most asinine thing ever.* People needed to protect themselves. We needed to stop eating, training, and sleeping in large groups.

"He doesn't want widespread panic." She lowered her voice. "This is a nasty variant, too. Previous canine flu exposure isn't offering much immunity." At my confused look, she added, "If you were sick with the canine flu before, you can still contract this." Her voice went hoarse, and she suddenly seemed to blink back tears.

I rubbed her arm. "Is everything okay?"

She sniffed. "No, Sam came down with it yesterday."

"Oh, no. I'm so sorry." I'd noticed her toddler wasn't at dinner last night. "How is he doing?"

"Okay for now. But this strain seems more severe than the original."

My stomach sank. Eden, Reed, and I had suffered through a nasty bout of canine flu at the beginning of the pandemic. Even though the three of us were in good health, it'd laid us all out for weeks. At one point, Eden had gotten so ill, I'd rushed her to urgent care.

But there were no urgent cares now. Or hospitals. Or medications.

Eden could get really sick again. *Hell*. We all could. And what would happen when children and the elderly—the groups most vulnerable to the virus—started dying?

There will be pandemonium around here.

Any conflicted feelings I had about leaving the school evaporated. *We need an exit strategy ASAP.*

Giving Olivia's arm a squeeze, I said, "I hope Sam fights it off and recovers quickly. Let me know if there is anything I can do to help."

She sucked in a shaky breath. "You can tell that sister of yours to get some rest or she'll be the next to come down with this."

"I'll do that." Thanking her, I walked over to the table set up in front of the nurse's office.

There, Isaac, the EMT, was running an infrared thermometer over Jerry Barnum's forehead. "A hundred and two point four, Nikki," he called out.

The dark-haired former college student jotted down notes on her clipboard.

"I didn't know you'd joined the medical team," I said, surprised at seeing her there.

Nikki pushed her glasses up the bridge of her nose as she looked over at me. "Hey, Lee. Yeah, Sharon let me switch teams to be closer to Baba. She's... under the weather." Her expression tightened with worry as she glanced at the nurse's office door and then back at me. "What are you doing here?"

"I came to see Eden."

"She's in the back with Rosie and the others," Isaac said over the top of Jerry's white hair. "Go on in."

I stepped around the table and reached for the doorknob.

"Hey, no cutting," Jerry Barnum barked through a hacking cough.

I gave the older man a sour look. "I just need to talk to my sister."

"You're fine." Isaac waved me on.

☙

I stepped inside the long rectangular room, only to stop short at the sight of Sharon.

The dark-skinned, middle-age nurse with salt and pepper hair glared at me from behind her desk. "Coming to steal more pain medication, Ms. Walker?"

Oh, crap. Technically, Eden had been the one to borrow Sharon's pain meds to treat one of her injured animals. But then, I'd taken some of them for Reed. Although the morphine seemed to have exorcized Hunter, I deeply regretted coercing Reed to take the drug. He'd quickly become an addict and detoxing had put him through pure hell.

The face mask helped hide my guilt. "I don't know what you're talking about. I'm here to see my sister."

"Mm-hmm." Sharon sucked noisily on her front tooth, not buying it for an instant. "She's in the back. And just so you know, I'm the only one with the keys to the medicine cabinet now." She patted the pocket of her powder-blue smock-shirt.

The door opened behind me, and Isaac popped his head in. "Jerry Barnum is presenting with symptoms."

"Send him in." Sharon gave me another critical look. "Move along, child. And tell that sister of yours her shift ended four hours ago. I'm going to ban her from the clinic if she doesn't rest some."

Nodding, I walked past her desk and the two empty exam tables.

At the back of the office, near the sink, was a doorway to another room. That space was dimly lit by battery-operated lanterns on the floor. As my eyes adjusted to the gloom, I looked over the row of cots. Three of them were occupied. Nikki's grandmother and Olivia's toddler were lying on the cots closest to the door. Both seemed to be napping, although their breathing was broken by fits of coughing.

The soft sound of Eden's voice drew my attention to the cot enveloped by a white curtain at the end of the room. It sounded as if my sister was reading.

"Today is your day. You're off to great places. You're off and away…"

Her words triggered bittersweet memories. Smiling, I snapped the curtain open. "Gran used to read us that book."

Eden gasped and jumped out of her chair. The Dr. Seuss book she'd been holding fell onto the lap of the little girl stretched out on the cot beside her. Not that the child noticed.

I gawked at Rosie, shocked by her appearance.

The poor thing looked terrible. Her blond curls hung lank, and her freckled face had a waxy sheen that brought to mind Gran's last days in the hospital.

As Rosie sucked in labored breaths through the oxygen mask taped over her tiny face, my heart ached with the unfairness of it all. The little girl had already gone through so much. She'd witnessed her mother's gruesome death and now had to battle a virus that never should have gotten into the school.

"Why are you here?" Eden asked, slipping on a pair of men's sunglasses that swallowed most of her face.

I looked at my sister and gasped. She looked almost as bad as Rosie. Not only was she wearing the same stained pink T-shirt and yoga pants she'd worn all week, her lips were cracked, and her brown hair hung in oily strands around her too pale face. "Eden, you look awful."

"Thanks," she said sarcastically. She yanked on the face mask that had been dangling from her ear.

She looked so terrible, I couldn't even bring myself to apologize. "My God. Your clothes are hanging off you. Have you been eating?" I'd been saving food for her at every meal, but I hadn't been watching to see if she ate it. From now on I would. "And you need to rest. Sharon said your shift ended hours ago." My tone came out harsher than I intended.

Eden stiffened. "I'm keeping Rosie company. She... she doesn't have much time." Her voice broke.

A softball lodged in my throat as I glanced back at the child. "I-I didn't realize it was that serious."

Tears leaked from under her sunglasses. "Why would you? You've been too busy breaking Reed's heart with Dev's brother."

Ouch. "I'm not here to talk about me. Although Reed and I are in an open relationship, by the way."

"Your choice, not his, I'll bet."

I opened my mouth to defend myself, but she didn't give me a chance.

"I can't believe you would do him so dirty. Reed is family, not some random hook up. He's been in love with you forever and you're treating him like garbage. You don't deserve him."

She straightened her spine, clearly bracing for a fight, but I wasn't in the mood.

"You're right. I don't deserve him. And as soon as we leave here, I'll make it up to him."

"Leave here?" she whispered.

"Yes, the three of us are leaving the school as soon as possible. It's too dangerous to stay here."

Baba's sudden hacking cough from the other side of the room underscored my words.

"I'm not going anywhere." Eden bent down and picked up a grey stuffed cat from the floor. "At least not until I have a cure for Rosie."

She nestled the stuffed animal next to the little girl. The gesture was so reminiscent of the way our mom used to tuck us in, it made my throat catch.

"You said it yourself. Rosie doesn't have much time left. She's beyond a cure."

Eden shook her head. "No. Mike is bringing back the serum and it will cure her."

Mike isn't coming back. I chewed the inside of my mask, wondering if I should break the news.

Eden continued. "We just need to keep Rosie alive until he gets back. Antivirals would help her immune system fight this, but Dominic won't authorize a supply run to the hospital to get them."

I made a choked sound. "Of course not. The hospital is overrun with Biters." Everyone knew Saguaro Valley General was ground zero for the Z-virus outbreak.

Eden shook her head. "I'm talking about the animal hospital. They have the antivirals too. It's not far away. Could you talk to Dominic and convince him to go?"

I took a step back, "He wouldn't listen to me—"

She grabbed my arm with surprising strength. "Lee, you're

the only one he'd listen to. If you can get him to approve the supply run, I'll do whatever you want."

I put my hands on my hips. "Does that include leaving the school with me and Reed?"

Her breath caught, and she looked down at Rosie. "Yes, I'll go wherever you want. Just help me get the meds for Rosie. Her life depends on it."

"What meds?" Grady demanded, stepping around the curtain.

Shit. How much did he hear?

Eden looked over at the burly man. "Antivirals. They'll help Rosie and anyone else who contracts this virus."

Sharon yanked the curtain completely open. "Eden, don't give Mr. Hoffer false hope. Antivirals have limited effectiveness in cases like Rosie's."

"But there's a chance they could help?" Grady's bloodshot eyes searched Eden's face.

Eden nodded.

Sharon sighed. "There's no use in discussing this. Sergeant Rosario already decided retrieving the medication would be too dangerous."

"More dangerous than letting the canine flu run rampant through the school?" I blurted out.

"It's not the canine fl—" Grady broke off as Sharon gave Eden a withering look.

Eden put up her hands. "I didn't tell her."

"You didn't have to," I said, coming to her defense. "It's obvious what's going on here. What isn't obvious is why Sergeant Pain in the Ass isn't doing anything about it?"

"Maybe because he hasn't been fully briefed on the situation," Dominic answered in a voice sharper than glass.

14

LEE

How many run-ins am I going to have with Dominic today?

As the sergeant stepped around the curtain, I braced myself for his anger.

He surprised me by turning his scowl on Sharon. "You said there were only two confirmed cases. Has that changed?"

Sharon nodded slowly. "We have four more."

"Does that number include the coughing people lined up in the hallway?" I motioned at the doorway.

"No," Sharon said with a heavy sigh.

Dominic cursed. "We did a full medical screen of everyone upon arrival. How the hell did this get in?"

Sharon pursed her lips. "Someone who'd recently contracted the flu could have escaped detection. Rosie is the first to show symptoms so we're considering her our patient zero."

Dominic's eyes narrowed. "The child brought it in?"

"No. She didn't," exclaimed Grady. "Rosie stayed at home with her mom. They rarely left the house. She had no contact with dogs or sick people."

Eden made a strange sound and glanced down at Rosie. She probably thought the shouting would wake the little girl.

Although Rosie didn't react to the noise, Sam whimpered in his cot and Baba shifted restlessly in hers.

Sharon scanned her sleeping patients and gave us all a hard look. "Keep it down."

Dominic lowered his voice. "The facts speak for themselves."

Grady's face turned red. "My daughter contracted this flu here. Under your watch—"

Sharon interrupted. "Gentlemen, arguing won't help. We need a containment plan and additional medical supplies."

Eden rubbed her hands together anxiously. "We can get supplies from the animal hospital along with the antivirals that can help Rosie... and everyone else who's sick. It's only eight miles south of here."

"Then what are we waiting for? Let's go." Grady turned as if to leave.

"No one goes anywhere without my authorization," Dominic said with a scowl. "This... dumb girl..." he pointed at Eden, "... has zero concept of how dangerous that area has become."

Eden wilted like a sun-baked rose.

No one insults my sister. "Don't you dare call her dumb. Her plan is good." I didn't really think so, but I wanted her to know I had her back.

Eden sent me a grateful look. "I know the animal hospital like the back of my hand. I can get in and out with everything we need in under five minutes—"

"Whoa. You're not going," I interrupted. "Dominic and his soldiers can go."

Dominic's tone frosted over. "Were you promoted to commanding officer, Ms. Walker?"

I lifted my chin. "Maybe we'd be better off if I was."

Dominic snorted. "You'd get everyone killed."

"No. That's what you're doing," I countered. "By ignoring the gang threat and this outbreak, you're hammering the nails into our coffins."

A muscle twitched in the sergeant's jaw. If looks could slay, I'd have died on the spot.

"I volunteer to go. I'll do anything to save my baby." Grady reached down and squeezed Rosie's foot through the blanket.

Maybe the guy isn't a total asshat.

"We really could use additional medical supplies," Sharon added. "We didn't get much out of the nursing home raid or the pharmacy supply run."

"Because other survivors beat us there," Dominic pointed out. "And they've probably already cleaned out the animal hospital."

Grady puffed out his chest. "It's a chance I'm willing to take."

Dominic gave Grady an assessing look. "Fine. I'll put a team together. You'll be on it."

Grady nodded, looking relieved.

Dominic pointed at Sharon. "You, put together a list of the supplies you need." He swung his finger in Eden's direction. "You, put together a diagram of the animal hospital. I'll need to see every entrance and exit."

Eden shook her head. "You won't need a map, because I'm coming with you."

The hell she is. Before I could argue, Dominic nodded. "Yes, you're on the team. But I'll still need the diagram in case something happens to you before we get there."

I felt all the blood leave my face. "No way. She's not going."

"She. Volunteered." Dominic drew out the words.

"Yes, I did." Eden gave me a dirty look. "And last I

checked, I was a fully responsible adult."

"You've never been responsible a day in your damn life," I spat.

She threw up her hands. "Because you never let me be. Sissy, I'm doing this. Deal with it."

Oh, hell no.

"It's settled." Dominic turned to Sharon. "I'll cancel the buffet and the community events planned for today. Tonight, we'll come up with a plan for social distancing."

"And masking," Sharon added.

Dominic nodded and turned to leave.

"Wait. I want to go on the animal hospital supply run, too," I called out.

Dominic stilled. "No."

"If Eden goes, I go." There was no way I'd let my sister go on a dangerous mission without me there to watch her back. Especially when she looked like death warmed over.

The sergeant whirled around with such a menacing look on his face, everyone but me took a step back. "Are you challenging me again?"

I popped my hip and glared back. "Why? Are you going to punish me with your knife again?"

The vein in Dominic's forehead throbbed, and I sensed he was barely holding in his rage. His jaw set in a hard line as he tried to incinerate me with his eyes. "This time I'll use my hands."

I know he meant that as a threat, but seeing him worked up like that ignited a bonfire between my thighs.

At that moment, I forgot all about the people around us and Darcy's death threat. All I could think about was Dominic and how I craved his punishment, his anger, his body...

"I think I'd like that," I murmured in a tone so husky it could have steamed the air.

Dominic's nostrils flared, and his death stare shifted into something that made me needy and breathless.

An electrifying heat crackled between us.

If we hadn't had an audience hanging on our every word, I'd have bet my life that the sergeant would have flung me down on an empty cot and introduced me to his monster cock.

Will I have to call it sir too?

My sister let out a cough that sounded suspiciously like, "Get a room."

Dominic blinked, seeming to come to his senses. "Fine. You can be on the team, Ms. Walker. But understand, this isn't another field test. If you screw up like you did this morning, it's your funeral." Then he stalked out, leaving me to face down three intensely curious sets of eyes.

"What?" I said defiantly, crossing my arms over my chest.

Eden shook her head.

Sharon harrumphed. "I need to get back to my patients."

As the nurse walked into the other room, Grady dropped into the empty chair next to Rosie.

"Let's give him some privacy." I tugged on Eden's arm.

She allowed me to drag her through the nurse's office, past Kiara and Jerry, who were now lying on the exam tables. But she stopped short when we stepped out into the hallway, and she saw Isaac taking Dev's temperature.

Zara stood next to her younger brother, a worried expression on her masked face.

"Dev! Are you okay?" Eden exclaimed.

Dev looked over at her. "Hey! I'm great! How are you?"

Zara punched Dev's arm. "You're not great. You've been coughing up a lung since we got back. Now you're running a fever."

"One hundred and three point two," Isaac called out to Nikki.

Dev gave me a sheepish look. "Guess it's not allergies." His gaze skipped back to Eden. "You aren't leaving, are you? I was hoping to see you... er... hoping that you'd be here."

Zara rolled her eyes. "Smooth. Real smooth, bro."

Dev's already flushed face turned a darker shade of red.

Eden shook off my hand. "I can stay a little longer. Let me show you to a spare cot. Sharon won't mind." She opened the door and beckoned Dev to follow.

"Eden, I still need to talk to you," I said in my big sister voice.

She waved me away. "Later."

Brat.

Zara shook her head as Eden and Dev stepped inside the nurse's office. "Ugh, younger siblings. Can't live with them. Can't kill 'em. Amirite?"

"Right." I turned and strode down the hallway, determined to find Reed. Not only did I need to tell him about the plan to leave, I also now needed to give him a head's up on the animal hospital supply run. Given how badly he'd reacted to me hiding my field test, I couldn't keep him in the dark about it.

What if Reed wants to go too? A sick feeling gripped me before I shook it off. *No. I'll make sure that doesn't happen.*

❧

"Hey, girl! Wait up!" Zara called after me.

Only the manners Gran drummed into me made me stop near the computer room door. I had no interest in talking with Zara after she'd betrayed my trust this morning. Even though I knew she'd been following Dominic's orders, I wasn't one to forgive easily. I'm sure Roger would say it all boiled down to my trust issues.

I tapped my foot impatiently. "What do you want?"

She stopped a few feet away and tugged off her mask. "To hang."

"Shouldn't you stay with Dev?" I motioned at the nurse's office.

She ran a hand through her short rainbow-hued curls. "He doesn't need me cramping his love life. He's crushing hard on Eden. I told him that ship already sailed into that beefcake Mike, but he's hoping she'll be open to multiple lovers like her big sister."

I knew she hadn't meant anything bad by it, but she'd hit a nerve. "Fat chance. She's not a whore like me."

Zara scoffed. "What's with this self-deprecating bullshit? You hangry or something?"

When I said nothing, she laughed. "Let's go check out that New Year's buffet."

I sighed. Zara took subtle hints about as well as her brother, Sai, did. "I'm not hungry. Besides, Dominic said he's canceling the buffet."

"Seriously? That's shitty. Everyone's looking forward to it."

"I can't imagine why." *Don't they remember how the last holiday meal in the cafeteria turned out?* "Anyway, I'll see you later." I turned my back on her.

"Wait. Are you still mad about this morning?"

I spun around. "Yes, I am. You totally set me up."

Zara held up her hands. "Dominic didn't give me a choice. I felt awful about it. You're like my best friend here."

I glared at her through narrowed eyes. "Best friends don't hide important shit about their siblings from each other." *Like the fact your brother is a damn werewolf.* I gave her a knowing look.

Her hazel eyes went wide. "I'm sorry, Lee. I wanted to tell you Eden was being field tested with us, but Mike ordered us not to. And then Dominic ordered us not to tell anyone that Danika attacked us in the auto shop."

I blinked in surprise. "Danika Bloom?" I'd thought no one had seen the woman since Dominic exiled her. The sergeant had been furious when she and her husband busted through the front gates trying to bring their dog to the school.

"Yeah." Zara leaned in and said in a low voice. "She was a zombie, but not like a regular zombie. She was fast, strong, and smart. Can you believe that shit? Mike called her a Howler."

Howler? I'd heard that term before. I wracked my brain trying to remember where.

"Dominic swore us to secrecy. He doesn't want it getting out that there are super zombies out there."

My stomach flipped. Dominic said we were facing much bigger problems than Javier's gang driving the zombies north. *Did he mean Howlers?* A chill raced down my spine. "Did Eden see Danika too?"

Zara nodded. "Danika attacked her and Mike. Dev and I totally thought Danika killed them. Can you believe those two assholes took out the Howler and then spent the entire night banging? They didn't even bother to let the rest of us know they were alive."

"What?" My voice went so high, it could have shattered the glass pane in the computer room door. "My sister had her field test, and you didn't tell me? You thought she died, and you didn't tell me?" What's worse, Eden hadn't told me either. I was going to have some serious words with the brat.

Zara's gaze darted around the hallway. "You were already so upset about Reed—that was the night he threw up for hours. And we didn't want you to completely lose it."

"Well, I'm completely losing it now," I shouted. "I'm so sick of people hiding things. You and Eden hiding your field tests. Avi hiding... his shit. Dominic hiding the gang threat and the fact there's a goddamn canine flu outbreak in the school."

"Canine flu?" Zara repeated softly. Lines of worry creased her eyes.

"I thought Dev just had a cold..."

Dammit. Zara wasn't a bad person. She cared about her family the way I cared about mine. I took a deep breath and reined in my temper. "Maybe Dev just has a cold. I'm sure Sharon will tell you one way or the other."

"Right." Zara glanced back at the nurse's office. "I'll talk to her, but not until we're cool." She motioned between us. "I know I haven't been a very good friend, but I promise from now on I will be. And I won't ever lie to you again. Even if it goes against orders. Okay?"

Deciding for once in my life to be the bigger person, I said, "Deal."

"Do you mean that?"

"Yeah. It's all water under the bridge." I took off my mask so she could see I wasn't bullshitting. "I'm sorry for being a bitch. I'm having a really crappy day. Reed found me with Avi and Dominic and lost his mind. Then later, Avi walked in on me and Sai and lost his mind."

"Fruitcake, Dominic, Avi, and Sai?" She let out a low whistle. "Damn, girl."

"Don't look so impressed. Both Avi and Reed hate me right now."

Zara made a dismissive noise. "No way. They're nuts about you. Avi just needs to wrap his mind around sharing you with his little brother and Fruitcake will be much more open-minded once those horny bitches have their way with him in the copy room."

I went motionless. "What?"

She laughed. "I heard Jacquie, Dawn, and Kelsey planning to seduce him. Poor Fruitcake. He's so drunk, he probably won't know what..." She caught the look on my face and trailed off. "Um. I thought you and Fruitcake had an open relationship."

"Not that open," I snapped.

Seeming to sense I was on the verge of exploding, Zara shoved her mask on and slowly backed away. "I'm going to check in with Dev. See ya."

As she disappeared down the hall, my emotions careened violently. I should have been okay with Reed and other women, but I wasn't. I really, really wasn't.

He's mine!

Logically, I knew that was totally unfair. But with every ragged breath, an image of Reed with another girl flashed into my mind.

Reed with Jacquie and her soulful brown eyes.

Reed with Dawn and her perfect bouncy tits.

Reed with Kelsey, who acted way too mature for her age.

Jealousy tore through me like a ravening zombie, shredding my insides and consuming my heart from within. A red haze fell over my vision.

Just then, Vincent pushed the computer room door open and stepped out. Catching sight of me, the bum raised his trash-filled hands and shouted. "The Queen is coming! The Queen is—"

"Going to die if she fucks with me," I snarled, "And so is every bitch who tries to take what's mine!"

An expression of reverence crossed Vincent's filthy, weather-beaten face. He dropped his trash and fell to his knobby knees before me. "Please, let me be *your* disciple." He pressed his dry, cracked lips to the top of my sneaker.

Ew! "No!" I scrambled back, then darted down the hallway in search of the man I actually wanted to kiss me.

I could only hope he wasn't kissing someone else.

15

REED

Every summer, Uncle Duncan used to take us out on the lake by his cabin. Eden and Lee always complained about the old rickety boat and the rotten fish smell that seemed baked into the wood planks, but I loved it. My favorite sensation in the world was sitting in that boat as it bobbed on the water.

Back and forth. Up and down.

Right now, I felt as if I was back on that boat. The table under me rocked while the copy machines and paper-filled shelves undulated around me.

Awesome.

It'd taken nearly an entire bottle of bourbon to get me to this state. But I was here. And nothing mattered now. Not Lee and all her lovers. Not Hunter and all his bitching. Not the apocalypse and all the zombies.

Nothing.

I hadn't felt this relaxed since... since the last time I'd injected morphine. Maybe I shouldn't have quit. It was quiet in my head without all Hunter's griping. And all the jealousy, pain, and heartbreak I'd been feeling seemed miles away.

The greatest hits of the seventies belted out of the old battery-operated CD player on the counter. Humming along to American Pie, I laced my fingers together under my head and let out a contented sigh.

This is perfect.

Dawn shifted next to me. "Can I have the rest of the bourbon?"

Well, almost perfect.

"Mm-hmm." Without opening my eyes, I pushed the bottle at her. Sai had gone to get more liquor, so there was no reason to be stingy.

Dawn swallowed noisily, then cuddled next to me.

I moved away. I didn't want her touch. I wanted Lee—Lee, who was probably boning some other dude right now. *Maybe Dev?* She seemed to be working her way through the Sighn brothers. Although I couldn't fault her for messing around with Sai. The rock star's charisma was so intense, it even had me jonesing for him.

Maybe I was being too hard on her. I mean, if Hunter was right, Lee wasn't in control of herself. Some jackass shifter made her a nympho.

A month ago, I never would have believed that, but that was before my crash introduction to zombies, body-snatching shifters, and super soldiers. Now, I could totally buy that my girl was under mind control. And it explained why she'd gone from refusing to even date a guy, to banging a bunch of random dudes.

I mean soldiers. Come on. Lee hates soldiers. Even from the time we were kids, she'd cross the street when she saw a soldier in uniform or shrink away from the national guard booth set up at our school. Soldiers reminded her of her father and the hell he put her through.

But this compulsion she was under made her want sex so

bad, she'd even gone after Dominic, who looked like my old G.I. Joe action figure come to life.

The shittiest part was that she'd probably only gotten together with me because of the compulsion. I was still in shock that she'd actually kissed me back all those weeks ago in her room. I'd expected her to shove me off her bed and throw one of Gran's porcelain frogs at my face. Normal Lee would have done that. Nympho Lee had shrugged off her towel and given me a taste of heaven.

I shuddered. That time with her had been the best moment of my life to date. But it didn't matter. We had to break this compulsion, even if it meant the end of our romantic relationship. It wasn't fair to Lee, and it wasn't right to take advantage of her uncontrollable urges.

"How do we stop Lee's compulsion?" I asked Hunter.

Hunter didn't respond. Or if he did, I couldn't hear him.

Oh, yeah. I'd forgotten he couldn't talk to me when I was high or wasted. I'd have to wait until I sobered up to get an answer.

"How are you feeling?" Dawn asked, drawing my attention to her.

"Like I'm on a boat," I blurted out.

"Yes!" She plastered herself even more closely to me. "This table is our boat. We should totally name it. That's what you do with boats, right?"

"Sure," I said, opening my eyes and scooting further away. Over the past hour, she'd been getting more flirtatious. All the girls were.

I made the mistake of glancing over at Kelsey and Jacquie, who were sitting on the copy machines across from us.

They caught my eye and giggled. They'd been doing that a lot since downing their third wine coolers.

Seeming to take my look for an invitation, they staggered off their copiers and stumbled over to the table.

Jesus no. I wished Sai would get back here so the girls wouldn't be so focused on me. When the rock star was around, he drew their attention, which I appreciated.

"Is it my turn to sit with Reed?" Kelsey asked Dawn.

Dawn sat up. "No. We're naming our boat."

"What boat?" Kelsey asked, slurring her words.

Dawn slapped her hand on top of the table. "This boat."

"Let's call it Slippery When Wet." Jacquie reached out to rub my thigh.

I jerked away. *These girls are something else.*

Dawn tossed back her curly hair. "I think we should name it Serenity."

"All aboard Serenity," Jacquie said, climbing onto the table with us.

"Hey!" Dawn tried to kick Jacquie off.

Jacquie slapped Dawn's foot away. "We promised to share him, remember?"

What?

"Right." Dawn slowly smiled. "Sharing is caring."

Letting out a husky laugh, Jacquie ripped off her shirt and straddled me. She wasn't wearing a bra and the sight of her large bare breasts temporarily short-circuited my drunk brain.

"Woo hoo!" Kelsey called out. "Let's get this party started!"

There was a rustling sound and suddenly all three females were topless.

I blinked, feeling dazed. *What the hell is happening?*

"Let's rock this boat." Jacquie grabbed my hands and brought them to her breasts.

"Ever had a threesome before?" Dawn leaned down to brush her pale pink nipples against my face.

Holy shit. Is this for real?

"It's a foursome," Kelsey blurted out. She started undoing her pants.

Isn't she like sixteen?

Dawn reached around Jacquie to cup me through my jeans.

My cock, greedy for any attention, hardened. I groaned, and for a split second, my fingers reflexively curled around Jacquie's breasts. But they didn't feel right.

They weren't Lee's.

"He's huge!" Dawn cried. "We'll need that lube Sai keeps in the drawer."

Hands were suddenly working my fly down.

I didn't have to hear Hunter's shouting in my head to know this was wrong.

Lee is my mate. Not them.

"Stop. This isn't happening." I shoved the girls away and rolled off the table. My equilibrium was shot, so I kind of crash-landed.

"Don't go!" the girls cried in a chorus.

Ignoring them, I staggered to my feet and headed toward the exit.

The woman of my dreams stared back at me through the narrow glass pane in the door.

Lee?

❦

HOPING IT WAS A HALLUCINATION, I BLINKED, BUT LEE'S face didn't disappear.

Jesus. She's seen everything.

That realization sobered me more than a punch to the jaw. I slowly pushed the door open, careful not to hit her with it. "What are you doing here?"

Lee looked from me to the topless girls. "Watching you turn down a good time."

"I don't want them," I said, feeling a little defensive.

"It's okay. You can be with other people." It looked as if it was costing her a lot to say that.

"I don't want other people. I only want you."

"Are you sure?" she whispered. I hated that her beautiful caramel-colored eyes were filled with uncertainty.

"It's the only thing I am sure about," I confessed. "I'm sorry I yelled at you earlier." The truth was there was nothing she could do that would change how I felt about her. No matter how many other dudes she boned, I would still love her. I might be jealous and pissy about it, but I'd still be hers. *Forever.* "I love you, honey."

She let out a soft cry and threw her arms around my neck. "I thought you'd broken up with me."

"Never," I said into her damp hair. It smelled faintly of chlorine and the vanilla body wash I'd gotten for her. *She must have taken the bath.* The knowledge that she'd enjoyed my gift filled me with pride.

Behind us, Kelsey sighed. "Aw! That's so romantic."

"No, it's not," one of the other girls said. "Everyone knows she's cheating on him with Avi."

Lee tensed.

"Ignore them," I whispered. "Let's go."

"No, the bitches can go." Lee pulled away and glared at the girls. "Get out or I'll tell your daddies I found you drinking and topless in here."

Kelsey let out a squeal. She and Jacquie quickly retrieved their shirts and ducked out of the room.

Dawn, who stayed on the table, gave Lee a look of challenge. "I don't have a daddy."

"No, but you have a grandfather who's really sick. Maybe you should check on Jerry instead of chasing after my man."

My man. I liked the sound of that.

Dawn slowly blinked. "Pop-Pop is sick?"

"He's with the medical team right now."

"If you're lying, there'll be payback." Dawn fumbled for her bra. It'd fallen over the laminator.

"I'm not lying, but it's been a whole three weeks since I've killed someone with a heartbeat. Bring it, bitch." The smile Lee gave Dawn was pure evil. I'd forgotten how scary Lee could be when she lost her temper.

Dawn, finally showing some sense, ran out of the room.

As soon as the door swung shut behind her, Lee sighed. "I can't blame them for throwing themselves at you. Holy hell, Reed! You're so hot, you're melting me like butter." She ran her hand over my smooth jaw and shorn hair, murmuring her approval.

An apology fell from my lips. "I know you liked the long hair and beard."

"Are you kidding? All I want to do right now is rip off your clothes and mount you like those girls were trying to do." She nuzzled my throat.

All the blood in my body pooled between my hips. I wanted more than anything to encourage her. But that wouldn't be right.

It's the compulsion. "Lee, stop. This isn't you. You don't really want me."

"The hell I don't. I've wanted you for years." Lee nibbled a path up to my ear and licked my ear lobe. "Do you know how many fantasies I had about you in your baseball uniform?"

I pulled away. "Wait. What?"

"And I won't even tell you how many times I'd touch myself to the sound of you jacking off through our bedroom walls."

I sucked in a breath. "You did?"

She gave me a sultry smile. "You tried to be quiet, but your waterbed would slosh all around, so I knew what was going on. It made me so hot." She ran her hands over my chest. "I always wondered what you were fantasizing about."

And just like that, any hang-ups I had vanished. I grabbed her and kissed her hard.

She moaned against my lips.

"You," I answered, thrusting my tongue into her welcoming mouth. "Always you."

The kiss got hotter and wetter as her hands moved over me. She yanked off my flannel shirt, and I was still drunk enough not to care that she was getting an eyeful of my scars.

She didn't seem disgusted by them as she broke our kiss to lick the mangled mess of my right nipple.

Lust pounded through me as she kissed her way down my stomach and undid my fly. I gasped her name as she shoved down my jeans and took me into her mouth.

The sensation of her lips and tongue was so mind-blowing, my knees buckled, and I nearly fell on top of her. "Jesus. Sorry. I—"

"You need to sit down," she said, tugging me forward.

I kicked off my pants and shoes as she steered me to the only chair in the room.

The exact moment Lee pushed my naked ass into the armless office chair, Slow Ride began playing on the CD player.

Lee let out a husky laugh.

"What's so funny?" I asked, feeling a stab of self-consciousness. I was totally naked—scars and erection on display—while she stood in front of me fully dressed.

"I had to dance to this song when Crystal called in sick a few months back. Max had me do her whole set, glitter bodysuit and all."

"Jesus. I'd like to have seen that."

"Yeah?" Her eyes sparkled. "I've been trying to think of how to repay you for the bath and gifts."

"You don't need to—"

She put her finger to my lips. "And I think I've figured it out. I'm going to give you a private show. And, from now on, no more open relationship. Just us."

Lee's words thrilled me, but I couldn't ask that of her. Not when I knew she had no control over her sexual urges. "I'm okay with the other guys, as long as I have a place at your side."

"Always." She kissed me. Then she grabbed some tape and a piece of paper from the shelf. As she secured it over the glass pane in the door, she said, "This show is for your eyes only. Are you ready?"

"Hell yeah." I stood and reached for her.

"Sit your ass down," she ordered.

Loving this bossy side of her, I sat.

She rewarded me by grinding to the beat of the song. "Oh, slow ride," she mouthed. "Take it easy." She danced seductively around my chair, the shake of her hips as mesmerizing as a metronome. Then she undressed, working off each bit of clothing so slowly I thought I'd die from frustration.

By the time she was finally naked, I was physically shaking. She was the most beautiful and sensual woman I'd ever seen in my life. Having her dance for me was almost a religious experience.

When I couldn't take any more, I tried to haul her into my lap.

She danced out of reach. "No touching, those are the rules in the club."

"Lee," I begged.

"What's the magic word?" she teased, rubbing her breasts together.

My eyes nearly crossed. "Jesus, please." I didn't know how much more of this I could take. She might not have realized it, but Hunter had been in the driver's seat all those other times we'd been together. Technically, this would be my first time, and I hoped I didn't embarrass myself.

She prowled over and straddled me. In the ultimate tease, she went motionless, with her bare feet on the floor, her pussy inches from my cock, and her nipples millimeters from my lips.

Unable to resist temptation, I licked one swollen tip.

She moaned, but when I tried to lick the other one, she pushed my face away. "No, touching, remember?" She rose on the balls of her feet, arching away from me.

"I'll be good." I forced my arms to my side, hoping she'd show some mercy.

Her eyes locked with mine as she aligned us. Then she dropped straight down onto me.

"Jesus Christ!" The shock of sinking into her tight, wet heat shook me to the core. And just when I'd decided I could die a happy man, she began to move.

Lust blanked my mind. Incredible sensations rolled over me, carrying me to a place I'd never been before. The high of being inside her was indescribable. No drug or alcohol could even come close. I was instantly addicted to this—to her. "Honey, what are you doing to me?"

"You've seen nothing yet," she panted. Using just the muscles of her toned thighs, she rose and fell over me. Slowly at first. Then faster and faster so that her breasts bounced with each stab of my cock.

The CD player went silent. But we made our own music. The wet slaps of our bodies mixed beautifully with my grunts and her breathless moans.

"You feel so good inside me," she cried. "So goddamn good."

I wanted her to feel better than good. Throwing my head back, I punched my hips up, trying to increase the friction.

She let out a ragged cry. "Yes! Yes!"

A hand reached between us.

I jerked my head up to see Sai standing behind Lee. The rock star was completely naked except for those gold chains around his neck.

He gave us both a heated look. "Am I late to the party?"

Since signing my first recording contract, the world had been mine for the taking. And I'd taken it all. Beautiful women. Beautiful men. Virgins. Whores. One at a time. Ten at a time.

All it took was the crook of my finger and they'd fallen into my bed. I'd gotten spoiled. Never was that clearer than now when the two people I desired most in the world turned to stare at me in surprise. And not a happy surprise. More the what-the-frack-are-you-doing-here surprise.

Awkward.

After Reed's invitation and my sizzling interlude with Lee, I'd assumed we were green light go for this.

"What are you doing?" Lee shouted.

"I-I thought the three of us were getting together." I yanked my hand from Lee's breast and backed away. "My bad."

Frack me.

"I asked him to join us," Reed explained, squirming under Lee. "You kept begging for a threesome."

"Do you want me to go?" I asked, hoping to hell they didn't.

Lee nodded, but then caught sight of my dick. "Holy crap! What is that?"

"Meet the dragon, darling." I swiveled my hips so she could better see the sleek black wings inked across my pelvis and the intricate black scales covering my throbbing dick. There were even yellow slitted eyes and sharp fangs inked around the tip.

"Jesus," Reed exclaimed. "And I thought my piercings were painful to get."

I winked at him. "It's a cautionary tale. Don't pass out at a tattoo parlor." Such bullshit. I'd lost a fracking bet to my old guitarist and had to get the ink of his choice. *Motherfracker.*

Lee licked her lips, clearly intrigued by my package. *And why not?* I was hung like a horse. "But I'm... we're not..." she trailed off, giving Reed a questioning look.

Reed's gaze licked across my body before he looked away. "I'd be okay with him... Um, with this... If you want."

I held my breath as Lee leaned over to whisper something in his ear. That movement shifted their bodies, giving me the million-dollar view of her bare pussy swallowing his dick.

Are those barbells? Frack.

I needed this. I needed them. So much my hands were shaking.

"But I want you to be happy," Lee whispered loud enough for me to hear.

"I'm happy if you're happy," Reed whispered back.

I'll make them both happy. Feeling my swagger return, I strode over to the drawer where I kept my stash of condoms and lube. It took me less than a minute to wrap my dick and grease it up. Then I made my approach.

Lee and Reed turned to look at me again, clearly still undecided.

I brushed my fingers lightly over her arm. "Don't you want to know what it's like to have two guys inside you... getting you off at the same time?"

"Yes," she breathed, her eyes going smoky.

"And Reed, don't you want to give your woman *everything* she desires?"

He nodded, slowly.

"Then let me rock your worlds. If you're not happy, there's a money-back guarantee."

The two of them slowly returned my grin, and I knew it was game on.

◌◌◌

"I'VE NEVER SEEN ANYTHING HOTTER THAN YOU TWO together." I ran my fingers over the sexy wings tattooed down Lee's spine.

She arched her back exactly as I hoped she would.

I reached around and cupped her large, firm breast. "Mouthwatering." Her tits were so much sexier than those fake silicone ones I was used to. I strummed her pert brown nipple in front of Reed's face.

He watched, seeming hypnotized.

"Isn't she beautiful, Fruitcake?"

"Yes," he gasped.

"Suck on this for me," I urged, pushing her stiff peak to his lips.

He suckled while I rolled the other nipple between my finger and thumb.

"Ooh!" Lee threw back her head, her hair tickling my chest.

"Frack, that's scorching. Kiss each other again."

Their mouths crashed together, her teeth nipping hard on Reed's bottom lip.

"Volcanic," I purred, urging them on.

As their kiss deepened, I arrowed one of my hands between their sweat-slicked bodies and found her clit.

She bucked against my fingers, her harsh cries swallowed by Reed.

"You're so wet," I crooned. I dipped my hand lower to stroke the slippery base of his cock. "And you're so hard."

Reed tore his mouth from Lee's and stared at me in shock. "Man, I don't—"

"Shh." I brought my fingers back to Lee's swollen nub. "Does that feel good, darling?"

"So good." She thrashed against my fingers, giving Reed the ride of his life.

"Jesus," Reed groaned, his hands white-knuckling the sides of the chair.

"That's it. Push him to his limit, darling."

She gripped Reed's shoulders and rode him harder, all the while bucking against my fingers.

Keeping the friction going, I pressed her closer to him. When she was nearly flat against his chest, I spread her gorgeous ass cheeks and rimmed her back hole.

She jumped but didn't stop moving over him.

Perfect. "That's it," I urged, my body torquing with lust. I touched my finger to the well-lubed tip of my condom, then slid it inside her.

"Oh, God!" she shuddered as I breached her tight ring.

"Relax for me, darling." I made sure to give her clit the attention it needed as I worked another finger in.

She thrashed her head from side to side. "Oh, yes. Yes!"

"You're amazing." I worked her clit and ass in tandem until her body tensed.

"Almost there," she gasped.

"Me too," Reed panted. His breathing was ragged as he tried to keep up with her frantic pace.

"Hold on." Not wasting any time, I pulled out my fingers and pushed my dick straight into that sweet little rose hole. The position was total shit on my knees, but it was so worth it when I felt her tight rim swallow me.

"Ah!" Lee flattened herself against Reed's chest.

I wanted to thank him for going motionless under us. It helped me slowly take possession of her virgin ass.

"It burns," Lee cried, instinctively pulling away.

I had to grab both her hips and hold her in place. "Just for a little bit, darling. Then it will feel amazing." I kissed the back of her neck and shoulders. "Doesn't it feel incredible to be inside her, Reed?"

"Yeah, but I don't want to hurt her, man," he answered in a strained voice.

"I won't go any further, if she doesn't want to," I said, even though every cell of my body demanded I bury myself balls deep.

"It's okay." Lee's voice quavered. "I want to try."

"It's going to feel so good." I slowly glided forward, the lube easing my way in.

"That's it, darling. You're doing it." I reached between them and strummed her swollen nub. "Feel that. Two cocks inside you, darling."

The moment I felt her relax into it, I gave one deep thrust and I was home, buried deep inside the ass of the woman I'd been craving for weeks. Even better, Reed was inside her too, sharing her with me.

Lee shuddered. "Oh, wow."

Wow, is right. I don't think I'd ever felt anything as sublime. "Now Reed and I are going to make you come so hard."

I snared his blue eyes over her shoulder. "Follow my lead."

He nodded, his expression a mixture of lust, confusion, and eagerness.

I eased my dick out and then thrust hard, driving her down onto Reed. "Now you move. Like we're playing catch." Weird analogy, but he was a baseball guy, so I knew he'd get it.

Reed punched his hips up, moving her back against me. I withdrew, then thrust, throwing her forward onto him. We moved back and forth, rocking her between us. It took only a few passes for them to get the rhythm, and then we were all three working together, our tempo getting faster and faster.

My thigh muscles shook from the strain of holding the uncomfortable position and sweat dripped from my chest onto her back. But I didn't give a frack. All that mattered was the sizzling lust building inside me.

This was just like my dream. Even better than my dream.

The need to come strung me tight as a bow, but I held out. Wanting her to go first, I rubbed her clit as if I was lighting a damn forest fire. "Come for us, darling. Come all over our dicks."

Lee thrashed and bucked, throwing off our dance. But it was fine because the next second she let out a loud cry and convulsed around us.

There was no holding back then. Her sweet ass milked my dick so hard I saw stars as I exploded inside her. "I'm coming, darling. I'm coming."

"I'm so... close," Reed grunted, his cock jerking against mine through the barrier of her body.

Wanting to push him over the edge, I threaded a hand through our spread thighs and cupped his balls.

He made a guttural shout and came.

I kept my hand there, stroking him as he unloaded everything inside her.

"Stop, man," he panted after a minute.

Chuckling, I pulled my hand away. Then I slowly withdrew from Lee's body.

She gasped when I tugged myself free.

"Congratulations, darling. You just earned your double penetration badge and your anal badge at the same time." I kissed the back of her neck and gently untangled a strand of her hair from around one of my necklaces. "You are the most amazing woman alive."

She gave a shaky laugh. "That would have been more of a compliment a month ago."

I slid the condom off and tossed it into the trash by the black copy machine. As I turned around, I caught sight of Lee stepping off Reed.

Frack. That man had a beautiful dick. I couldn't wait to stroke those barbells while I pounded into his virgin ass.

Just the thought made me hard again.

Still quivering, Lee stumbled her way over to the table. She winced as she tried to sit.

Concerned, I called out, "Are you okay, darling?"

She nodded, but it was clear she was a little sore. I grabbed some baby wipes I kept on hand and one of the wine coolers from off the counter. "Here. These are for clean-up and that's for taking the edge off. I promise the sting will fade with practice." I kissed her forehead, hoping she'd be open to more practice with me.

"Thanks," she said, looking a little shell-shocked.

She wasn't the only one. Reed was pulling on his pants with shaking hands. I hadn't paid too much attention to his body beyond his amazing dick, but the sight of all his scars had me doing a double take.

"Frack. What happened to you?" I walked over and stroked my hand down the mangled skin of his chest.

Reed shoved me away and turned his back on me.

"What's wrong?"

"He was in an accident a long time ago," Lee explained. "He's sensitive about his scars."

"He doesn't need to be. They only make him more interesting... more unique." I reached out and touched his shoulder.

Reed whirled around. "Jesus. Stop it, man. I'm not into dudes."

Cue the sound of a record scratch in my head. "B-but the threesome was your idea?" I stammered.

"Yes, but only with her. Not you and me. I'm straight."

There was no mistaking the ring of uncertainty in his voice. "So, you don't want this?" I ran my hand down my body, proud of my lean muscles and rock-hard abs.

Lust flared in his eyes before he looked away.

Ah. I get it. He's ashamed of wanting me. "Fine then. Kiss me and prove me wrong." I grabbed the back of his head and pressed my mouth against his. As I suspected, his resistance went up in smoke the second I swiped my tongue against his bourbon-flavored lips. With a groan, he opened his mouth and dragged me into his arms.

As his tongue danced with mine, I shoved my hand in his still open pants. Then I stroked that glorious, pierced dick that was still sticky and wet with their desire.

He pushed me away again. "I don't... I don't..." His gaze went to Lee, who was watching us with rapt attention.

"Don't stop," she begged, dropping the baby wipes. She slid her hand between her thighs and touched herself. "That's such a turn on."

"Yes, darling. Start warming up that motor again. Cause we're about to take her for another spin."

"But... but..." Reed's confusion was adorable.

"This next time, you're the one in the middle. Her pussy on your dick. My dick in your ass." I reached out and stroked him again. "But first, I'm going to warm you up." I slowly dropped to my knees, taking his jeans to the floor with me.

He shook his head, but his dick hardened and bobbed in front of my lips.

"Tell me you don't want this?" I teased, blowing a hot breath over him. "Tell me, you don't want Sai Sighn to suck your dick."

"I don't—" The first swipe of my tongue had him moaning. "Jesus," he threw his head back.

"More?"

His groan of surrender was a beautiful thing. "Yes. More."

"More," Lee echoed. Her husky moans increased as she worked her jewel faster and faster. Clearly, seeing me with Reed excited her.

She really was the perfect woman, and he was the perfect man.

And they're mine.

Digging my fingers into Reed's tight ass, I deep throated every fracking inch of him, barbells and all.

Reed's harsh groan was drowned out by a loud knock on the door.

"Stop screwing around. Dominic wants the three of you on the next mission. We leave on the hour," Avi shouted.

Frack. Buzzkill strikes again.

❧ 17 ❧

LEE

*B*ang.

The dead woman slapped the front window. The glass rattled, and the brightly colored tinsel hanging over the dusty wood blinds danced in the hazy afternoon light.

"What's that?" Grady shouted as he white-knuckled the crowbar in his hands.

"Shh. It's a Biter," I whispered, peering over the front counter.

"Just one?" Reed asked from where he crouched near my feet.

My stomach flipped as I looked down at him. Reed had been gorgeous before, but with his new clean-shaven look, he was mesmerizingly beautiful. Even hungover, he had to be the sexiest man alive.

"Yes," I answered, forcing my gaze back over the counter.

The dead woman's filmy white eyes rolled in her desiccated skull as she tottered back to the sidewalk in heels and a dazzling purple sequined dress. The Biter, who I immediately dubbed Ms. Sparkle, lifted her head like a dog sniffing the air and then hurled her body against the glass a second time.

Bang.

I jolted at the sound of the impact.

Why won't she go away?

Reed tensed, lines of strain bracketing his bloodshot eyes. "I don't like this."

That made two of us. *Neither he nor Eden should be here.*

I glanced over at my sister, who knelt by the display case filled with rotting pastries. She hadn't moved a muscle in twenty minutes. Her strange mannequin impersonation was as unsettling as her too-pale skin, and the way her pink T-shirt hung on her thin frame. She was also wearing those huge dark sunglasses again. Probably to hide the circles under her eyes.

Bang.

Ms. Sparkle hit the glass again.

The sound will draw the others. Tension climbed up my back. *Where the hell is Dominic?*

I leaned further over the counter so I could scan the street outside. There was no infuriatingly handsome soldier in sight. But I'd bet Reed's basket of treats that the sergeant was watching to see how we'd handle ourselves. Everything was a damn test to that man.

Screw his tests and screw him for dragging Reed along on this mission. I knew Eden, Grady, and I were here because we'd volunteered. And I could understand why Dominic made Avi and Zara our scouts and Sai our driver—they were among the most skilled fighters in our group. But he shouldn't have made Reed come in his hungover state. Now, in addition to keeping Eden out of harm's way, I also had to worry about keeping him safe.

And there was plenty to worry about. I leaned further over the counter so I could see the legions of dead filling the

Heritage Square Plaza. Most of the rotting remains of Saguaro Valley's finest shuffled around the Canine Memorial Fountain directly in front of the animal hospital. Some dragged half-torn limbs in their wake.

There were hundreds of them out there.

Swallowing hard, I moved into a crouch next to Reed. "We're going to be fine, honey. Dominic, Zara, and Avi will be back soon." Then we'd all hightail it out of here. There was no way Dominic would have us approach that wall of death outside. He might be a sadistic asshole, but his orders were to keep us alive, not kill us.

I bit off a muffled groan as I sat down. Being with Sai and Reed at the same time had been incredible, but it'd left me with a lingering soreness in delicate parts of my body. The slight discomfort wasn't enough to keep me from wanting to repeat the experience, though. In fact, I couldn't wait to try it again.

Maybe with Dominic and Avi this time?

No sooner did I have that thought than I remembered how frosty Avi had been to me on the trip down here. The werewolf barely looked at me since I'd walked out of the copy room with Sai and Reed. I hated the tension between us, and I missed the way his steady strength had calmed my nerves. I could also really use one of his reassuring whole-body hugs right about now.

Bang.

The Biter hit the window again.

I looked over at Grady, who was finger combing his greasy mullet. "Can you take care of it?"

"You take care of it. I'm saving my energy for the animal hospital." He dragged a flask out of his back pocket and drank from it.

I stared at the man in disbelief.

"I'll handle it." Reed reached for his shotgun. Dominic

had secured a long, sharp blade to the tip of the barrel, turning it into a pretty decent spear.

"No." I couldn't let Reed risk his life out there when he could barely walk in a straight line. "I need you to watch Eden. Can you find her something to eat?"

Reed gave me a frustrated look. "I can protect us."

Not in his current state. I didn't want to injure his pride or point out that his complexion was sallow, and he was sweating bullets. Still, I couldn't let him walk out into danger. Thinking fast, I said, "I know you can. But this is another one of Dominic's tests. I screwed up my field training test this morning and want to redeem myself. Please let me do this. It's just one Biter and she's in freaking high heels. I could take her out blindfolded." I squeezed his leg through his jeans.

"I'll go with you," he said, not easily swayed.

I gritted my teeth. Grady couldn't be trusted to watch over my sister, and I didn't want Reed leaving the safety of the coffee shop. Deciding to switch strategies, I fluttered my lashes. "If you stay here and watch out for Eden, I'll make it worth your while later." I brushed my lips against his.

His grimace melted into a smile. "Yeah?"

"Oh, yeah." I slid my hand up his thigh. "Just you and me this time."

"Um, maybe we could invite Sai," he said, sounding nervous. "I mean, if you don't mind..." He searched my face as if he was unsure of my reaction.

"Not at all. I loved seeing you together." I'd never known Reed was into guys, but then again, I'd never known I'd be so aroused watching two guys together. As long as they included me in the action, I was totally on board with it.

Reed grinned and kissed me.

As I greedily sucked the whiskey flavor from his tongue, the window rattled again.

I reluctantly tore myself away. "So, we have a deal?"

Reed sighed and nodded.

"Good." I kissed him one more time and then strode around the counter to the door. The bells tied to the handle jingled as I stepped outside into the stifling afternoon heat.

❧

"Hey, you!" I called out in a low voice.

Ms. Sparkle turned away from the front window and shambled in my direction. Back when she had a heartbeat, she might've been an attractive young woman or an elderly bag lady. Her rotting skin made it impossible to know for sure. Her milky white eyes locked on me, and she let out a loud wailing moan.

Crap. What if she's calling the others over?

The idea of the undead mob in the plaza turning in my direction made sweat bead on my forehead.

Can't worry about that now.

Taking a deep breath, I summoned my training and raised my knife.

She was three feet away.

Two.

One.

I waited until her perfume of death burned the back of my throat. Then, dodging the skeletal hands reaching for me, I swung my knife at her head.

Two feet of razor-sharp military-issued steel sliced through her cloudy eye in a stomach-turning squelch.

She crumpled like a rag doll at my feet.

I stared at the lifeless body, waiting to feel something. But my reservoir of sympathy for these creatures was bone-dry.

I bent down to retrieve my knife, only to find it stuck in the Biter's skull. I gave it a futile tug and heard another loud window bang. Startled, I looked up to see Reed slap his hand against the café window and point to my right.

Three men in tattered evening wear stumbled around an abandoned car and headed straight for me.

My mouth dried.

Shit. Where did these Biters come from?

I tried frantically to free my knife.

As they lumbered closer, their blackened lips peeled back to reveal bloodstained chattering teeth. The sound was like bone on chalkboard, and it sent an involuntary tremor through me.

The guy in the white tux was closing in. I gave up on my knife and fumbled for my handgun. Yanking it free of my holster, I aimed it between his rolling pearlescent eyes. Just before pressing the trigger, I remembered the reason for rule of survival number five.

Gunshots attract Biters. Dammit, I can't fire on them. Not with the mob in the plaza right there.

The guy in the tux lunged.

Instinct had me jumping back, barely avoiding gnashing teeth.

"Eat dirt!" Dominic shouted behind me.

Weeks of training conditioned me to drop to the ground.

I didn't hear the knives zinging through the air, but the guy in the tux and his friends collapsed one by one with Dominic's blades embedded in the centers of their foreheads.

I slowly picked myself up, stiffening at the sound of Dominic's combat boots stomping down the weed-choked sidewalk.

"What the hell was that? Are you trying to get yourself killed?"

Ignoring his harsh tone, I bent down to retrieve my knife from Ms. Sparkle's head. This time, a hard yank pulled it free.

"Don't you remember the third rule of survival?" Dominic's deep voice rumbled like thunder.

He was close enough that I could smell the cinnamon gum on his breath and the masculine scent that was his alone. I fought hard to keep my suddenly haywire hormones from clouding my mind. "Don't get bitten?" I stayed kneeling as I wiped my blade clean and tucked it back into my thigh sheath.

His massive shadow fell over me. "No. That's a given. The third rule of survival is to be aware of your surroundings at all times. Something you just failed to do."

Great. I failed another test.

I glared up at the six-and-a-half-foot wall of muscle. "She's dead, isn't she?"

"And what were you going to do about them?" He pointed at the guy in the tux and his pals.

My stomach curdled.

Honestly, if Dominic hadn't shown up, I didn't know what I would've done.

"They would've surrounded you." Dominic's large, warm fingers curled around my wrist. He unceremoniously hauled me to my feet.

I stumbled and crashed into him. The feel of his hard muscles sent frissons of heat pulsing through me. Forgetting who I was dealing with, I wrapped my arms around him.

He thrust me away and took two steps back.

Oh, yeah. I'm not supposed to touch him. Trying not to feel rejected, I said, "I would've figured something out."

His neck muscles bunched up like they did when he was warming up for a fight or a lecture. "If you don't start paying attention, you'll end up like them." He jabbed his finger in the mob's direction.

I sucked in a shallow breath. "We're not really going to try to get through them, are we?" I couldn't even see the animal hospital through the throngs of zombies.

When he didn't answer, I continued. "We'll die if we try to take on that herd."

"That's my call to make."

My gaze slid back to the coffee shop. No way would I allow him to risk my family over some meds that probably wouldn't make one iota of difference to poor Rosie. "I won't allow Eden or Reed to go."

The tic in his jaw jumped. "They'll go if I say so."

This is all some stupid training exercise for him. I jabbed my finger into the center of his tactical vest. "Understand this. If anything happens to them, I will make you pay for it every day for the rest of your life."

The edges of his lips curled in amusement. He opened his mouth as if to say something, but suddenly cut off and glanced at the sky.

"What is it?" I followed his gaze, seeing nothing but a few clouds.

He pushed me in the direction of the coffee shop. "Get inside."

"Why? Did you see something?" I scanned the abandoned cars in the street and the boarded-up store windows. "Dominic?"

When he didn't reply, I turned to see him pulling knives from the heads of the Biters. It was impossible not to notice how the well-defined muscles of his shoulders strained against his short-sleeve T-shirt as he retrieved his blades.

Holy crap. The man is fine.

He looked up and caught me gawking.

No way would I let him think I was mentally undressing him. I pretended to shudder and scrunched my face up in disgust. "You've got brains on your vest."

He flicked the zombie goo away. "Inside. Now."

"After you, oh mighty leader," I said, with a mock bow.

He glared at me until I gave up and walked ahead.

But I had the last laugh. As soon as I felt his gaze on my back, I put some extra sway into my hips.

His muffled groan told me all I needed to know.

Sergeant Pain in the Ass put up a good front, but he was totally into me. It wouldn't take much to push him over the edge. I just needed to be sure I didn't fall over with him.

18

LEE

The moment I stepped into the coffee shop, Reed swept me into his arms. "Are you okay? I was so worried."

Dominic snorted behind me. "If you really cared about her, you'd have put your ass on the line to protect her. Not the other way around."

Reed flinched.

Snapping to Reed's defense, I said, "I asked him to stay here. I thought you were testing me again."

"If I was, you failed. And you failed too, Hippie." The sergeant glared at Reed. "Maybe you do belong on green team." Shaking his head, he pulled out his radio and strode to the back of the coffee shop.

"No, you're not getting in the driver's seat," Reed muttered under his breath.

I gave him a sharp look, but he seemed lost in thought. Trying to bring his attention back, I tugged on his arm. "How is Eden?"

"Not good."

I followed his gaze to where my sister still knelt, staring at her reflection in the display case. She still hadn't moved a muscle.

Something isn't right with her. And it was more than working too much and missing her soldier boyfriend. Unease trickled through me as I walked over and put a hand on her forehead.

Eden's skin felt cool to the touch.

Weird.

"Are you feeling sick?" I whispered, hoping Dominic wouldn't hear.

Fortunately, the sergeant was busy talking to Sai on the radio. The rock star was waiting back with the SUV because Dominic wanted him ready to pull us out at a moment's notice.

Eden snapped to awareness and grabbed my hand in a shockingly strong grip. "I'm fine." She pushed me away and used the display case to pull herself up. "I haven't been sleeping much since Mike left. I'll be fine once he gets back."

It's time to break it to her.

"Edie, Mike isn't coming back." If the stories about Javier's gang were true, the soldier was either dead or wishing for death.

She pressed her bloodless lips together and shook her head in denial. "No. He'll be back."

I let out a heavy sigh. I wanted my little sister to find happiness, but the end of the world was no time to fall in love.

Eden swayed unsteadily on her feet.

Concern blossomed into worry as I forced her to sit down and grabbed her icy hand in mine. "You've got to take better care of yourself."

She pivoted her head around, and her sunglasses slipped. Pale silver eyes stared out at me from her gaunt face.

What the hell?

I blinked in confusion. Eden had brown eyes like me. "Are you wearing colored contacts?"

She quickly pushed her sunglasses back up the bridge of her nose. "Don't be ridiculous."

It must be a trick of the light. Maybe a reflection of the tinsel. I glanced at the window and back at Eden.

"Sissy, stop fussing over me. I'll be fine once Mike gets back with the serum."

"Serum? What Serum?" Reed asked, leaning over the counter.

She looked down at her hand. "It's nothing."

I wasn't about to let that go. "Is this serum what you were talking about back in the nurse's office? You said it could cure Rosie."

She nodded. "Yes. It can cure anything. I got... hurt during my field training test and Mike gave me the serum. It completely healed me." She held up her palm. "See."

"See what? Edie, you're not making any sense."

"I should have died and turned into a Biter, but I didn't. I'm fine."

A Biter? I sucked in a breath. "Edie, were you infected?" Zara said Danika attacked Eden and Mike during their field test. But that had been days ago, and the Z-virus always killed an infected person within twenty-four hours.

Eden didn't answer. Instead, she rubbed her hand on her pant leg anxiously. "Mike went back to base to get more. It'll fix Rosie and everyone at the safe house. Everyone. Yes. Everyone will be fine. Better than fine." She let out a high-pitched laugh.

Oh, God. She's completely lost it. I exchanged a helpless look with Reed.

Eden tugged on the ends of her hair. "But we need to buy them more time. Rosie needs more time. More time until

Mike gets back. That's why getting the antivirals is so important."

I could hear Dominic stomping back in our direction. There was no way Eden could go anywhere in her condition. She needed to eat, sleep, and pay visits to Sharon and Roger back at the school.

"Look, Edie. Reed is going to stay here with you. I'll go with Dominic and Grady to get the supplies."

Reed opened his mouth to argue, but I wasn't hearing any of it.

"I'll be fine." I patted my knife with the kind of bravado that would have made our Uncle Duncan proud.

Eden shook her head. "But you don't know where to find the medicine."

"It's in the cabinet inside the supply room. Remember, I visited you at the animal hospital dozens of times. I'll get the meds for Rosie."

She grabbed my arm. "Promise?"

The desperation in her tone startled me.

"I promise." I went as far as crossing my heart the way we'd done when we were kids.

She gave me a relieved smile that faded as she caught sight of something over my shoulder.

⬩

I TWISTED AROUND TO SEE SERGEANT PAIN IN THE ASS glaring at us. "What?"

"We're aborting the mission. Get your gear. We're moving out as soon as Avi and Zara check in."

Finally, he's showing some sense.

Eden made a choked sound.

"The hell we are," shouted Grady, spitting a stream of chewing tobacco on the tile.

Dominic's gaze narrowed. "I heard a drone outside. The Calaveras are monitoring this area."

So that's why Dominic was in such a rush to get me inside.

Grady huffed. "I don't care about some gang bangers. I'm not leaving."

"Well, we're getting the hell out of here." I tried to grab Eden's arm, but she pulled away.

Dominic scanned our faces. "I want everyone in formation back to the vehicle just like we practiced. Remember, where do we stab the dead?"

"In the head," Reed and I replied in unison.

Grady put his hand on the mother-of-pearl butt of the handgun holstered at his waist. "The Calaveras don't scare me."

"Then you're an idiot," I said, remembering the way Javier's men attacked us at our house.

"We're leaving." Steel underlay Dominic's words.

Grady rocked back on the heels of his boots, as if digging them into the ground. "Not until we get the medication for Rosie." He nodded in Eden's direction. "She said the animal hospital has what my daughter needs."

Eden nodded slowly. "The antiviral will be there. We stocked up to treat the epidemic last spring, but then Order 1537 went into effect..." Her voice trailed off as she rubbed the dog collar she wore around her neck.

Eden never took the damn thing off. It was her way of remembering her pet, Sasha. Unfortunately, the pit bull mix had been one of the many casualties of the controversial canine flu legislation mandating the euthanasia of all dogs.

Dominic shook his head. "The infected are blocking access to the building."

Grady paced in front of the counter. "We'll use the back entrance."

"And if it's blocked?"

Grady's eyes lit with ferociousness. "I'll kill everything that stands in my way. The Biters won't stand a chance." He flexed his arm and the Confederate flag tattoo on his bicep danced.

Dominic held up a hand. "It's not up for discussion."

Grady straightened his shoulders. "I promised my wife that I'd watch over Rosie, and I'm going to keep that promise."

"We're *all* leaving," Dominic growled.

Grady narrowed his moss green eyes. "I'm getting those antivirals today. If you're too much of a coward, you can run your pussy-ass back to the school."

Dominic's expression sharpened like the blades he carried.

Seeming unaware of the danger he was in, Grady continued. "It's time a real man took charge."

Oh shit. Other than me, no one challenged Dominic and got away with it.

As if sensing an impending explosion, Reed tried to step between them. "Grady, we get that you're worried about Rosie, but you need to chill, man."

Grady shoved Reed. "Back off."

Reed stumbled into a coffee tower display. Bags exploded, and beans skittered across the floor.

I threw Grady a dirty look as I rushed over to Reed. "Are you okay?"

"No. Stay in the back seat, asshole," Reed muttered, dusting a handful of beans off his jeans.

Back seat? What's he talking about?

"Think before you act, Grady," Dominic warned.

I spun around in time to see the biker raise his fist.

"You don't care if my daughter dies." He punched Dominic square in the jaw.

Dominic didn't even flinch. "Get a hold of yourself."

Grady drew back to punch Dominic again. "You don't give a shit whether any of us dies."

Dominic caught the punch, trapping Grady's hand in the air. "That's why I've been training you all to protect yourselves," he said dryly.

Grady's lip quivered, but he quickly schooled his face into a grimace. "Then help me get the medicine for my little girl."

Dominic dropped Grady's fist. "It's too dangerous." His gaze searched out mine and held it. "I won't risk your lives. You're too important."

My heart skipped a beat.

The sound of Grady drawing his gun sucked the air out of the room. Grady aimed the gun at Dominic's head. "I'm doing this my way—"

Before he finished his sentence, Dominic knocked the gun away. He seized Grady's throat and lifted him into the air.

Wow. Grady had to be close to three hundred pounds. I marveled at the strength it'd take to deadlift that much weight with one arm.

Dominic didn't even look winded.

Grady's boots kicked wildly. His face turned a deep shade of red as he clawed at Dominic's hand.

"If you want to live under my protection, you follow my rules." Dominic released his hand, and Grady fell to the floor, panting.

Eden cleared her throat, breaking the awkward silence. "There's a window in the supply room. Could we try to break in from the alley?"

Dominic glared at her. "No."

Grady fought to catch his breath, his Adam's apple bobbing spastically. "We just need someone to draw the Biters away," he wheezed. "I can do that. I can distract them, and you guys could get into the animal hospital."

Eden shook her head. "It's too dangerous. You're all that Rosie has left."

"We're all leaving." Dominic's tone offered no room for argument.

Grady's suicidal behavior must've been catching because Eden shook her head. "I'm staying."

Over my dead body.

I stalked over to my backpack and slung it on. "Grab your stuff, Eden. We can try the Urgent Care on 4th Street tomorrow." I invoked the big sister no-nonsense tone into my voice.

She shook her head. "It has to be today. Rosie doesn't have much time. If you need to go, I understand. But I have to get the medication. Are you with me, Grady?"

"Damn straight, girlie." His eyes flashed fire at Dominic as he retrieved his weapon and stood.

I threw her backpack in her face. "Hell no."

She's leaving even if I have to carry her out.

She caught the pack and clutched it to her chest. "I have to do this, sissy. This is all my fault."

"What are you talking about?"

"Rosie's sick because of me. Remember when the Blooms tried to bring their dog to the safe house?"

It would have been impossible to forget. Dr. Bloom didn't survive his attempt to ram through the front gates of the school and Danika Bloom had been exiled. Given what Zara told me, the stupid woman hadn't survived long on her own.

Eden sniffed. "Well, I found their dog outside. Kona was badly injured. The soldiers were going to shoot her, but I begged them to let me euthanize her humanely."

"And did you?" I held my breath, hoping against hope Eden hadn't done what I suspected.

A tear slipped from under Eden's sunglass lens. "No. I tried to nurse her back to health."

A sinkhole opened in my stomach. "You didn't..."

Oh, hell. Who am I kidding?

This was my sister. The girl who'd left her dream job at the animal hospital and quit her first year of college to lead canine rights protests. She'd turned our home into an underground dog rescue, for Christ's sake. Of course, she'd try to save the first mongrel she came across.

Her breath came out in a hiccup. "I kept Kona in the shed outside. That's who I was sneaking off to see all the time."

"Tell me you didn't take Rosie to see the dog."

Eden lowered her head. "Kona didn't initially show any signs of being sick. I thought it'd brighten Rosie's spirits..."

Grady, who'd walked over, looked at Eden as if she'd sprouted another head. "You exposed my daughter to a dog?"

Dominic turned to look at Eden. "What?"

Eden chewed her lips. "Kona was recovering, but then she started showing signs of the canine flu. It was right around the time Rosie got sick. Kona... died last night."

Grady cursed and sat down heavily.

Dominic froze, his expression terrifying.

"Oh, Eden," Reed said, shaking his head.

Eden rubbed her arms. "The antivirals can give Rosie a fighting chance until Mike gets back." She paused and took a deep breath. "There should be enough to treat anyone else who gets sick."

"The medicine isn't a cure," I pointed out. If it had been, the government wouldn't have pushed forward its divisive dog-killing legislation. And the vaccination that doomed the entire world would've never been created.

Eden slung on her backpack. "If taken early, it can significantly reduce the complications of the flu. And even taken late, it could mean the difference between life and death. Rosie needs the medicine now. We can't wait."

A low rumble sounded in Dominic's throat. The corded muscles in his neck stretched taut, and the tic in his jaw worked overtime. "Not only did you endanger that child, but you've also put every civilian in the safe house at risk."

The feral note in his voice had me taking a step back. I'd never seen him come so close to losing it.

"I'm sorry," Eden whispered through tears. She looked from the sergeant to Grady. "I'll make things right."

Grady looked up and glared at her. "If my daughter dies, you die." He grabbed his crowbar from off the counter and jabbed it in Eden's direction.

This is bad. Very bad.

We were going to have to leave the safe house as soon as we got back. There was no way we could stay once news of this got out to the rest of the survivors.

Eden gave me a pleading look. "Please don't be mad, sissy. I had to help Kona. I just had to help her."

Feeling dazed, I could only stare at my sister. *Is this my fault?* I'd always protected Eden. Looked out for her. Swooped in to save her from the consequences of whatever terrible choice she'd made. I'd also encouraged her love for animals, from that first little field mouse she saved in Gran's driveway, to her job at the animal hospital. Never did I think it would result in this.

Did I help create a monster?

"Sissy, don't look at me like that—" she broke off as the coffee shop door flew open.

Avi rushed in, carrying Zara. Both of them were covered in blood.

19

AVI

Lost in shock and grief, I carried my sister's body to the coffee shop counter.

I barely registered Eden's gasp of surprise and Lee's pained cry as I strode by them.

It occurred to me I hadn't carried my sister like this since she was a small child. Back then, Zara demanded I carry her everywhere. Sai and I called it her princess phase, although Zara insisted, she was a queen, not a princess.

Even nowadays, when she'd throw a bucket of sass my way, I'd see her as that little girl—fake tiara perched on top of her curls, plastic scepter clutched in her tiny hand. *"Take me over there, Abi!"*

She'd thought the world of me then. She'd listened to me then.

And now. Now…

A ragged sob rattled my chest as I gently set Zara down. Blood poured from her ravaged thigh and ran over the side of the counter.

"Christ! What the hell happened?" Sarge shouted.

I stared at him, unable to form words.

If only I could go back ten minutes before the attack. Five minutes.

Grief shredded me as I played it back in my head. Zara and I had been perched on the side of the overturned ambulance near the gas station. It'd given us an excellent view of the animal hospital across the street, along with the legions of dead blocking access to it.

"Dominic isn't crazy enough to send us over there, is he?" Zara had asked.

When I didn't answer, she'd laughed and said, "Well, I did say it's a good day to die."

I should have told her to shut up. To take it back. You didn't throw shit like that at the universe and expect nothing to happen.

Why did she say that? And why did she put her leg over the open driver's side window?

How many times had I told her to watch her six? To always look twice before making any move. If only she'd glanced down, she would have seen the Biter strapped in the seat before it grabbed her thigh and... and...

No. It wasn't her fault. *It's mine.* I should have noticed the dead fucker there. Even with my senses dulled from the silver, I should have been aware of the danger lurking right below us.

Sarge had warned us that Biters could go into stasis and wake when they smelled food.

But I hadn't paid attention to the creature rousing below us because I'd been too pissed about Lee getting it on with my good for nothing, party-boy brother, who turned everything into a competition between us.

My anger made me blind to the danger. And Zara paid the price with her life.

Letting out a wounded cry, I hugged her body tightly to my chest.

A puff of breath slipped from her blue-tinged lips and her head lolled back against my chest. How many times had she fallen asleep on me like this after demanding more bedtime stories?

"Read one more Abi!"

"Read one more."

I should have read more stories.

Tears clouded my vision as I pressed my lips to her wildly colored hair. Hadn't I told her it looked like clown hair? I wished I could take it back. All the harsh things I'd said over the years. All the lectures. All the punishments I'd doled out for skipping school and sneaking out. I should have been more understanding. More supportive of her crazy lifestyle with those loser boyfriends of hers.

"No! Not Zara!" Lee cried behind me. She sobbed against my back. "How? Why?"

I wanted to yell that it was her fault. I wanted to spew my pain onto my mate like battery acid. But it wasn't Lee's fault, it was mine.

And Zara's.

"She wasn't paying attention." My voice shook. If only Zara had been Lykos like me, she could have shifted and healed. But she was human.

Lee wrapped her arms around my waist.

And although she'd wounded me, I needed my mate's touch. I needed my oak tree.

"Why are you all standing around? Grady, give me your belt," Eden shouted. "We can make a tourniquet."

"There's no point," Sarge said softly. "Zara's been infected. You know what has to be done Avi."

The sight of him unsheathing a knife made my throat

close up. I leaned down and whispered in Zara's ear, "I'm sorry, Z. I love you and I'm so damn proud of the woman you've become."

Zara's body convulsed in my arms.

"She's turning!" Grady shouted in a panicked voice.

"Set her down, soldier," Sarge ordered. "I have to do it now."

I let out a shuddering breath and slowly released Zara. Then I stepped away as Sarge moved in.

I turned to look out the front window. I couldn't watch him end her life—a life I'd seen slip into the world. The first thing my mom had done after giving birth was hand her to me. "A sister for you, Avi."

A sister for you.

My knees gave out.

Lee was there the moment I hit the floor. Her long hair fell over us like a curtain as she wrapped her arms around me. Her tears splashed my face, mingling with mine.

"No! You can't do this!" Eden shrieked. "Zara just needs the serum. Give her the damn serum and she'll be fine. I know you have some on you, Dominic."

"Stand back." Sarge's tone was sharper than the weapon he held over Zara.

"Get out of the way, girlie," Grady shouted.

"Edie, please," Reed pleaded in a softer tone.

"No. Don't, Dominic. The serum can heal her. Mike used it on me when I—"

A wet crunch interrupted Eden. Her plaintive wail marked the end of my sister.

Zara is gone.

Lee tightened her arms around me. "We'll see her again, Avi. We have to believe that."

If only I could. I looked over at Sarge. He'd bowed his head over my sister's body. As if feeling my stare, he snapped to attention. "The blood will draw the dead. We leave now."

"I told you, I ain't leaving," Grady spat.

Reed shook his head. "Don't be stupid, man. Look what happened to Zara."

Grady slung on his backpack. "I'm getting those meds for Rosie. Some stupid slut getting herself killed doesn't change that."

In an instant, all my emotions coalesced into a rage so intense it felt as if my skin was on fire. "What did you just call my sister?"

Lee tried to hold me down. "Avi, don't."

I pushed her away so I could approach the male who'd dare disrespect Zara moments after her death.

"You heard me," Grady spat out a wad of chewing tobacco. Some of the brown juice spattered onto Zara's hand draped over the counter.

Sarge cursed and tapped on the machine grafted to his arm. "Stand down, Avi."

But I wasn't going to fucking stand down. I ripped off the silver band and let out a bestial roar.

ॐ

Kill him, my wolf urged.

Yes. My body contorted, my bones crunched, and dark hair sprouted through my pores.

"Jesus, you weren't lying, man," Reed murmured to himself.

Grady's jaw dropped as he scurried back. "What the hell are you?"

"Death," I wanted to answer, but I couldn't speak through a mouthful of fangs.

Sarge was suddenly in my face. "Activate handler pairing."

It felt as if a slingshot suddenly hit me square in the chest and my skull cracked open. Pain drove me back down to the floor. My partially transformed body reverted to its human shape, and an invisible tether snapped between me and Sarge.

"Avi!" Lee cried.

It's the bond. He's enslaved me!

Steely determination drowned out my shock and horror.

It wasn't my emotion. It was Sarge's. *Shit. I'm feeling what he's feeling. He's my handler now.*

"What are you doing to Avi?" Lee tried to run over, but Reed grabbed her and locked his arms around her.

Sarge crouched down over me and said in a low voice. "You left me no choice, Avi. You'll follow my orders now."

Some unseen force made me lower my head and parrot back. "I will follow your orders." *No!* I shook my head, fighting his control. "I won't be your slave."

Sarge grimaced. "You're my beast now. You do what I tell you. Understand?"

I gritted my teeth, trying not to answer. "Yes, sir," slipped out anyway.

"Good."

It wasn't good. It was a fucking disaster. *I have to break the bond.* But as far as I knew, only the handler could do the unpairing. That meant Sarge and I would be linked until he broke the bond or one of us died.

"Look at me," Sarge ordered. The moment our gazes locked, he said in a low voice. "You will not fight this. You will accept me as your handler. You will feel no emotion and you will follow all my orders. Understand?"

An almost tranquil stillness fell over my mind. "Yes, sir," I said in a toneless voice.

Lee pushed out of Reed's hold and glared at Sarge. "What did you do to him?"

"What had to be done," he answered, rising to his feet. "Everyone, fall in behind me."

With no conscious thought on my part, I stood and positioned myself behind Sarge.

Grady sputtered. "D-did you all see that? Camel jockey here just turned into a monster." He pointed a shaking finger at me.

"He's a shifter, not a monster, you racist pig." Lee gave him a scathing look as she glanced around the coffee shop. "Where's Eden?"

I scanned the room, feeling nothing as my gaze moved over the corpse on the counter. Sarge had left his knife in Zara's skull. I wondered if he would retrieve it. It wasn't wise to leave weapons behind.

Sarge cursed. "Eden isn't here."

Reed motioned to the rear of the coffee shop. "She must have slipped out the back door."

"There she is." We all followed Grady's finger to the front window and the view of Eden sprinting toward the plaza.

"Oh, God! No!" Lee cried, rushing for the door.

Sarge grabbed her arm. "Stay here."

"Get your hands off me!" Lee tried to shake him off. When he didn't release her, she pulled her knife.

I tensed, but my handler quickly restrained her.

Seeing my mate pinned by the larger male should have enraged me. But it didn't. I felt nothing. Not even Sarge's emotions. It was almost a relief. No more jealousy, anger, or pain. No more unrequited feelings for the female thrashing in my handler's grip.

"I need to get to her!" Lee yelled, her normally sweet scent spiking with sour notes of fear.

"Let her go, Dominic." Reed pointed his knife-tipped shotgun at my handler's head.

The instinct to protect Sarge had me running over and

ripping the weapon away. Given our previous encounters, I expected a knock-down fight.

Reed surprised me by backing away.

Sarge scoffed. "Hippie won't shoot me. Give him his gun back, Avi."

I thrust the weapon at Reed's chest, but gave him a warning look.

He didn't notice. His gaze was locked on Lee and Sarge.

"You don't want to do this," Sarge said to Lee.

I wondered if he was trying to use mind control on her. It wouldn't work. Titans couldn't compel humans the way Alpha shifters could. I'd always wished I'd been born an Alpha. Then I could have compelled my siblings to listen to me.

Zara never listens. I glanced over at my sister's body, feeling nothing. Not even a faint echo of grief.

"Eden will die out there!" Lee cried.

"So will you," Sarge said in a pained voice.

She increased her struggles. "Either help me or get the hell out of my way."

Grady roughly pushed past us. "That girlie is distracting the horde so we can get to the hospital. She has more balls than any of you."

Sarge didn't stop the biker from shoving open the door and running toward the plaza, but he did release Lee. "Christ. If we do this, we do it my way. You and Reed head to the front of the hospital. Get the front doors open, understand?"

Lee stared at him blankly.

Reed stepped around me to get to her side. "We'll take care of it, sir."

Sarge looked over at me. "Avi, protect Eden."

I nodded, yanking my sais out. It was unfortunate that my favorite melee weapon shared a name with my brother, but the sharp metal prongs were excellent for stabbing Biter skulls.

"Remember rule of survival number five. Guns are only used as a last resort," Sarge warned.

I doubted Lee heard him as she'd already shoved open the door and rushed outside. I also doubted any of us would survive the next hour, but that didn't bother me.

As Zara said, it's a good day to die.

❦   20   ❦

LEE

Reed followed me out of the coffee shop and stayed close on my heels. Together, we navigated around debris and abandoned cars in the street. My heart hammered a frantic beat as we stepped over bloody piles of bones and tattered clothing.

Eden!

I could see her in the distance, standing in the parking lot, waving her hands like a traffic controller. "What's she doing?"

"Trying to draw the dead to her," Reed whispered.

"She's insane." Fear speared through me as we watched her beckon the Biters.

"This way," Eden called out to the enthralled masses. "Come and get me."

As I desperately searched for some way to reach my sister, Avi rushed by us at a dizzying speed.

"Avi!" I sprinted, trying to catch up with him, but something snagged my backpack and sent me flying backward.

Dominic's voice growled in my ear, "Your orders were to get to the steps." He locked a muscular forearm across my chest.

I balled my hands into fists. "Goddamn it, Dominic. Let me go."

Reed made a sound of frustration behind us. "This is getting old, man."

Dominic loosened his hold but didn't let go. "You both need to get to the front doors."

Panic gripped my heart and squeezed. I'd lost sight of my sister. "Eden needs our help."

"Avi has it covered."

I gasped as I caught sight of Avi plowing through the crowd of Biters. *Oh, God! They'll attack him!*

Just as the zombies turned in his direction, Avi vaulted onto the roof of a red sedan. Body after body slammed into the car, but he'd already bounded onto the next vehicle. Using the tops of cars like stepping stones, he jumped through the ocean of dead toward Eden.

But what if he is bitten?

As if reading my mind, Dominic said, "He can shift and heal himself from most injuries."

Grady's shout broke through the cacophony of moaning and chattering teeth. A pack of zombies surrounded him by the fountain.

Dominic shook me, bringing my attention back to him. "Avi will save your sister. Now get those doors open!" He released me and took off in Grady's direction.

I fell forward, barely catching myself from face-planting on the asphalt.

Reed grabbed my arm. "He's right. We need to open the doors."

"No." *If anything happens to Eden, I'll never forgive myself.*

"You're not driving!" Reed shouted, tugging me in the direction of the animal hospital.

What the hell is he talking about? I dug my feet in. "I'm not driving to her." *Although maybe that isn't a bad idea.*

Reed gave me a frustrated look. "We can't help Eden if we're dead."

As if to underscore his point, two Biters—a thin, blonde woman in a pencil skirt and an elderly man in a stained hospital gown—stumbled toward us. Most of the left side of the woman's face was missing, leaving the ghastly white of her skull and teeth exposed.

"Let's go hot." I motioned at Reed's shotgun. If anything, the loud noise would help Eden by drawing Biters to us.

Reed lifted his weapon, but his finger froze on the trigger. "Dominic said not to use guns unless absolutely necessary."

"Screw that." I drew my handgun and fired.

The side of the old man's head blew off. The Biter's frail body flew back, the IV tubing still attached to his arms streamed after him like pale ribbons.

The blonde stumbled over his body. Then she righted herself.

Oddly enough, she looked a lot like my high school English teacher.

I hated that teacher.

"I'm not a pussy," Reed shouted.

Ignoring his weird ramblings and the ringing in my ears, I fired again. The first shot winged the blonde in the shoulder. She canted to the right, but kept coming.

Reed ran up to her and speared her in the face with the bayonet-like end of his shotgun. "Glad you approved, asshole," he muttered.

There was no time to question his odd behavior because more creatures were turning in our direction. They blocked my view of Avi and Eden. "Where are they?" Fear clogged my throat.

"We can see them from the steps." Reed grabbed my arm and dragged me toward the animal hospital.

Together, we darted around the undead stragglers. As we passed them, they turned and shuffled after us.

The memorial fountain loomed ahead.

We ran around the edge of the enormous, white marble monstrosity city council commissioned as a tribute to the euthanized dogs of Saguaro Valley. Unfortunately, instead of pacifying the animal rights groups and bereaved pet owners, it had become the focal point for their protests.

Remembering the news footage of Eden's animal rights group going toe-to-toe with police in riot gear made a tremor run through me. The two groups had clashed in the very spot where Grady and Dominic were currently battling for their lives.

Reed and I skidded to a halt fifty feet away.

The fountain teemed with undead. Throngs of Biters thrashed against each other in a shallow pool of stagnant water inside the fountain basin. The ones that fought their way to the edge hurled themselves at the two men.

With their backs to the animal hospital, Grady and Dominic fought side by side. The blood-soaked pair looked like demented serial killers. Grady whacked Biter after Biter with his crowbar, while Dominic threw his blades with almost preternatural speed.

My eyes tracked the airborne knives. Every one of them hit a flesh-eater in the center of their forehead.

Damn. He's good.

But his skills with the blade weren't enough. Zombies continued pouring out of the fountain, and the men were dangerously close to being surrounded.

They need to use their guns.

Dominic left Grady's side to retrieve his knives. As he bent down, a whale-sized Biter in a floral muumuu jockeyed to the edge of the fountain.

He didn't see her.

A violent surge of panic kicked my feet into action.

"Lee," Reed shouted.

Ignoring him, I ran toward Dominic. I got close enough that the smell of rotting flesh slapped me across the face, but not close enough to shoot with any accuracy.

The female Biter launched herself at Dominic.

"Dominic, behind you," I shouted.

The sergeant spun around in time to block the creature's attack. It was no small feat given the flesh-eater probably outweighed him by two hundred pounds. He roundhouse-kicked the thing to the ground and stomped on its bloated, wet face.

Dominic lifted his gaze to mine and gave me a curt nod of thanks. Then a new group of zombies stumbled out of the fountain, snaring his attention.

Reed caught up with me. "We need to go," he panted.

Indecision grounded me. *Do we stay and help?* The men were grossly outnumbered. *What if something happens to Dominic?* The thought twisted me up inside.

As if sensing my hesitation, the sergeant called out, "I've got this. Get to the doors."

Fighting my instinct to run to his side, I turned and followed Reed up the single flight of wide cement steps leading to the main floor of the clay-colored animal hospital.

Reed yanked on the handle of the front door.

It swung open.

"It looks deserted," he said, peering into the lobby.

"Looks can be deceiving." Eden's former coworkers were sticklers for following protocol. If they hadn't locked up, it meant that either something made them leave in a hurry, or they hadn't left at all. Neither explanation gave me the warm fuzzies.

"Should we go in?"

I scanned the parking lot. "Not without Eden." A flash of pink caught my eye.

There.

Immediately, my relief at spotting her turned to panic.

Eden looked like a movie star swarmed by adoring fans as she slowly walked backward. Each step brought her closer to the end of the parking lot. With her back to the street, she couldn't see more zombies approaching from the other direction.

"Where is Avi?" The shifter was nowhere to be seen.

Fear for them suffocated me.

The new arrivals filled the street behind Eden. The Biters closing in on her shook their broken limbs with frenzied anticipation.

We have to help her.

Before I could barrel down the steps, Reed grabbed my arm.

"Look." He pointed at a silver truck parked at the end of the lot.

Something moved on top of it.

"Avi," Reed said, with more than a hint of awe.

The shifter clambered over the truck roof, cupped his hands to his mouth, and shouted at my sister.

Eden twisted around. An expression of horror crossed her face as she glanced at the zombie-filled street behind her.

Giving up all pretense of calm, Eden raced in Avi's direction. As she reached the truck, she threw her hands into the air.

Avi hauled her onto the hood.

He's got her.

"Thank Jesus." Reed let out a relieved breath.

The galloping of my heart slowed to a canter.

Dominic and Grady dashed up the steps toward us.

Grady wiped a streak of brackish blood from his mustache. "They just keep coming and coming." He motioned at the packs of Biters heading for the steps.

Thankfully, the zombies lacked the coordination to climb stairs. But there was still the wheelchair ramp to worry about.

As I turned to look at the ramp, Dominic stalked over to me. "Are you okay?"

I gave him a jerky nod.

He raised one hand as if to touch my face. It hung in the air for a second before he dropped it to his side.

Reed looked from Dominic to me, an inscrutable expression on his face. "I'm fine too, by the way. The building is unlocked."

"Fucking A." Grady rushed over to the door. "I've got to find the meds."

"Stop," Dominic shouted. "We haven't cleared it."

Grady darted into the lobby.

Biting off a curse, Dominic glanced at me, and then at the building. Indecision flashed in his eyes.

Avi's voice crackled through his radio. "Sarge, we're boxed in."

I turned my attention back to the parking lot. The sight of the Biters closing in on the truck chilled my blood.

Dominic's gaze zeroed in on Avi and Eden. "Can you get inside the vehicle?"

"Negative." Avi's way too calm voice was barely audible over the chattering teeth of the bloodthirsty horde.

"There's a tree overhanging the truck. Help Eden climb it. Then you jump to safety."

"This?" Avi pointed to the spindly Palo Verde shaking tiny yellow petals down on the truck.

"Yes. I'll create a distraction and draw the infected. When the mob disperses, take Eden back to the SUV."

"Ten-four." Avi grabbed Eden's arm and led her toward the roof of the truck.

The mob slammed into the vehicle.

The truck rocked wildly. Avi and Eden, precariously perched on the edge of the windshield, fought for balance. They were barely out of reach of the grasping hands.

Dominic turned to me. "Get inside. Help Grady."

Right. Like I'll abandon my sister for that jackass.

"No. I can help you. What's the plan?"

Reed made a choking noise.

I twisted around in time to see Eden's sneakers slipping on the flowers coating the windshield. Biters snagged her leg and dragged her to the edge of the hood. The air in my lungs froze.

No. No. No.

Avi yanked Eden's arms, trying to keep her on the vehicle.

The mob surged. A naked male Biter clambered onto the hood. He charged Avi. As Avi tried to hold him off, Eden was wrenched out of his grasp.

As if in slow motion, I watched her fall into the mosh pit of death. "No," I shouted, my heart exploding in my chest. "Nooooooo!"

Forgetting about my own safety, I ran down the stairs. I couldn't see what was going on, but I could hear my sister's bloodcurdling screams.

Oh, God. They're tearing her apart!

A primitive part of my brain took over. Darting past the zombies, I fired at anything that moved in my direction.

As I neared the fountain, I saw a frenzy of motion near the truck. Biters covered the vehicle. There was no sign of Avi.

Eden's cries cut off.

I shook my head, refusing to accept what the silence meant.

Bloated, wet zombies swarmed me.

I pumped the trigger of my gun and realized the magazine was empty.

Reed appeared next to me, his face ashen. "Lee, we have to get inside."

"Go," I screamed, reloading.

He shook his head. "Not without you."

Biters surrounded us.

He fired off several deafening rounds.

Dominic rushed over, firing his gun into the oncoming mass of undead. He pointed at the animal hospital. "Get inside."

I shook my head. "I have to get to Eden."

He stepped in front of me. "She's gone."

A bubble of hysteria rose in my throat.

He's wrong.

She's not dead.

She can't be dead.

Eden!

I tried to push past Dominic.

He grabbed my arm. "Move."

Tears blurred my vision. A hurricane of grief tore through my soul.

Rotting skeletal faces seemed to spin around me.

She's dead.

My hand dropped to my side, the gun dangling by my fingertips. My knees weakened, threatening to give out.

Dominic grabbed the straps of my backpack and shook me. "Do you want to join her? Hippie too?"

I glanced over at Reed. The panic in his eyes brought me back to my senses.

I still have to protect him.

Dominic released me and emptied his firearm into the wall of undead closing in around us.

More came. Wave after wave of them. As one fell, two others seemed to take its place.

"Christ, I'm out." Dominic patted his vest, searching for a knife, but he was out of those too.

We were completely surrounded. Out of options, we moved back-to-back as the dead pushed forward from all directions. The sound of their clicking teeth was the only thing I could hear until Reed shouted, "Yeah. Okay, man. You can drive."

As Dominic and I gave him a sharp look, Reed let out a war cry and rushed straight at the lumbering wall of death. Showing no fear, he used the bayonet end of the shotgun to stab every Biter in reach straight through the eye socket. He didn't even wait for them to fall, just jabbed them in the face, yanked out the blade, and impaled the next one.

As the bodies collapsed like dominos, Reed spun in a circle, impaling the Biters stumbling over their fallen comrades—stab, yank, stab, yank, stab, yank. In the space of a minute, the stacks of corpses were high enough to act as protective barriers for us.

Holy crap. We'd gone from certain death to having a fighting chance. I blinked, too shocked to believe my eyes.

Dominic seemed stunned too, until Reed shouted, "Dom, get her the fuck out of here." Then, the sergeant snapped to attention, grabbed my arm, and hustled me toward the stairs.

Reed ran with us, stabbing anything that lunged in our direction.

As we made our way up the stairs, I cast a quick glance down at the parking lot. Biters swarmed over the truck. I couldn't see my sister or Avi, but in my mind, the zombies feasted and fought over their bodies like sharks.

A wounded cry escaped my lips as my legs gave out.

"Survive now. Grieve later," Dominic shouted, sweeping me into his arms.

But it was too late. The overwhelming terror and anguish triggered the darkest of my memories. As Dominic carried me into the tomblike lobby of the animal hospital, I tumbled into the nightmare of my past.

DOMINIC

I had a big problem. Bigger than us being trapped inside the animal hospital with Lee catatonic and hundreds of infected trying to beat down the door.

Hunter is here, wearing the hippie's skin like a damn suit.

In the half an hour since we'd barricaded ourselves in here, I hadn't taken my eyes off my beast.

After ripping Lee's limp body out of my arms, he'd carried her to one of the empty exam rooms to inspect her for injuries.

I watched him from the hallway, cursing my stupidity.

How did I not see it before?

Hippie's takedown of Avi back in my office should have tipped me off—those were classic Hunter moves. But after seeing zero indication Reed had been under Hunter's influence this past week, I'd bought Reed's assurances Hunter was gone.

It'd been a bad call. Seems I was making a lot of those these days. Case in point, me dragging these civilians on this FUBAR mission.

Sighing, I dropped the back of my head against a framed poster of a basket of kittens.

Bringing Lee and Avi's families here had been reckless and self-serving. I'd wanted to show them how unprepared they all were, so they'd never consider leaving the safe house. Instead of proving my point, I'd gotten their family members killed. And, given the crashing vitals displayed on my biometric scanner, Avi, too.

Shame washed over me. Not only had I paired with Avi against his will, my first order sent him to his death. I deserved to drown in the pain of his last moments on earth, but all I sensed when I reached for our link was an absence of emotion. Me ordering him not to feel anything turned out to be a mercy for me—a mercy I didn't deserve.

Christ. What a goddamn joke of a handler I'd turned out to be. If the colonel could see me now, he'd probably throw my ass back in the slammer to rot for all eternity.

I sighed again, eyeing the reason for my initial imprisonment.

Hunter's stance and mannerisms were unmistakable, even wearing the hippie's body.

Just look at the way he cracks his knuckles as he paces around Lee. How many times have I yelled at him for that annoying habit? Hundreds? Thousands?

For years, I'd gone to bed and woken up to that cracking sound. My complaints hadn't made one iota of difference and when I'd finally used my handler power and ordered him to stop cracking his knuckles, he'd bared his fangs and promptly cracked his neck.

Insufferable bastard.

But it wasn't as if I didn't have my own irritating habits. Hunter frequently griped about me sharpening my knives all the time. And yet, ironically, his last gift to me had been a sharpening stone.

My lips curled as I remembered that morning—one of the last mornings we'd spent together. I'd awoken to him dropping the stone on my chest.

"Happy birthday, handler," he'd said in his gravelly voice.

"It's not my birthday," I'd shouted once I'd caught my breath. I, like the other Titans, didn't have birthdays. Our superiors preferred to keep us in the dark about our age.

He'd frowned. "Do you want the present or not?"

I warily inspected the shirt he'd wadded around the stone. "Is it a grenade?"

He'd chuckled, sending a rush of amusement through our bond. "If I wanted to kill you, you'd be dead. Nah, you're stuck with me for life, handler."

Those words thrilled me. For how many beasts wanted to stay with their handlers? None that I knew of. And most handlers eagerly anticipated the mandatory three-year beast rotations. Not me. After Hunter and I were paired, I'd refused to bond with any other beast.

I'd always wondered why the colonel hadn't forced the issue. Maybe Hunter and I reminded him of his bond with General Brooks. Or maybe it was because Hunter and I were an unstoppable force. No other beast-handler teams could claim over a hundred successful ops.

Too bad our track record hadn't been enough to save us after the shitstorm in Afghanistan...

"Wake up, dirty dancer," Hunter crooned, trying to rouse Lee.

She stared unblinkingly up at him from the metal exam table he'd set her on. It physically hurt me to see her in that near comatose state again. Only decades of self-discipline kept me from rushing over and dragging her back into my arms.

It seemed her spell over me had grown even stronger. My feelings for her went far beyond lust and attraction. I was obsessed with her. When I wasn't watching her sleep, or screw, or eat, I was training her harder than any of the other civilians. I needed her to be stronger... fiercer... tougher. I needed her to survive this world because I couldn't imagine existing in it without her.

And that scared me. Because Lee was human and weak. So damn weak.

She'd fallen apart like this after the Christmas Eve training exercise. I'd been half out of my mind until Avi finally snapped her out of her trance. I didn't know exactly how he'd roused her, but it apparently involved fellatio.

It's worth a try. "Put your dick in her mouth," I called out.

Hunter spun around. "The fuck?"

I shrugged. "It might have woken her up last time."

Something clattered to the floor in the room down the hall. I glanced over to find Grady ransacking the supply room in his search for the antivirals. I hadn't told him they were in the locked cabinet over the counter. Best to keep that one busy and out of trouble.

My heightened senses warned me of something coming at me hard and fast. I ducked to the side.

Hunter smashed his fist into the kitten poster, shattering the glass.

"Shit," he yelled, looking down at his bloody knuckles. Or rather, Hippie's bloody knuckles.

"You should take better care of that kid's body," I warned.

He bared his teeth and punched me in the jaw with his other fist.

I took the hit, hoping it would ease some of his anger. "Feel better?"

"No!" he roared. "What were you thinking, dragging my mate out here?"

"What are you thinking, hijacking that kid's body?" I threw back.

As his nostrils flared with anger, I noticed his irises were darker than the hippie's were normally. It was a tell I'd have to remember. Although as close as we'd been, I shouldn't have needed any external clue to recognize him.

"Did you think I wouldn't figure it out, Hunter? You're my beast."

"No, I'm not," he spat, pointing at my biometric scanner. "You're paired with the little Lykos now." He stopped, blinked slowly, then gave me a shit-eating grin. "You broke our bond."

My gut rolled as I realized he was right. I had to sever our connection to pair with Avi. It'd been an in-the-moment decision made only to prevent Avi from going on a rampage after the death of his sister.

Hunter chuckled. "Now, if Reed dies, I can jump back to my old body. I'll be free from your motherfucking control and..." he glanced back at Lee who hadn't moved a muscle.

"And what?" I pressed. "Run off into the sunset with the human statue?" I waved at Lee, fighting the urge to move closer to her. Something inside me demanded I go to her side... touch her... protect her. I battled the overwhelming compulsion. I didn't know how or why she had this power over us. Hunter thought it was because she was his mate. I didn't agree, but I'd sure as hell leverage it against him.

I stepped closer to my beast. "Look at how she reacts to losing her sister." I motioned at Lee. "What do you think will happen after she loses Reed? You know how attached she is to him." She'd barely left the hippie's side this past week.

Hunter paled, no doubt realizing the impossible situation he was in. He couldn't have his freedom without killing his host body, and he couldn't kill his host body without hurting his mate. Shifters, as a rule, would choose death over harming their mates. It was a trait shared by us Titans.

My gaze was drawn to Lee before I snapped it back to Hunter.

"You can't put her through that," I announced confidently. "And it doesn't matter anyway, because Avi isn't long for the world." I lifted my scanner so he could see Avi's readings.

He gave me an outraged look. "Why aren't you out there trying to save him? Don't you care about your beast?"

Yes, and he's standing right in front of me.

When I didn't answer, he snorted. "Oh yeah, I forgot for a second who I was talking to—the beast killer."

The pain in his voice cut me to the quick. I'd given everything to save him, and in return, he hated me. It wasn't the right time or place, but he needed to know the truth.

❧

I EXHALED, MY MIND TURNING TO THE NIGHTMARE IN Afghanistan. "Hunter, your brothers had to be terminated."

Hunter shook his head. "Something went wrong with their programming."

That much was evident. Every Typhos at the military outpost, apart from Hunter, had simultaneously turned on their handlers. After killing the Titan soldiers—something that should have been impossible—they'd gone after the civilians and enlisted soldiers. They'd slaughtered hundreds of humans.

Hunter swallowed hard. "My brothers needed to be reconditioned, not assassinated. And for you to order me to kill them—" his voice choked off.

"I was following *my* orders." I'd hated giving that command, but I had no choice. The colonel was emphatic that the remaining Typhos die by Hunter's hand.

"You should have told the colonel to fuck himself,"

Hunter raged. "They're gone. My brothers are gone because you couldn't stand up to that piece of shit Lyk—"

"I did stand up to the colonel," I interrupted. "He ordered me to kill you. I refused. And he made me pay dearly for my insubordination."

Hunter went motionless. "So, your court martial wasn't for my brothers' deaths..."

"No. It was for letting you live. And to further ensure your survival, I made Jen pair with you." As General Brook's daughter, she was untouchable and, by extension, so was her beast.

A mixture of emotions played out over Hunter's borrowed face. I wished I could sense what he was feeling, but I wouldn't be able to do that until we were bonded again.

"T-they stripped you of your rank. They gave you a life sentence."

I nodded.

"For me?" he whispered.

"For not following my orders," I clarified.

"But you always follow orders. Every fucking order. You're the goddamn order guy. Why would you do that for me?"

I didn't answer.

"W-why didn't Jen say anything?" he finally sputtered.

Ah, Jen. She'd always been loyal, even though I could never give her what she wanted. "Because I told her not to tell you. I knew you'd go after the colonel if you knew."

"Fuck!" Hunter shouted. He punched the damn kitten poster again. Bones cracked.

Hoping he hadn't broken Hippie's fist, I cleared my throat. "I'm sorry for the way it all went down with your brothers. And if you need to hate me for it and exact your vengeance—"

"I don't hate you. Even though I wanted to," he interrupted. "And I couldn't kill you even when... I had the chance."

"Why?" I'd always wondered why Hunter hadn't turned on me when his brothers had turned on their handlers.

His eyes clashed with mine and his breath sawed in and out. "Because..."

And it hit me like a blade to the chest. *He feels for me what I feel for him.*

Christ. I should have expected it. Hunter and I had been bonded far longer than any other active-duty teams. Training together. Fighting together. Living together. Sharing our minds, emotions, and sometimes our dreams, although we never talked about those.

Somewhere down the line, our bond had morphed into something it was never intended to become.

I'd first suspected it when Jen tried to claim me and couldn't. My suspicions grew when Hunter refused visits with the breeders—something all other beasts eagerly awaited. And I'd known for certain after severing my bond with him. The pain and grief I'd experienced after losing our connection had nearly driven me mad. When the colonel offered me an early release from prison, I'd agreed only on the condition they return Hunter to me.

"Dom," he said, staring at me with eyes that were the wrong shade and color, but somehow still his. "I've missed you."

I grunted, unable to tell him I felt the same.

His brows knitted as he glanced over at Lee. "But I need to be with her. She's my mate."

I followed his gaze to the beautiful, stubborn human who'd captured my interest in a way no other female ever had. "She calls to me too..."

A lock of dark hair had fallen over her open eyes and my hand itched to smooth it back. I tore my gaze away before I forgot myself and ran to her side. "But I don't trust it. What are the chances she is my mate, your mate, and Avi's mate?"

Hunter looked stunned.

"Think about it? This power she has over our kind isn't natural."

He shook his head. "It has to be."

"It feels real," I admitted. "But what if it's not? What if she's been engineered to make us want her?" The colonel told me once that only a few lines of genetic code separated Titans from shifters. As much as I hated to admit it, we really weren't that different.

"Alpha Diaz wanted her too," Hunter added slowly. "You know the fucker who killed Jen."

"I remember." My hands reflexively clenched into fists. Alpha Diaz's faction had also captured Mike. I'd have to deal with him soon.

Hunter let out a deep breath. "So, you think she was created by army scientists, too?"

I shared a troubled look with him. "I don't know. She appears human, and yet...."

"Her scent is different," he blurted out. "She doesn't smell fully human. But she also doesn't smell like a shifter or a Titan. She's something else."

Something else? What else is there?

The sound of glass breaking distracted me. *Grady is really tearing up the place.* "We'll figure out what she is after we get back to the safe house."

"Okay." Hunter wiped his bloody knuckles on his shirt in an unsuccessful attempt to stop the bleeding.

"Here." Without thinking, I grabbed his injured hand, lifted it to my mouth, and ran my tongue over the torn skin to heal it.

His breathing went shallow as his gaze locked on my lips.

Hunter's reaction took me back to those dreams we'd

shared—the ones we'd never acknowledged. I dropped his healed hand and stepped away before my body could betray me.

He grabbed my arm. "Dom—" Then, seeming to realize he'd touched me without permission, released me. "Sorry."

I should have told him it was okay. That I'd give him, and only him, permission to touch me. But I didn't. A lifetime of repressing emotion wasn't easily undone.

Hunter closed his eyes. "Not now, cocksucker." He opened them and gave me a frustrated look. "Reed is trying to regain control."

"Don't let him. I need you with me." *Now. Always.* "Are you with me, beast?"

He snapped to attention. "Yes, handler."

The heaviness in my chest eased. "When we get back to the safe house, I'll figure out a way to return you to your body without killing the hippie." *Then I'll reforge our bond.*

"Really?"

I nodded. *And nothing will separate us again.*

A whimpering sound drew my gaze back to Lee. Her eyelashes fluttered.

Once more, I warred with the urge to go to her... comfort her... protect her.

Hunter looked as if he was wrestling with the same compulsion. He gave me a tense smile. "I guess she didn't need a dick in her mouth to wake her after all."

"Pity," I murmured.

"False alarm," I announced to Dom when Lee didn't wake. "Guess we're going to have to go with your plan." I was only joking. No way would I take advantage of my mate in her current state.

It killed me to see her looking so small and vulnerable. She'd curled into a fetal position on the exam table, with her legs bent and drawn up to her chest.

Resisting the urge to be at her side hurt like a bitch, but I didn't want to cut this discussion with Dom short. Not when he was staring at me as if I actually mattered to him.

"It's good to have you back, Hunter," he said in a low voice. He seemed to force out his next words. "I missed you."

Dom never says shit like that. My world rocked on its motherfucking axis.

For years, I'd hated him. I'd sworn he'd pay in blood for what I'd thought was his ultimate betrayal of our bond. I'd wanted him to experience as much suffering and pain as I could possibly inflict before giving him the mercy of death.

And now?

Now I knew Dom wasn't to blame. He'd only been

carrying out the colonel's orders. And when that big Lykos bastard wanted me dead, Dom gave up his position, rank, and his motherfucking freedom to save my sorry ass.

I couldn't wrap my mind around the depth of that sacrifice.

He must care about me a lot.

And I'd be lying if I said I didn't feel the same. In the space of a minute, I'd gone from wanting to kill Dom to wanting to...

I immediately strangled that thought.

Dom glanced down at his forearm. "I'll re-pair us when you're back in your body."

I looked over at his biometric scanner and frowned. Avi's heartbeat was so low, he had to be hovering near death. That shouldn't have bothered me, but it did. I mean, I didn't care that the little Lykos would die—he was a dickwad after all. But Dom's lack of concern bothered me. Handlers were supposed to look out for their beasts.

"What if I don't want to be bonded to you?"

Dom slowly bared his teeth. "Tough shit. You're mine." Taking me by surprise, he grabbed my arm, flipped me around and threw me face first into the wall.

I could have fought him—I knew dozens of ways to break the hold—but I didn't. In fact, as he crushed my body between him and the wall, all I felt was deep satisfaction and want. And for the first time, I didn't feel any shame about it. Riding backseat during Reed's threesome with Lee and Sai had been eye opening in more ways than one.

"Say I'm your master. Say you belong to me." Dom cranked my arm higher into my back, sending sharp spikes of pain through me. For Dom, pain and pleasure would always tied together.

"No," I gasped, not making it easy for him.

"No?" He kicked my legs apart, rolled his hips forward, and ground himself against my ass.

I groaned. We'd done this before in dreams I'd replayed a thousand times. First, we'd fought until we were bloody. Then he'd shoved me down and... *Ah fuck.* My cock turned to stone.

"Say it," Dom demanded, his breath hot against the nape of my neck.

There was no point in fighting what I wanted. "You're my master," I said in a rush of breath. "I belong to you. But I also belong to her." I flicked my gaze over to the exam room. "She's my mate." *Even if she hates me.*

Dom cursed. "What you feel for her isn't real, Hunter. She's not—"

I reared back, shoving him off me. Then I spun around. "It feels fucking real. And that's good enough for me. If you want me, you need to accept that we are a package deal." *Me. Her. And unfortunately, that cocksucker Reed.*

As if on cue, Reed roared, *"Hunter!"* in the back of our mind so loudly, I cursed.

Dom's black eyes drilled into mine. "What is it?"

I shut my eyes and focused inward. *"Not now, cocksucker!"* I didn't know how long I could keep Reed suppressed, but I wanted to stay in control as long as possible.

Reed's rage blasted at me like a flamethrower. *"It's my body, asshole. Not yours."*

"I saved your life," I reminded him.

"Oh, please. I heard your plan. You want me to die so you can jump back into your old body. Screw you, man."

Shit. He heard that?

"Shit is right," Reed shouted. *"You can bet your ass I'll never let you in the driver's seat again."*

I didn't doubt he meant that. *"I won't hurt our—your body. I swear."*

"Why would I take your word?"

"Because losing you would destroy Lee." I opened my eyes and let him see her curled up on the exam table.

The violent shift in Reed's emotions gave me whiplash. *"What happened? What's wrong with her?"*

"We don't know. She's been like that since we got here." I didn't realize I'd spoken out loud until Dom put his hand on my shoulder.

"Status, soldier?"

Reed shoved me into the back seat so fast I didn't have time to react.

Jerking away from Dom, he yelled, "The status is Lee is in shock and you two assholes are standing around rubbing your dicks together."

Dom glared at us. "I need Hunter. Bring him back. That's an order."

His words lit me up like a flash grenade.

"No way, man," Reed shouted. "I'm not letting that psycho take control ever again."

Dom grabbed us by the collar. "Listen up, Hippie. We're trapped inside this animal hospital with an army of infected trying to beat down the door. If you want your girlfriend to survive this, you'll let the soldier with decades of tactical training take point."

"Please, Reed," I'd never begged for anything before, but I was begging now. *"I swear on Lee's life, I'll let you take over any time you ask. And after we're back at the safe house, you won't hear from me again."* I threw out that last bit to sweeten the deal, but I meant it. Dom said he was going to get me out of this body and my handler always delivered on his promises.

Reed was silent for a beat. *"You won't try to get me killed?"*

"Fuck no. I'll do everything I can to keep us—you alive."

"Fine," Reed snapped, allowing me full control again.

Dom somehow knew the moment I stepped in because he let us go.

I gave him a sharp nod. "Thanks, handler."

Reed huffed. *"Don't thank him. I only agreed because you swore to leave me alone once we get back home. Now let's try to wake Lee up."*

❧

"YEAH, WE SHOULD TRY TO WAKE LEE UP," I SAID OUT LOUD for Dom's benefit.

Dom followed us into the exam room and watched as we gently shook Lee.

"Wake up, dirty dancer."

Lee let out a soft moan, but her eyes didn't focus.

"She's not hurt, is she?" Although Dom's tone was neutral, the slight shifting of his brow and the pinch of his mouth told me he was far more worried about her than he let on.

"I checked her over. I didn't see any injuries." And thank fuck for that. A Typhos having a human mate had to be a cosmic joke. We, like the Titans, were nearly immortal. Humans were anything but. So many things could end them in an instant. A fall. A blow to the head. A bite from an infected... It made me want to roll my dirty dancer in bubble wrap and hide her in some heavily fortified tower somewhere.

"So, what's wrong with her?" Dom asked as he ran his gaze over her body.

"Obviously, she's having a PTSD episode," Reed said, sounding exasperated. *"Eden's death must have triggered it."*

"But why does she have PTSD in the first place?" I asked out loud.

Dom snapped his head in our direction. He was apparently as interested as I was.

Unlike all the other times I'd asked the same question, Reed actually answered. *"Gran told me that when Lee was little, her dad—who was some big shot Special Forces soldier like you two assholes—flipped out and attacked his family with a knife. He killed Lee's mom and older sister, but only wounded Lee. Lee stopped him from going after Eden."*

I caught Dom's eye. "So, Lee's dad, who was a snake-eater, stabbed most of the family to death. But Lee was able to protect Eden."

Dom asked the burning question. "How did Lee protect her sister?"

"By killing him," Reed said slowly. *"The military police said she'd stabbed her father over a hundred times."*

"How does a child stab a Green Beret a hundred times?" I exclaimed.

Dom looked impressed.

"I don't know. Lee never talks about it. Not even to the shrinks Gran made her see. And occasionally, she has these space-outs—that's what she calls her flashbacks. Although they've never been as bad as this." His sadness mixed with my shock.

My poor dirty dancer. She was so much stronger and braver than I'd ever imagined. I rubbed the side of her face, wishing I'd been there to protect her.

Although she stared up at me, there was no recognition in her eyes. Wherever she was, it was far from here.

I wanted so badly to reach her—to comfort her—but I didn't know how. And even if I did, she wouldn't want to see me. *She hates me. She thinks I'm a rapist.* Even though I know she loved being with me. *Fuck.* She'd nearly ruptured my eardrums with her screams of pleasure. *How can she think I abused her?*

"Because you possessed me to have sex with her," Reed said, reading my thoughts. *"She thought she was with me. She didn't consent to having sex with you. That's rape."*

I still didn't understand. *"But I told her I wasn't you. I even made her call me Not-Reed. How more clear could I have been?"*

"You're hopeless, asshole."

Dom made a choked sound. "Lee is covered in infected blood."

"So are we." I shrugged, wondering his point. It'd been a bloodbath out there.

Dom shoved me aside and yanked Lee's shirt up to her neck.

"What the hell is he doing? Stop him," shouted Reed.

I grabbed Dom's arm. "Hey! Dom, we're not fucking her awake."

"You're damn right!" shouted Reed.

But Dom looked panicked, not excited, as he shrugged off our hand and flipped her black sports bra up, exposing her breasts. "Thank Christ. The blood didn't get through the fabric." He sounded relieved as he traced his finger down a small cut over her heart. "I should have healed this back in my office."

"He did that to her," Reed snarled. His anger made mine burn hotter.

I glared at my handler. "What the fuck, Dom? How could you use a knife on her after what she's been through?"

Dom winced. "I didn't know..."

"Bullshit. He knew enough," Reed snarled.

Dom scrubbed a hand through his hair, something he only did when he was tired or frustrated. "I'm not in my right mind when I'm around her. I screwed up, okay."

I sighed, my anger evaporating. "Join the club." Just thinking of all the ways I'd fucked things up with Lee made me want to slam my head into the wall.

Dom licked his thumb and rubbed it over Lee's wound.

As we watched her skin knit together and all traces of the wound disappear, Reed made a sound of surprise. *"Dominic can heal people?"*

"Titan saliva has restorative properties, but don't get too excited. It won't do shit for serious injuries," I answered,

admiring my mate's gorgeous breasts. *Will I ever get to touch them again?*

"Don't bet on it, asshole," Reed quipped. This ability he had to read all my thoughts sucked balls.

As Dom pulled his hand away from Lee's chest, his fingers grazed her nipple.

Lee moaned and grabbed his wrist. "Yes," she murmured. "Touch me. Pleasure me."

Dom went motionless. "Is she conscious?"

"I'm not sure," I said, watching her move restlessly.

Her gaze seemed to briefly focus on Dom's face as she pushed his hand between her legs. "Please, Dominic... I need... I need..." She rocked herself against his fingers, seeming frustrated. Then, keeping his hand shackled, she shoved her jeans and underwear down to her thighs and brought his hand to her bare sex.

Fuck.

A sharp burst of arousal surged through Reed and I, making our heart race and our cock throb.

Dom looked dazed as Lee ground herself against his palm.

"More," she cried. "I need more, Dominic. Please."

Dom let out a pained groan. He wore the anguished expression of an outgunned soldier. "I can't fight this, Hunter. I can't fight her..."

"Then don't. Accept that she is our mate." He had to accept her. Because I needed them both.

"Our mate," Dom echoed softly. Then he turned and rubbed his thumb over her sex.

"Oh, God. Yes!" Lee arched off the table, tossing her head back and forth.

"Stop him!" Reed roared in our mind. *"She's out of it."*

But I refused to interfere. One, because Lee was begging for this. And two, Dom—the male who could usually only touch if he was inflicting violence—was gently caressing our mate.

As Dom's thick fingers slipped inside Lee, stroking her—giving her exactly what she was seeking—the Titan lowered his head and sealed his mouth over hers.

"He's never done that," I said to Reed, sharing with him my shock and awe. Dom told me once he'd choose death over kissing. His abject refusal to lock lips with Jen at their wedding had made for a very awkward moment.

Lee rocked against Dom's hand, shrieking, "Yes! Yes!"

"Come for me, baby," Dom ordered, plunging his fingers deep inside her.

She howled his name as she orgasmed.

Dom stayed with her as she shuddered through her aftershocks. Then he slowly redressed her. When he smoothed her shirt and stepped away from the exam table, I knew things would never be the same between any of us.

Dom must have realized it, too. The Titan looked as if he'd taken a mortar round to the chest as he dropped onto the bench seat across from Lee.

Reed groaned. *"Jesus. I'm going to have to share her with G.I. Joe too, aren't I?"*

"Yeah, it's getting crowded at the dinner table, huh?"

I glanced at Dom's biometric scanner, noticing Avi's vitals had improved. *The little Lykos might just make it after all.* "Real crowded," I added out loud.

Lee suddenly gasped and sat up. She looked around the room, her forehead scrunching in confusion. "H-how long did I space-out?"

"Long enough," Dom answered in a gruff voice. "Long enough."

23

LEE

It'd been a half an hour since I'd come to my senses, and the four of us still hadn't found the damn antivirals. It didn't help that my brain was replaying the memory of Eden and Avi's deaths over and over. I stared down at the bottles of pills in my shaking hands, unable to read their labels through my tears.

"We need to hurry this up," Reed said in a low voice from across the supply room.

Startled, I jerked my head up and smacked it into the open cabinet door. The bottles flew out of my hand. I dove for them, forgetting I was standing on a counter four feet off the ground. As I pinwheeled my arms, trying to regain my balance, Dominic grabbed me.

"I've got you." His hands wrapped around my waist, steadying me. The heat of his long fingers burned through my shirt.

"Thanks," I said, pushing him away. "I'm okay now."

"Are you?" he asked, looking as if he actually cared. *That's a first.* Maybe Sergeant Pain in the Ass had been hit on the head during the fight outside. That would explain why he'd been acting so strange. Ever since I woke on the exam table feeling strangely relaxed and blissed out, he'd looked at me differently—almost tenderly. And he was more overprotective than ever, not allowing me to get more than a few feet from him.

I'd probably be thrilled by it if my heart hadn't been shattered.

Eden's dead. Avi's dead. Zara's dead.

Tears clogged the back of my throat as I stared down at the pill bottles I'd dropped. They rattled as they rolled slowly back and forth on the floor.

An insane tendril of hope flared inside my chest for a moment.

Maybe Eden and Avi are still alive. They could've fought back and found safety inside one of the cars.

I'd turned to look out the window when the echo of Eden's horrific screams rang in my ears.

No. They're dead.

Anguish flooded me.

Grady slammed a drawer shut. "I haven't found jack shit. Tell me you got something?"

"Lee?" Dominic stared up at me, streaks of dried blood covering his handsome face.

I wiped away my tears and scanned the room that was smaller than the kitchen in our old rental house.

How many times did I come here with Eden? Six? Seven?

She'd adored the head veterinarian. He'd written one of her letters of recommendation.

Is he outside right now feasting on her remains?

I choked on my breath.

Dominic reached up and grabbed my arm. "You have to breathe. In and out."

I glanced down.

His coal-black eyes burned into mine. "Stay with me, baby."

A hysterical laugh bubbled from my lips. "Baby? You're calling me baby? What have you done with the real Sergeant Rosario? The one who makes me run laps until I puke and tells me what a piss-poor soldier I am?"

Some unnamed emotion flashed in his eyes. "I'm sorry for mistreating you."

He's apologizing? I must be in some alternative reality.

Reed turned his head in our direction. "Dom, hostiles inbound. We need to move out."

Dominic returned his grim look. "Ten-four."

I looked between them in shock. "So what? Reed is telling you what to do now?" None of this made sense. Nothing made sense anymore.

Eden is dead. Avi is dead. Zara is dead.

My breathing came faster.

Dominic's grip on my arm tightened. "Focus, Lee. Find the meds."

My stomach twisted itself into knots as I scanned the shelves again. "Give me a second." *It must be here.*

If we left without finding the antivirals, this trip would have been for nothing.

Eden would have died for nothing. Avi would have died for nothing. Zara would have died for nothing.

I swallowed back a sob.

Sunlight filtered through the decals covering the window, leaving distorted shadows on the floor. The pill bottle rocking in and out of a paw-shaped shadow caught my eye.

Elation ran through me as I recognized the name of the medication. "There it is!" I jumped down and reached for the bottle at the same time as Dominic.

An electric spark arced through our skin when we touched. I expected the sergeant to jerk away like all the times before. Instead, he curled his large hand around mine, entwining our fingers.

I stared at him in shock, wondering if he'd been possessed.

"The antivirals!" Grady shouted, running over. "Give them to me."

Dominic dropped my hand and snatched the bottle. "Lee found them. She'll carry them." He stepped behind me, his cinnamon scent rising above the faint odor of wet fur and disinfectant.

Grady looked as if he was going to spit nails.

"You have to stay alive to get these pills back to the safe house," Dominic said, his hot breath tickling the nape of my neck as he tucked the pills into a side pocket on my backpack.

It was obvious what he was doing—trying to give me a reason to stay alert and alive. But he didn't need to.

I still have a reason to live.

I glanced over at Reed. He was crouched by the door, shotgun in hand.

I won't lose him too.

Dominic straightened his broad shoulders, seeming to snap into drill sergeant mode. "Hustle up. Grab what supplies you can."

I bent down and scooped up bottles of antibiotics, painkillers, and other meds I didn't recognize. We'd figure out what they were later. I slung my pack off and began stuffing the bottles inside.

"It's go time," Reed said, urgency eating a hole in his words.

Stopping only to shove a pile of bandages inside my pack, I followed Grady and Dominic to where Reed stood sentry.

"The back exit is that way." Dominic pointed to the south end of the building.

Reed slowly opened the door. The sound of breaking glass traveled down the hallway.

The Biters are breaking in. My blood turned to ice.

"Fall in." Dominic stepped in front of Reed.

Reed grabbed my hand and dragged me to his side. "Stay close to me."

Not about to argue, I squeezed his fingers. *Whatever happens. At least we'll be together.*

Dominic glanced back at us. I expected him to sneer—he'd never liked Reed—but he only nodded. "Keep her safe."

"Yes, sir." Reed tightened his fingers around mine.

Together, we followed the sergeant out into the long hallway. It became darker and harder to see as we walked toward the back of the building.

Dominic clicked on his flashlight. The beam of light refracted off of the empty metal kennels up ahead. Some had been ripped apart and were covered with bits of torn flesh. I quickly averted my gaze.

"This hallway should take us through surgery into the back exit," Dominic whispered.

"Yes," I confirmed, remembering the layout of the animal hospital.

A guttural howl came from behind us.

Grady glanced back. "What was that?"

"Move," Dominic ordered.

The four of us broke into a run. Reed gripped my hand as we tore down the hallway.

The horrible noise got louder and so did the pounding of footsteps behind us.

We finally came to the double doors leading to the surgery rooms, but they'd been chained shut.

"Christ," Dominic gritted out.

My sneakers squeaked as I skidded to a stop, narrowly avoiding the muscular wall of his back.

The chains rattled violently as rotting hands reached

through from the other side. They grasped and clawed, seeking live flesh.

"Fall back," Dominic shouted.

We all spun around.

The beam of the sergeant's flashlight illuminated the Biter at the end of the hallway.

Even covered in blood, I would have known that oval face and cleft chin anywhere.

Eden.

THE SHOCK AND PAIN OF SEEING MY SISTER—MY DEAD sister—paralyzed me.

Her sunken eyes, the same fish-belly white as her skin, skittered from side to side as she sniffed the air.

Given the limited visible damage to her body, she must have died quickly. The dead only fed on the living. Once she joined their ranks, they must've lost interest.

Grady lifted his crowbar and took a step forward. "I'll put the bitch down."

"No." Dominic grabbed Grady's arm. "It's a Howler."

Eden is a Howler?

"They are strong, fast, and nearly impossible to kill," Reed said in a low voice.

How does he know that?

Eden let out an inhuman, bone-chilling sound and rushed toward us at breakneck speed.

Oh, crap!

Reed threw me at Dominic. "Protect her."

"Get behind me!" Dominic shoved me backward. The motion sent me careening into the doors behind us. One gnarled hand pushed past the chain and grabbed the bottom of my shirt.

I screamed.

Dominic spun around and yanked me free. As he dragged me to his side, he shouted, "Hit first and hit hard, soldier."

"Hooah." Reed lifted his knife-tipped shotgun and fired. I'd thought he was out of ammo, but a resounding boom reverberated in the narrow hallway.

The middle of Eden's torso exploded outward, painting the sea foam walls crimson.

Seeming unaffected by the gaping hole in her stomach, Eden increased her pace. As she ran, her body knitted back together until the visible skin of Eden's stomach was smooth as porcelain.

She's regenerating. How is that possible?

Grady jostled into my side. He said something, but I couldn't hear him over the ringing in my ears.

I did hear Dominic though.

"Body shots? Pathetic. Are you even trying?"

Reed flipped the sergeant off, pumped the shotgun, and pressed the trigger.

Nothing happened.

Eden was only a few yards away.

The door chains jangled behind us.

I trembled.

Death ahead of us.

Death behind us.

Eden bounded into the air.

"She's going to kill Reed!" I screamed, trying to pull away from Dominic.

I have to protect him. Even if it meant sacrificing myself.

Dominic held me in place. "He's got this."

Right before Eden reached him, Reed jabbed the knife end of the shotgun into her mouth.

Eden went limp.

A cry escaped my lips as Reed flung her body down.

Wrenching away from Dominic, I fell to the floor as if I'd been impaled too.

Eden!

Grady gaped at Reed. "You nailed her right in the face. You get bonus points, you son of a bitch." He lifted his hand and waited for Reed to slap it.

Ignoring him, Reed strode over to me. "Dirty dancer, are you okay?"

I couldn't tear my gaze from my sister's body to answer him. Pain coiled tight around my heart. *"I'm so sorry, Edie."*

Even bathed in blood with a gun sticking out of her face, she was beautiful. Out of the three of us girls, she'd looked the most like my mother.

Maybe they're all together now. Mom, Angel, and Eden. Maybe they're waiting for me...

Reed cursed. "Dom, I think she's about to have one of her PTSD episodes."

Dominic crouched next to me. "We need you to be strong, baby. You've got to stay with us. Fight with us. Can you do that?"

But I couldn't. The echoes of my mother's scream rang in my ears. My vision began to waver. Then, out of the corner of my eye, I saw Grady kick Eden's corpse.

"No!" I shrieked, my rage bringing me back to full focus.

"Don't touch it, Grady," Dominic ordered.

It. My sister had become an it.

"I'm just making sure it's dead." Grady whacked Eden's face with a crowbar so hard he dislodged the shotgun and sent it skittering across the floor.

My vision went red. Without a conscious thought, I pulled my knife and jumped to my feet. "Touch my sister again and I'll end you."

"Whoa. Watch it, little lady. You don't want to bite off

more than you can chew." Grady twirled his crowbar and flashed me his yellow-stained teeth.

I'd taken a step forward, planning to slice that bastard's horseshoe mustache right off his face, when Dominic's arms banded around me.

"Now's not the time." The sergeant yanked the knife out of my hand and stuffed it back into my thigh sheath. Catching sight of Reed stalking over to Grady, he called out, "Down boy."

Reed stopped in his tracks and gave Dominic an irritated look. "Woof."

Dominic shook his head. "Don't play that card. I can't let you kill him."

I didn't remotely understand the strange way the two of them were communicating. But without saying another word, they switched places.

Reed slung his arm around my waist while Dominic marched over to Grady.

Faster than I could blink, the sergeant had the burly biker pinned to the wall in another chokehold. I couldn't hear what Dominic was saying, but Grady was definitely getting his ass chewed.

"If that fucker ever threatens you again, I'll turn him into a stain on the ground," Reed promised.

I gave him a watery smile and promptly burst into tears. "She's dead, Reed. She's dead." I threw my arms around his neck, sobbing.

Reed cursed. "Uh. Yeah, you take the wheel, cocksucker."

I was crying too hard to care that he was mumbling gibberish again. And it didn't matter because the next moment Reed dragged me into his arms. "I'm so sorry, honey. So sorry." He pressed his lips to my forehead. "Our Edie didn't deserve to go out like this."

"No," I sniffed. "She—"

A loud crash interrupted me. It'd come from the front of the building.

Dominic threw Grady down. "Fall in." He motioned us to follow him back down the hallway.

Grady scrambled to his feet and hustled after the sergeant.

"Come on, honey," Reed dragged me after them.

I glanced back at Eden's body. We were taking the light with us. "B-but we're leaving Edie in the darkness." She'd always been afraid of the dark.

"She's already moved on. She's with Gran and my mom now." Reed tugged my arm. "And unless we want to join them, we need to stay with Dominic."

He's right. My steps were jerky and awkward as I tried to keep up. I tripped over the shotgun in our path, but Reed caught me before I fell.

"Rule of survival number nine, never leave a weapon behind," I muttered. For some reason, thinking of Dominic's stupid rules calmed me. Taking a steadying breath, I stopped and grabbed the shotgun.

"We have to hurry," Reed whispered.

I let him steer me to the front of the animal hospital, where we joined Dominic and Grady crouched behind the reception desk.

Dominic raised a finger to his lips.

I lifted my head high enough to see Biter after Biter shuffling into the lobby. Somehow, they'd pushed through the chairs stacked against the doors. As they filled the space, so did their grotesque smell.

How do we fight our way out of this?

Seeming to have a similar thought, Dominic ripped the shotgun from my hands and handed it to Reed.

Reed looked down at it blankly.

"Hippie?" Dominic clenched his jaw. "Christ, I need Hu—"

Grady interrupted him. "They're swarming. They've caught our scent."

He's right. The Biters were moving erratically—like fire ants whose nest had been crushed. There was a crash as one of the zombies knocked over a display of cat food.

"There are too many of them," I whispered.

Dominic apparently agreed because he motioned us to retreat to the hallway.

As we backtracked, Grady's boot crunched on broken glass.

Every head jerked in our direction. A chorus of teeth chattered in excitement.

Oh, shit.

Dominic grabbed my hand and took off.

It took all my concentration to keep up with his long strides. The pills in my backpack rattled as we careened into the supply room.

Reed and Grady followed us in, slamming the door behind them.

My heart pounded as I stared at the thin piece of wood standing between us and them.

It won't hold.

"Barricade the door!"

Dominic knocked bottles and lab equipment off one of the shelves. Then, in an impressive display of strength, tore it free from the wall and wedged it between the door and the counter. It wouldn't hold, but it would buy us time.

Panting, I spun in circles, looking for salvation in the small room.

The glass-paned window on the door shattered, and skeletal arms shot through.

Glass. Window. Of course! The window over the counter. "Look. There!"

Following my pointed finger, Dominic grunted in approval. Without a word, he grabbed my hips and lifted me onto the counter.

The window slid open easily.

"Is it clear?"

I peered through the opening, down to the empty alley below. "Nothing in sight." Finally, our luck was improving.

"Good." Dominic's voice sounded tight. "Now climb through."

Gladly. I tossed my backpack out the window. As I shimmied through the small opening, the realization that a larger person wouldn't be able to get through hit me like a kick to the stomach.

Oh, no. I pushed myself back down.

"What are you doing?"

"You can't fit." There was no way Dominic, with his massive build, could get through. Grady couldn't either, although I could give two shits about that asshole.

Dominic's face was carved in grim resolve. "I know."

"They're breaking through," Reed cried. "Get out of here, honey."

It'd be tight, but maybe Reed could squeeze through. "Reed, come with me."

"Go. I'll follow." Reed's eyes didn't meet mine. He'd never been a good liar.

"Reed!" I screamed over the sound of fists pounding on the door. I refused to leave without him.

He and Grady struggled to keep the shelf against the door.

"We can't hold it," Grady shouted. "Lee, get those pills to my daughter. Tell her I love her and that—"

He was interrupted by the sound of wood splintering.

"I love you, honey. Go! Get out of here!" Reed shouted.

No. This can't be goodbye. I can't lose him. Suddenly, all the suppressed emotions I had for Reed exploded to the surface. There was no time to deny my feelings or hide from the truth. I loved Reed so much it hurt. And I didn't just love him as my only surviving family member. No. I loved him romantically and wanted to spend the rest of my life with him —even if we only had minutes left together.

"I'm in love with you, Reed Jarin Marshall," I shouted.

Reed gave me a grim smile as he strained to hold the shelf. "I'll love you from this life to the hereafter. Now go. Live. For me and Eden."

I shook my head. "No. I can't live without you." *And so I'll die with you.* Decision made, I prepared to climb down.

"Enough." Dominic jumped up on the counter, blocking my view of Reed. "You're leaving." He shoved me back toward the window.

"Take this." He pushed the radio into my hands. "Get in range of Sai and radio him. He'll come for you."

"No. I'm staying." I tried to push my way around him, but it was like shoving a brick wall.

Dominic gritted his teeth and hauled me over to the window. "Why can't you ever follow orders?"

"I'll follow all your orders if you let me stay. Please let me stay, sir!"

Dominic gave me a searching look, as if he was trying to memorize my face. Then he slanted his head and kissed me.

I was too shocked to do anything other than gasp as his sharp, sweet cinnamon flavor invaded my senses.

Surprise quickly gave way to burning desire. For weeks, this dark, smoldering heat had been building between us. The sexual tension had become a powder keg, and his kiss lit the match.

My body went up in flames. A frenzied cry escaped my

lips as I grabbed him by his vest and kissed him as if my life depended on it.

All other emotions were obliterated by the savage, all-consuming hunger I had for this man. My vision tunneled. Nothing mattered but this moment. Nothing existed except this...

His tongue mating with mine. His hands gripping my ass. His erection throbbing between us.

And just when I was certain his ironclad control had finally snapped, Dominic suddenly jerked away.

"Pass the final test. Survive," he ordered. Then he picked me up and tossed me out the window.

❦ 24 ❧

LEE

Pain exploded from my right ankle as I landed hard in the alley. I lost my balance and fell into a dense patch of chin-high oleander muscling its way along the building. Disoriented, I lay there panting.

It took me a full second to realize Dominic had just kissed me stupid so he could chuck me out the window like last week's garbage.

That son of a bitch!

Inside the building, someone screamed.

My irritation quickly turned to panic. *Oh, no! Did the Biters get in?*

Trying to block out the pain in my leg, I called out, "Dominic! Reed!"

The silence was deafening.

Shouting their names again, I willed the men to appear in the window over my head. A fist-sized knot formed in my stomach when they didn't.

Oh, God. They're gone.

A storm of emotions threatened to overwhelm me. My breathing went choppy and black edged across my vision. Just when I felt myself falling into darkness, Dominic's last words rang in my ears.

Pass the final test. Survive.

Knowing I had to calm down if there was to be any chance of that, I focused on the breathing technique I'd learned from Roger. With every inhale and exhale, I pushed away the anguish and grief. Only when I felt centered and emotionally numb did I try to stand. My ankle pulsed with so much pain, I fell back on my ass.

Crap. Is it broken?

I quickly rolled the cuff of my jeans halfway up to my shin and slid my sock down. Although my ankle was turning the color of an overripe tomato, it didn't appear to be broken.

Just a sprain. Thank God for small favors.

A bald zombie in an Armani suit staggered around the trash bin at the back end of the alley. There were probably more where he came from.

I have to call for help!

I looked around for the radio. *It must've fallen into the oleander.* Keeping the weight off my injured ankle, I stood. As I leaned over to peer deeper into the bushes, my hair fanned out and tangled in the branches.

Dammit.

My frantic tugs sent dozens of pale pink flowers cascading to the ground.

Click-click.

The unmistakable sound of gnashing teeth made the hair on my neck dance on end. The terrifying noise seemed to be coming from right next to me.

That's impossible unless the bald zombie is one of those fast zombies like Eden...

Panicked, I twisted my head far enough around to see Baldy lurching past the trash bin at a snail's pace. It'd be at least a few minutes before he caught up to me.

Still. I need to get free if I don't want to become zombie chow. Gritting my teeth, I pulled hard against the branches.

My hair yanked free at the same moment there was a sharp, tearing pain in my lower calf.

I looked down, and my heart stopped.

A shriveled husk of a zombie, wearing faded blue medical scrubs, lay at my feet. The bottom half of its body was missing, and most of its raven hair had sloughed off. Its skeletal arms twined around my leg.

A primal scream ripped from my lips as its jaws clamped around my bare calf.

My scream turned into a shriek. I tried to kick it loose.

Oh, God no!

The thing bit down harder. Its emaciated arms tightened around my leg like a boa constrictor.

With a burst of adrenaline, I drew my knife and swung it into the top of the creature's skull. The blade made a crunching sound as it broke through brittle bone.

I swung at it again.

And again. And again.

My hand stilled only when the back of its skull caved in, and the Biter went limp. Gasping for breath, I finally shook my leg free.

The creature slipped to the ground, one milky white eye mocking me from its shattered face.

Shit.

It'd probably been there, half concealed by the bushes, the whole damn time. I'd completely missed it. In my mind, I heard Dominic chiding me.

Rule of survival number three, be aware of your surroundings at all times...

Dammit. With a roar, I kicked the thing into the alley wall.

A dozen yards away, Baldy tripped over something and fell to the ground.

I sheathed my knife with shaking hands.

Please, please, don't let the Biter have broken the skin.

The acrid taste of fear burned my tongue as I slowly looked down.

Blood welled in three places where teeth had sunk into my flesh. As far as injuries went, it was nothing. I'd had paper cuts that sliced deeper. But harmless-looking or not, the bite would infect me.

The area around the wound seemed to tingle as I realized what that meant.

I've failed the final test.

Game over.

I collapsed on the asphalt, desperately searching the empty window for a familiar face.

Who am I kidding? The guys are dead. And now I am too.

Swallowing back a sob, I looked down at my leg.

If only I'd been paying closer attention, I might have noticed the zombie in the bushes. If only I'd rolled back down my pants, maybe it wouldn't have been able to puncture my skin. If only Dominic hadn't thrown me out the window. I let out a moan of frustration. Playing the what-if game wouldn't change a goddamn thing.

Down the alley, Baldy stumbled to his feet and shuffled closer in bloodstained Gucci loafers. Black flies buzzed around his head like a halo.

In twenty-four hours, I'll be like him.

First came the black veins that marked the infection's progress throughout the body. Then came numbness, dizziness, unconsciousness, and death. Moments after that, I'd rise as a flesh-eater.

No. I can't let that happen.

My hand pressed my gun against my head before I'd even registered the thought. The barrel was cold against my temple. "Goodbye," I whispered to the empty window. I shut my eyes, imagining the faces I hoped would greet me on the other side.

"*No!*" a deep baritone voice shouted.

❦

I BLINKED IN CONFUSION. THE VOICE HADN'T COME FROM the window or the alley. It'd come from inside my head.

Just a figment of my imagination. I put my finger on the trigger.

The voice spoke again. *"This is not the part where you die, anassa."*

"My name is Lee and yeah, this is the part where I die," I said out loud. "I'm infected." I looked down at my leg and shuddered. "I'm doing this."

There was no response.

Great. Now I'm talking to myself. Maybe the Z-virus was already infecting my brain, making me hear voices.

In that case, there's no time to waste.

Taking a deep breath, I steadied the gun and pressed the trigger.

Click.

Dammit. I'd forgotten I was out of ammo. Snarling in frustration, I threw down the useless weapon.

"I told you this isn't the part where you die." The voice sounded smug.

"Who the hell are you?" I called out. "And where the hell are you?" Other than the corpse I'd mutilated and Baldy slowly lurching in my direction, the alley was empty.

Oh, God. Am I talking to Baldy? My stomach pitched. *Have I suddenly become the zombie whisperer?*

A velvety chuckle rippled through my mind. *"No need to panic. I'm not here physically."*

I stiffened, immediately thinking of Hunter. "You're not going to possess me, are you?"

"*I wouldn't dream of it, anassa.*" His low, rich voice made my stomach flip.

I gave my hormones a mental bitch slap. This was so not the time to get all hot and bothered over some voice I was probably hallucinating.

He laughed again, increasing my suspicion he could read my mind. "*They call me Ghost.*"

"What kind of name is that?" I snapped, feeling irritated by the seductive pull of his voice.

"*What kind of name is Heaven Lee?*" he replied in a mocking tone.

The hairs on the back of my neck rose. "I didn't tell you my first name. How do you know it?"

"*I know everything about you.*"

"Really? What's my favorite color?"

"*Brown, because it reminds you of your mother's eyes.*"

Oh my God. "How can you possibly know that?"

"*I know e—*"

"Everything. I got it."

The sound of shouting came from the window. A tingling spark of hope jolted me. *Are the guys still alive?*

Answering my unspoken question, Ghost said, "*Yes. And you can still save them.*"

"How?"

"*First, deal with that.*"

"That?" I echoed in confusion.

Gravel crunched near my head.

I looked up to see Baldy standing over me.

With a flash of horror, I realized Baldy wasn't bald after all. The Biter's scalp had been ripped off, exposing the white of his skull. Tiny white worms wriggled in the space where his eyes should've been.

Baldy pounced, half leaping, half falling on me.

I moved to the side, barely escaping its gnashing teeth. I tried to roll to my feet, but in my rush, I accidentally put weight on my bad ankle. It crumpled under my weight.

Baldy tackled me, pinning me to the ground.

Oh, no! My arms shook as I strained to keep the creature's snapping jaws from my throat.

"Stab it!" Ghost shouted in my mind.

As Baldy thrashed over me, several maggots dropped onto my face.

Ahh! I fought the urge to bat them away. *No. I have to keep focus.* This was my field training test all over again, except there was no Zara here to save my ass. I did still seem to have a personal cheerleader though.

"You can do this. Save yourself," Ghost chanted.

Finding some hidden reservoir of strength, I held the creature off with one hand, and drew my knife with the other.

"That's it."

Letting out a muffled cry, I thrust my blade straight into Baldy's empty, maggot-filled eye socket.

The flesh-eater went lax and collapsed on me.

"Ugh." Gagging on the rotten stench, I used my good leg to kick the Biter off. Then I yanked my knife free and wiped it on the corpse's two-thousand-dollar suit.

"Well done, anassa."

"Thanks, buddy," I said, shaking the disgusting little white worms from my hair.

"Boo," he said quickly.

"What?"

"You call me boo, not buddy. It's an inside joke between us... because of my name..."

I froze. "Wait. Do I know you?"

"Not yet, but we'll meet soon."

That threw me for a loop. "So, are you from the future or something?"

He chuckled. *"No. I can see the future."*

I rubbed my temples. This was beyond insanity, but of course, I had to ask the mother of all questions. "Then tell me. Do I survive this?" I motioned at the bite on my leg.

"All will be revealed in time."

"Is that the best you've got?"

"So it was. So it is. So it will be."

I gritted my teeth in frustration. It figured the figment of my dying imagination would be cryptic as hell.

"How about you focus on helping them, anassa?"

"Them?"

More shouts came from inside the building.

"Dominic! Reed!" I called up to the window.

"They can't hear you."

"I'm getting you out!" I yelled. "Ghost, how do I save them?"

"You'll have to figure that out for yourself. I can't directly interfere..."

"Interfere with what?"

"Your destiny."

I glanced down at my leg. "News flash. I'm fresh out of destiny."

The figment of my imagination had the nerve to laugh.

Annoyed, I crossed my arms over my chest. "Seriously, boo. Either help me or fuck off."

"You need to remember your training."

"Right." *Okay.* I could work with that. I took a deep breath and let it out.

Rule of survival number nine, never leave a weapon behind.

I picked my gun off the ground and holstered it. Then I yanked up my sock and rolled the cuff of my jeans down, completely covering the bite.

Rule of survival number eight, travel with backup.

Ignoring the pain from my ankle and calf as best I could, I stumbled over to the bushes and fished out the radio.

I pressed the tall button. "This is Lee, over. Sai, are you there?"

Silence.

"Sai, do you read me?" I pushed the talk button several more times, trying to hail the rock star. All I got for my effort was radio static.

"Sai is out of range."

"Thank you, Captain Obvious. I don't suppose you could tell him we're in trouble."

"No."

"You can't or you won't?"

"He can't help you. He's busy saving his brother."

"Avi is alive?"

"Yes."

Thank God. A dizzying relief shook me. Maybe my willow tree would survive, and I'd get the chance to apologize to him before I died. I hated the way things ended between us. But first, I had to focus on saving Dominic and Reed. I stared down at the radio. "Should I bother trying the school?"

"You're out of range of the safe house too."

"What am I supposed to do? I can't save the guys from hundreds of zombies by myself."

"Yes, you can."

"Come on. You've got to help me. Please," I pleaded.

"Ghost helps those who help themselves."

I gritted my teeth so hard I was surprised I didn't crack a molar. "Anyone ever tell you you're super annoying?"

"Only you, anassa."

Panic and frustration clawed at me as I limp-jogged down the alley. My overstuffed backpack lay on its side in the middle of the asphalt. I'd stumbled past it when Ghost cleared his throat.

"What?"

"Aren't you going to grab that?"

"No." It'd be idiotic to carry another ten pounds when I could barely walk as it was.

"What about the promise you made to Eden?"

Crap. I'd almost forgotten I'd promised to get the meds for Rosie. "How do you know about that?"

"I know e—"

"Everything. Yeah, I remember." I backtracked, picked up the backpack, and stuffed the radio inside it. The pills rattled cheerfully as I slung it on.

Once the weight settled on my shoulders, I felt a new sense of determination.

I don't know how, but I'm going to save Dominic and Reed, reunite with Sai and Avi, and bring the meds back to Rosie.

"You can do this. Just believe in yourself." I could hear the smile in Ghost's voice.

"At least one of us is enjoying this," I muttered.

"Yes," he said, not sounding the slightest bit apologetic. *"What comes next is my favorite part..."*

❧

The adventure continues with Claiming Her Beasts
Book Four

IT'S GETTING REAL NOW. WE'RE STRANDED IN THE deadliest part of the city, being hunted by the living and the dead. My beasts need me to give them a reason to fight—to survive.

One problem.

I'm running out of time.

There's no way I can tell my guys I have one foot in the grave. Not when they are finally working as a team and agreeing to share me—making all my wicked fantasies come true.

But a violent shifter gang and a terrifying new creature are closing in. And to defeat the monsters, I may have to become one...

ABOUT THE AUTHOR

Dia wanted to be a writer from the time she could hold a pencil. A lover of paranormal romance, reverse harem, science fiction, urban fantasy, and horror, she writes action-packed stories featuring kick-butt heroines and the alpha male heroes who fall for them.

You can find her books on amazon.

If you want to be notified when the next book in the series releases, please sign up for Dia's newsletter.

You can follow Dia on:
https://diacole.com/
or
Join her reader group:

https://www.facebook.com/groups/1082971415136332